THE PURSUIT

BY JANET EVANOVICH

The Fox and O'Hare novels
with Lee Goldberg

The Heist

The Chase

The Job

The Scam

The Pursuit

The Stephanie Plum novels

One For The Money	Twelve Sharp
Two For The Dough	Lean Mean Thirteen
Three To Get Deadly	Fearless Fourteen
Four To Score	Finger Lickin' Fifteen
High Five	Sizzling Sixteen
Hot Six	Smokin' Seventeen
Seven Up	Explosive Eighteen
Hard Eight	Notorious Nineteen
To The Nines	Takedown Twenty
Ten Big Ones	Top Secret Twenty-One
Eleven On Top	Tricky Twenty-Two

The Diesel & Tucker series

Wicked Appetite	Wicked Business

Wicked Charms (with Phoef Sutton)

The Between the Numbers novels

Visions of Sugar Plums	Plum Lucky
Plum Lovin'	Plum Spooky

And writing with Charlotte Hughes

Full House	Full Speed
Full Tilt	Full Blast

JANET EVANOVICH

AND

LEE GOLDBERG

THE PURSUIT

headline
review

The right of Janet Evanovich and Lee Goldberg to be identified as the Authors of the Work has been asserted by them in accordance with the Copyright, Designs and Patents Act 1988.

Published by arrangement with Bantam Books, an imprint of Random House, a division of Penguin Random House LLC, New York.

First published in Great Britain in 2016
by HEADLINE REVIEW
An imprint of HEADLINE PUBLISHING GROUP

1

Cataloguing in Publication Data is available from the British Library

ISBN 978 1 4722 2560 3 (Hardback)
ISBN 978 1 4722 2561 0 (Trade Paperback)

Offset in Minion Pro by Avon DataSet Ltd, Bidford on Avon, Warwickshire

Printed and bound in Great Britain by Clays Ltd, St Ives plc

MIX
Paper from
responsible sources
FSC
www.fsc.org   FSC® C104740

Headline's policy is to use papers that are natural, renewable and recyclable products and made from wood grown in well-managed forests and other controlled sources. The logging and manufacturing processes are expected to conform to the environmental regulations of the country of origin.

ACKNOWLEDGMENTS

We'd like to thank Dr. D. P. Lyle, cataphile extraordinaire Gilles Thomas, and Alan Blinken, former U.S. ambassador to Belgium, for sharing their expertise with us.

THE PURSUIT

1

Nicolas Fox, infamous con artist and thief, woke up in a coffin. His ability to stay calm was partially due to the lingering effects of the tranquilizer shot he'd been given eighteen hours earlier, in Honolulu. It was also due to his belief that if his abductors had really wanted him dead, he would already be dead instead of napping in a high-end casket. Especially after he had thrown one of the kidnappers through a glass coffee table and tried to choke another with a kukui nut lei. So despite the dire nature of his present situation, Nick was optimistic about his future.

He lifted the heavy lid of his coffin and sat up to find himself in a bank vault. Concrete walls were lined with hundreds of safe-deposit boxes. The ceiling was low, outfitted with strips of fluorescent lights. The floor was white tile. A twelve-inch-thick steel door was ajar, as was an iron-barred gate that opened into the vault.

It took Nick only a second to realize that it was all fake. The iron bars of the gate were PVC pipes that had been painted black. The wall of safe-deposit boxes was a large photograph. The floor was linoleum, the steel door made of painted Styrofoam. It was the equivalent of a movie set. Someone was training for a heist and Nick had a good idea which vault they were planning to hit—the basement diamond vault located in the Executive Merchants Building in Antwerp, Belgium.

A man walked onto the set. He was dressed like a fashion-conscious Angel of Death in a black turtleneck sweater, black jeans, and black loafers. He was in his fifties, but had the athletic build of someone thirty years younger. It was his strikingly angular face, and the thinning, pockmarked skin glued like yellowing wallpaper to his sharp cheekbones, that betrayed his age.

Nick had never formally met the man, but he remembered him from Hawaii. He had led the abduction team. He spoke excellent English with a slight accent. Nick knew he was Balkan.

The man tossed Nick a cold bottle of mineral water. Nick caught the bottle and noted that it was Valvert, a Belgian brand. Nick was pretty certain he wasn't in Hawaii anymore.

"How are you feeling?" the man asked.

Nick took a long drink before he replied. "I suppose

traveling to Belgium in a coffin is better than flying coach these days. At least I was able to lie flat."

"And sleep like the dead."

"The afterlife looks surprisingly like the diamond vault in the Executive Merchants Building in Antwerp," Nick said.

"You're very good."

"I'm assuming that's why I'm here and not buried in this coffin."

"For the time being," the man said.

FBI Special Agent Kate O'Hare closed and locked the door on the high-end Oahu beach house. Her maverick partner Nick Fox had rented the house, and last night he'd disappeared. His red Ferrari was still parked in the driveway. His blood was also left behind. Okay, maybe it wasn't *his* blood, but it was *someone's* blood. And the blood trail led to the front door. Not such a shocker since a lot of people probably wanted to kill Fox. He was a world-class thief, con man, and an international fugitive. For the past couple years he'd been secretly working with Kate to take down bad guys that the FBI couldn't touch. Not that he was doing it out of the goodness of his heart. It was either help the feds or go to jail for a very long time.

And lucky me, Kate thought. I got stuck with him. Not only was she stuck with him, but she was also sort of hot for him. Could it possibly get any worse?

The beach house was at the end of a cul-de-sac. Houses

to either side were hidden behind gates and tropical hedges. The sound of the surf was a constant murmur in the distance.

Kate walked down the driveway and cut across to one of the neighboring houses. She rang the bell and pulled the FBI badge case from her pocket. She flipped it open beside her head for the benefit of whoever looked through the peephole. The homeowner would see a blue-eyed woman in the vicinity of thirty with a slim, athletic build, her brown hair currently cut in a rakish, chin-length bob that not only met FBI requirements but also was practical. Her hair didn't require much care and didn't give an assailant a lot to grab in a fight. She wore a white permanent press polyester shirt, skinny jeans, a holstered Glock clipped to her belt, and a thin-bladed knife in a sheath just above her ankle.

The door was opened by a short woman in her midfifties wearing a purple halter top, colorful floral shorts, and flip-flops. She was more charred than tanned, her skin like tree bark. She held a Bloody Mary in her left hand, her long, polished fingernails as red as her drink.

"Do we really have to do this again?" the woman asked.

"Again?"

"Just because I signed a petition demanding to see a president's birth certificate doesn't mean I'm going to take a shot at him from my bathroom window while he's bodysurfing. When's he coming?"

"I'm not here about a presidential visit, ma'am. I'm investigating a possible crime that occurred next door."

"You'll have to narrow it down. Crimes occur there all the time. It's party central. That's why I have a camera aimed at the house. It's so I have proof of the drunken tourists who drive over my grass, vomit on my flowers, and let their kids pee on my palms. But does anybody care? No."

This brought a smile to Kate's face. The woman had security cameras. And one of them was aimed at the beach house Nick had rented. This was good.

"I'd like to look at the footage," Kate said.

"Hallelujah! You know how long I've been waiting for someone with a badge to ask me that?"

Kate edged past her and tried not to scrape herself on the lava-rock wall in the process. The woman closed the door, opened a coat closet behind her, and swept aside some windbreakers on hangers to reveal a shelf holding a DVR, a flat-screen monitor, a keyboard, and a mouse.

"Ta-da," the woman said. She turned on the monitor and typed in a password. The image on the screen was divided into six squares showing different angles of her property. One angle was a clear view of the rental house, and she clicked on the feed to expand it to full screen. "You can rewind using the backspace key. I got this at Costco. Great, isn't it?"

"Wonderful," Kate said.

"Can I get you a Bloody Mary?"

"Sure," Kate said. She didn't want a Bloody Mary, but it was the easiest way to get rid of the woman.

It took Kate only a few seconds to scan through the

footage on the DVR and find what she wanted. Yesterday, late afternoon, a Ford Explorer drove up to the beach house, and four men got out. They drew guns and fanned out around the house. Kate could tell from the way they moved and handled their weapons that they were trained soldiers, just like her. This was a professional strike team. And yet they didn't try to disguise their faces.

Moments later, Nick emerged from the house, his hands zip-tied behind his back, a gun held to his head by a man with a pockmarked face. Nick was six feet tall, brown-haired and brown-eyed, and even now, in this dangerous situation, he moved with the relaxed grace of a man confident in his ability to take care of himself. She was relieved to see that Nick was alive and uninjured, but she still felt a pang of anxiety in her chest. He was far from safe. Behind Nick and his captor, two other men carried out a third man who was covered with blood, his clothes shredded. A glass coffee table had been shattered in Nick's rented house. She suspected this bloody guy was the unfortunate missile that had destroyed the coffee table.

The pockmarked man shoved Nick into the backseat of the Explorer while the two other men opened the rear door, hefted their injured comrade inside like a sandbag, and slammed the door closed. The men piled into the car and drove away, giving Kate a good view of the license plate. That sloppiness intrigued her.

The woman returned with a fresh drink in each hand and

held one out to Kate. Kate's drink had a big pineapple wedge on the rim. "Here's your Bloody Mary."

"Sorry, I have to pass. I can't drink on the job." Kate unplugged the DVR and tucked it under one arm. The last thing she wanted was new footage of Nick Fox, one of the FBI's Ten Most Wanted fugitives, floating around. "I'm going to need to take this with me as evidence. Is that okay with you?"

"Be my guest."

"It might be a while before you get it back. In the meantime, I'll have a forceful talk with the owners of the rental house about taking responsibility for the bad behavior of their tenants."

She'd also return to the beach house later tonight to clean up the blood and take Nick's suitcase, clothes, and toiletries. She wanted to be the only law enforcement agent on Nick's trail.

"Thank you so much," the woman said. "Bring back the DVR when you're off-duty, and I'll make you the best Bloody Mary you've ever had."

"Deal," Kate said. She'd never be back, but she'd make sure the woman got a new DVR.

Kate got into her Jeep, took out her cellphone, and found the phone number for the duty agent at the FBI field office in Honolulu. She identified herself and asked the agent to run the Explorer's license plate for her. The response was almost immediate. The car was registered to the same airport-based car rental agency as her Jeep. That was great news, because she knew that most rental car companies tracked their cars, either with GPS units or theft prevention devices that, in some cases, could even be used to remotely disable the vehicle. She thanked the duty agent and called the rental company.

"This is FBI Special Agent Kate O'Hare. You rented a Jeep to me yesterday afternoon. I need you to ping the locator on a Ford Explorer of yours with the following license plate number and tell me where I can find it. I'll be stopping by shortly with identification, and I'd appreciate it if you had the information ready for me."

The Ford Explorer was parked under a broken streetlight where Lagoon Drive came to a dead end against the eastern fence of the Honolulu International Airport runway. The road got its name from the Ke'ehi Lagoon that ran the length of its south side and faced Waikiki. On the north side of the road was a line of general aviation terminals, cargo carriers, and tour operators. It was a remote spot and was virtually deserted, the silence occasionally broken by jetliners, fat with tourists, coming in for landing.

Kate drove up to the SUV slowly and parked. She got out of the Jeep, drew her weapon, and approached the Explorer. Abandoned and empty. No surprise there. There was blood all over the cargo area, along with glass shards, soiled gauze, and torn wrappers from bandages and other medical supplies. She holstered her gun, went back to the Jeep, and retrieved her go bag. It contained everything she needed for a few days in the field, including clothes, extra ammo, rubber gloves, and an evidence-collection kit. She took the rubber gloves and kit and returned to the SUV.

It bothered her that whoever had snatched Nick didn't feel it necessary to properly dispose of the Explorer. It suggested that they were either stupid or already out of the country. She didn't think they were stupid. She meticulously searched the SUV and found a Walgreens receipt and a disposable cellphone. The cellphone had been wedged into a cranny by the back wheel well. It could have been in the wheel well for weeks or months, or it could have fallen out of the injured guy's pocket when they tossed him into the cargo area. Kate dropped the phone and the receipt into the evidence bag. If every person called from the phone was also using a throwaway phone, it created a completely closed network. If she lucked out and the phone belonged to the injured guy and he had made at least one call to a nondisposable phone, she had a lead.

If the phone didn't give her anything, she'd have the fingerprints she was going to lift from the car, the photos of the bad guys she was going to pull from the DVR and the security camera at Walgreens, and the list she was going to get of every private jet or cargo plane that had departed the airport in the last twenty-four hours.

2

"Why don't you stretch your legs?" the pockmarked man said to Nick, with a sweeping wave of his hand to express his generosity. "What can you tell me about this vault?"

"Just some useless trivia," Nick said.

Nick got up stiffly, cracked his back, and began walking slowly around the set, shaking his arms to get the blood flowing again. Still wearing a red aloha shirt with a surfboard motif, khaki shorts, and flip-flops on his otherwise bare feet, Nick stood in colorful, casual contrast to his host.

"Indulge me," the man said.

"The building was constructed in the mid-1970s and is occupied exclusively by individual diamond merchants who store their inventory in safe-deposit boxes in the vault, which is two floors underground."

As Nick spoke and continued circling the room, three more men and one woman came in to listen. The men had the demeanor of thugs. The woman was young, graceful, and stunning, with natural blond hair and emerald green eyes. She would have looked elegant even if she'd been wearing a garbage bag instead of Gucci.

"The vault door weighs three tons, has a lock with a hundred million possible combinations, and can withstand twelve hours of sustained drilling, not that it would ever happen, since it's protected by an embedded seismic alarm that will go off the moment the drill bit touches the steel. Even if you could get the vault door open, it's protected by a magnetic field." Nick pointed to a plate on the door that aligned with another, matching, plate on the wall. "If the field between the door and the wall is broken, the alarm goes off at the police substation, which is only half a block away."

"That's true at night," the man said. "But during business hours, the vault is wide open so the merchants can get to their diamonds."

Nick nodded his head. "But the interior gate remains locked. It's opened remotely by security guards stationed in a command center upstairs who watch from a video camera mounted outside the vault door. After hours, opening this gate requires a special key that is impossible to duplicate."

"The bars could easily be cut with a torch."

Nick reached up and tapped a matchbox-sized unit on the ceiling. "Sure they could, but that's not an option. The vault is also protected by a light detector as well as a combination heat and motion sensor."

"So you don't come through the door," the man said. "You tunnel in."

"The room temperature is maintained at sixty degrees Fahrenheit at all times," Nick said. "An increase of more than five degrees in the ambient room temperature will trigger the alarm." Then he added: "Oh, and there are also seismic sensors in the floor and the walls to prevent tunneling your way in."

The man nodded, impressed. "You've studied this vault before."

"It would be professional negligence if I hadn't. I could lose my license to steal." Nick winked at the woman then looked back at the man. "Frankly, I'm surprised you're even interested in this. It's not your style. You're more of a smash-and-grab guy."

"You know who I am?"

"It's not a big secret. Your face is on the wall of every law enforcement agency from Stockholm to Perth. You're Dragan Kovic, leader of the Road Runners, an international gang of diamond thieves who've pulled dozens of jewelry store robberies across twenty different countries in the last decade, stealing two hundred million dollars' worth of diamonds."

"Closer to two hundred and fifty million," Dragan said. "But who's counting?"

"Your gang's trademark is driving a vehicle, often an Audi, through a storefront. You've also used a FedEx truck, a bulldozer, an ice cream truck, a motorhome, a cement truck, and my personal favorite from your repertoire, a police car. Then you smash the display cases with pickaxes, grab the diamonds, and speed off. You're in and out of the stores in four minutes and out of the country within two hours." Nick pointed to the vault door. "But this is different. You can't drive an Audi through that."

"That's why you're here," Dragan said. "There's at least five hundred million dollars' worth of diamonds in that vault, and we've already got clients lined up, waiting impatiently for the stones. You're the only one with the skills to get us inside. It's taken us more than a year to find you, and we're running out of time to pull off the job."

Things weren't adding up for Nick. Why would Dragan be interested in a heist that he knew was beyond his team's skill level? He had been doing the same routine for the past ten years. Why change now? Nick was about to pose the question when a fifth man limped onto the set. His face was covered with stitches, making him resemble a scarecrow stuffed into loose-fitting Versace sweats instead of burlap sacks. His flat eyes looked like they'd been ripped from a doll and glued onto his face. It was the guy who'd attacked Nick in Hawaii, and been tossed through the coffee table.

The scarecrow made eye contact with Nick, did his best to ball his meaty hands into fists, and took a step forward. Dragan cut him off, placing a halting hand on his chest.

"Easy, Zarko," Dragan said. "You can't blame a man for defending himself."

"I don't blame," Zarko said, staring at Nick. "I kill."

"How did you find me when the FBI, Interpol, and just about everybody else on earth with a badge hasn't been able to?" Nick asked.

"They would have much more success finding crooks if they were crooks themselves," Dragan said.

The deputy director of the FBI had come to the same conclusion. That was why Nick was now secretly teamed up with Kate.

"We found the forger in Hong Kong who made the 'Nick Sweet' passport you've been using lately," Dragan said. "He's done a few of ours, too. He was an excellent craftsman."

"'Was'?"

"Sadly it took some persuasion to convince him to help us find you . . . persuasion which unfortunately left him incapable of forgery or tying his shoes again. However, in the end he was quite generous with his information."

Nick sighed and shook his head in disappointment. "I'm a thief. Instead of abducting me and threatening me, did it ever occur to you to just politely invite me to participate in one of the biggest diamond heists in history?"

"I like leverage," Dragan said.

"Five hundred million dollars in diamonds is plenty of incentive for me," Nick said.

"That's our money."

"Minus my fifteen percent commission as a creative consultant."

"I'm not used to negotiating," Dragan said. "I'm used to taking what I want."

Nick turned to the blond woman. "I assume you've rented offices in the building, posing as a diamond merchant."

She smiled, like a child witnessing a magic trick. "How did you know that it was me occupying the office and not Borko, Dusko, or Vinko?" She gestured to the other men in the room besides Dragan and Zarko.

"The Road Runners always use a beautiful, seemingly rich woman to case the jewelry stores that they're planning to hit, often months in advance," Nick said. "Why would it be any different now that the target is a vault?"

Her smile widened. "You think I'm beautiful?"

Dragan rolled his eyes. "Litija's been a tenant in the building for nearly a year. She can go in and out as she pleases during business hours."

"I have an empty office where I do nothing but sit and watch *House Hunters International* and *Love It or List It* from America on my laptop," she said. "I have a safe-deposit box in the vault that I visit at least twice a day, though all that's in it is some makeup."

"But it's thanks to her that we've learned every detail of their security system," Dragan said, "and were able to construct this accurate re-creation of the vault to try to devise a way in."

"Impressive, but overkill. Getting in is easy," Nick said.

Litija was skeptical. "You just told us all of the reasons why it can't be done."

"Let me kill him," Zarko said.

Nick looked at one of the remaining men, who'd said nothing so far, and had a face only a turtle could love. "What's your opinion?"

"I think we spent too much on your coffin. When Zarko is done with you, it will be easier to bury you in bags."

"I'm sorry I asked," Nick said. "What about you, Litija?"

"I'd really like to see you do it, because you're cute, funny, and are the only person besides Tom Selleck who has ever looked good in that outfit," she said, gesturing to his aloha shirt and shorts. "But I don't believe that you can."

Nick turned to Dragan. "I guess you didn't share my résumé with them."

"I don't ask for advice on my decisions," Dragan said.

"I'm relieved to hear it, considering the consensus of the room. So let's make a deal, shall we? Think of me as a willing and eager participant. I'll even overlook how you got me here."

"Very gracious of you," Dragan said. "It's been a pleasure watching you try to turn this situation to your advantage. I can see why you're a world-class con man, but it also makes me worry that I'm being swindled. So here's my one and only offer. You will remain as our guest. If you get us into that vault and out safely with the diamonds, we'll give you a ten percent cut. But if anything goes wrong, you die. How does that sound?"

"Fifteen percent would sound better," Nick said. "But I'm in."

"Excellent," Dragan said. "What do you need?"

"A car, for starters," Nick said.

"Cars are not a problem. That's how all of our robberies begin."

"I thought you'd appreciate being in your comfort zone."

"What kind of car would you like?"

"One that can fit in Litija's purse," Nick said.

Kate's dad, Jake O'Hare, was in shorts and flip-flops when Kate handed him his boarding pass.

"I'm going to Antwerp and I might need help," Kate said. "We have just enough time to get to the airport."

"Andy's not going to like this," Jake said. "We have a one o'clock tee time."

"Since when would you rather play golf than execute an unlawful extraction?"

"You didn't tell me the part about the unlawful extraction," Jake said. "The answer is never."

Kate had grown up as an Army brat, following her father around the world while he performed "extraordinary renditions" with his Special Forces unit. He was retired now, living with Kate's sister in Calabasas, enjoying the good life and missing the old one.

"Are you traveling in those clothes?" Jake asked. "They look like you slept in them. Not that I mind, but the TSA might pull you out of line thinking you're a vagrant."

Kate looked down at herself and smoothed out a wrinkle in her navy blazer. She hadn't slept in the clothes, but they weren't exactly fresh either. She'd kicked through the dirty laundry on her floor this morning and chosen some clothes that looked the freshest.

"I just rolled in from Hawaii and didn't have a lot of time to put myself together," she said. Not to mention she wasn't all that good at the whole pretty-girl thing. She didn't have time. It wasn't a priority. She had no clue where to begin. Her father had taught her forty-seven ways to disable a man with a toothpick before she was nine years old, but he hadn't exactly been a fashionista role model. And clearly she was lacking the hair and makeup gene.

The ten-story Executive Merchants Building was a major repository of the world's wealth. The building looked like just another 1970s-era concrete and glass box, a place somebody might go to have a cavity filled, a car insured, or a tax return completed. The complete absence of style was the style. The only ornamentation on the building was its array of big, boxy surveillance cameras.

The main entrance was on the southern side of Schupstraat, one of three narrow streets that comprised the "special security zone" in the heart of Antwerp's diamond district and Jewish quarter. The three streets, Rijfstraat, Hoveniersstraat, and Schupstraat, formed a rigid "S" that began on the northeast corner of the district and ended on the southwest edge. Both ends of the "S" were closed to free-flowing vehicle traffic by retractable steel columns in the pavement that were lowered after vehicles passed police inspection at adjacent kiosks and then raised again after the inspected cars entered the secure zone.

On a Thursday at 11 A.M., three days after Nick's abduction, Litija walked into the Executive Merchants Building. She sashayed through the marble-paneled lobby and blew a playful kiss to the elderly guard who sat in the control center behind a thick window of bulletproof glass. He waved back at her with a friendly smile as she approached the turnstile that controlled access to the first-floor offices, the elevators, and the stairwell. Litija swiped her tenant ID card over a scanner and walked through the turnstile as it unlocked.

She bypassed the elevator and took the stairwell. She paused on the landing just inside the door for a moment, listening for voices and looking around to make sure she was alone. There were no cameras in the stairwell. No footfalls of anyone else climbing the stairs.

She hurried down to the next landing, crouched beside an air vent near the floor, and took a screwdriver out of her purse. She quickly unscrewed the grill, reached into her purse again, and pulled out a radio-controlled red Lamborghini with a tiny camera taped on top of it.

Litija placed the car into the vent, and it sped off.

3

Nick and Dragan sat in the back of a panel van parked directly across the intersection from the police kiosk on the southwest corner of Schupstraat and Lange Herentalsestraat, which also happened to be the northwest edge of the Executive Merchants Building. Borko and Vinko were in the front seats, trying very hard to look anywhere but at the uniformed, heavily armed officers they were facing.

"Do we really have to park here?" Borko asked.

"Any further away and we wouldn't have a signal," Nick said. He used a joystick to steer the Lamborghini while watching the camera's view on an iPad that sat on his lap.

"But we're parked right outside the building we're going to rob," Vinko said. "The police can see us and our van."

"Relax," Nick said. "A thief planning to rob that building would have to be insane to sit here to do his recon."

Dragan gave him a hard look. "You're reading my mind."

"That's what makes this spot the safest place to be," Nick said. "Besides, the police aren't on the lookout for thieves plotting to break in. Everybody knows it's impossible. The police are for show." Nick steered the Lamborghini past several air vents and around a tight corner. "How long have the guards worked in the building?"

"One guy just got his thirty-year pin. The others have been here nearly as long."

"That proves my point," Nick said. "They've stayed so long because it's a very cushy job. Nobody has tried to break in to the vault since the day the building opened, and they know that nobody ever will."

Nick parked the Lamborghini at the end of an air vent that gave their camera a view down into the vault foyer. They could see the open vault door and the closed gate. Something caught Nick's eye. He zoomed in on a door a few feet from the vault.

"You don't have that door on your set," he said.

"Because it's a supply closet," Dragan said. "We aren't interested in stealing toilet paper and file folders."

Litija came in, and Nick adjusted the camera view to a wider angle. She walked past the open vault door, stood in front of the inner gate, then turned to wave at the security camera and the guards watching in the control room. It looked like she was waving at Nick and Dragan.

"The security camera that's mounted outside the vault is only watched during business hours, when the door is open," Nick said. "But at night and on weekends, there's nobody watching the monitors. The feed is recorded and taped over every thirty days. In fact, there isn't a single guard in the building after hours. Do you know why?"

"Because a break-in is impossible," Dragan said.

"You're catching on," Nick said.

Litija was buzzed through by the guards upstairs. She pushed the unlocked gate to let herself in and stumbled a moment after the gate swung closed behind her. She dropped her purse in the process and crouched down to pick it up.

"When the vault is open during the day, the heat and motion sensor is deactivated, of course, or everyone who walks in would set off the alarm," Nick said. "More important, to protect the privacy of the tenants and the contents of their safe-deposit boxes, there aren't any cameras in the vault."

So nobody saw Litija take a tiny bottle of hairspray from her purse and spritz the combination heat and motion sensor, coating the surface with a thin, milky film. She got up, tugged on her miniskirt, and presumably went to her safe-deposit box, disappearing entirely from view.

A few moments later, Litija walked out of the vault again, closed the gate behind her, and, before she left, offered a parting wave to everyone who was watching.

"That takes care of the heat and motion detector," Nick said. "In the morning, our camera will be parked right here, so we'll be able to see the building manager enter the combination and open the vault. Then we can do it, too."

"We're still using a car to open the vault," Dragan said. "I love it."

"You have a reputation to maintain."

"You have style, Nick, I'll give you that." Dragan pointed to the magnetic plate on the vault door and the matching one on the jamb beside it. "But the instant we open the vault door, we'll break the magnetic field, setting off the alarm in the police station. And if we cut the power to the magnets, that will activate the alarm, too."

"Don't worry," Nick said. "I've got that covered."

"How?"

"If I tell you now, it would ruin the surprise."

Nick was sharing details only as they were needed so Dragan couldn't proceed without him. It was a way to extend his life expectancy for as long as possible. He figured if he hung in there long enough, Kate would track him down and rescue him. He'd been under constant watch and hadn't been able to contact her, but he knew she was like a dog with a bone when she had a job to do. And right now, like it or not, her job was to retrieve him. He was government property.

"What about the gate?" Dragan asked. "It can only be opened with a key that can't be duplicated."

Nick smiled. "We'll rely upon human nature for that."

· · ·

While Nick and Dragan were parked on Lange Herentalsestraat, Kate O'Hare and her father were standing on Schupstraat, outside the Executive Merchants Building. They were lost amid the stream of tourists, police officers, and bearded men in yarmulkes carrying attaché cases full of diamonds chained to their wrists.

Kate had identified the men who grabbed Nick by running their pictures and fingerprints through FBI databases. She had pinpointed their location when she gleaned a non-cell number from the throwaway phone. The call had been to an office in the Executive Merchants Building. The number was no longer in service, but it was a credible enough lead to get Kate and her father on a plane to Antwerp, the medieval Belgian port city that was home to 80 percent of the world's trade in rough diamonds. Their first stop was Stadspark, a triangular park in the city center, where they picked up two Glocks and plenty of ammo that an arms-dealing friend of Jake's had hidden for them in a prearranged spot. From there they went to Schupstraat.

Kate's phone rang and she recognized the number as coming from the Federal Building in West Los Angeles where she was currently based.

"O'Hare," Kate said.

"Hey, Katie Bug. It's Cosmo Uno. Whatcha doin'? What's shakin'? Haven't seen you in forever. Heard you zipped in here and zipped out. Like you were here for a nanosecond, right?

And I must have blinked and missed you. Bummer, right? Am I right?"

Kate stared at her phone. Cosmo Uno was the annoying idiot in the cubicle next to her. He was shorter than her, single and desperate, slicked his hair up with what looked like goose grease, and was a foot jiggler. All day long when she was in her cubicle she could hear him jiggling his foot.

"Why are you calling me?" Kate asked him. "And how did you get my number?"

"You're gonna love this. Wait until I tell you. Like I thought I was the luckiest guy in the building to get the cubicle next to you, and now we're working together."

"*What?*"

"That's over the moon, right? I mean, we're practically partners. Do you love it? I love it."

Good thing she wasn't in the building, Kate thought, because she'd have to shoot him.

"See, here's the thing," Cosmo said. "Jessup thought it would be a good idea if you had someone to help you keep track of expenses."

Kate narrowed her eyes. "Un-hunh."

"So I'm going to be your expense guy. For instance, there's an item we just received for a rental car in Hawaii. That's a mistake, right?"

"I'm busy," Kate said. "Good talking to you."

She disconnected, turned to her father, and pointed at the building directly in front of them.

"The office that one of the Road Runners called on the throwaway was in this building," Kate said. "A building, incidentally, with a vault that holds a fortune in diamonds."

"A vault that's impossible to break in to," Jake said, holding up the Antwerp guidebook he'd bought so they'd look like tourists. "Rick Steves says so right here."

"That's one mystery solved," Kate said. "Now we know why a gang of international diamond thieves kidnapped Nick."

"We don't actually *know*," Jake said.

"Okay, we *think* we know."

"Good enough for me," Jake said. "What's the plan?"

"We'll get a room at the hotel across the street." Kate pointed in the general direction of Lange Herentalsestraat, where, unbeknownst to her, Nick had been sitting in a panel van only a few minutes earlier. "Then we'll watch for an opportunity to rescue Nick. We need to be ready to take it when it comes."

"I'll call my friend who left the guns for us in the park," Jake said. "He can get us a rocket launcher."

"We don't need a rocket launcher."

"Sure we do," Jake said. "Nothing creates opportunity like a rocket-propelled explosive."

"It would also create an international incident. I'm going to be in enough trouble as it is."

Kate hadn't informed her bosses, Special Agent in Charge Carl Jessup or Deputy Director Fletcher Bolton, that Nick had been taken, or that she was pursuing him to a foreign country. She couldn't take the risk that they wouldn't let her go.

"Not if we don't get caught," Jake said.

"We aren't blowing up anything, Dad. Whatever we do will have to be quick and quiet."

"We're dealing with the same thieves who drove a bulldozer through a jewelry store in Saint-Tropez in broad daylight and escaped in a speedboat," Jake said. "So this might end quick, but it won't end quiet."

Kate's phone rang again. Same L.A. number. "Oh for the love of Pete," Kate said, opening the connection. "Now what?"

"You haven't filed your form S-Q-zero-zero-niner," Cosmo said.

"I'm pretty sure I filed that," Kate said, having no idea what he was talking about.

"We can't find it."

"If you call me again I'll have you killed," Kate said. "I can do it. I know people."

And she disconnected.

4

Shortly after 1 A.M. on Saturday, a panel van drove up to the Executive Merchants Building's underground parking garage on Lange Herentalsestraat, half a block down from the police kiosk at the intersection with Schupstraat.

Nick was one of five men in the back of the van. Zarko, Vinko, Borko, and Dusko were on the team. Dragan was not. They were all dressed in regular street clothes.

Zarko took a remote control out of his pocket, aimed it at the garage door, and pressed a button. The garage door rolled open. Even before they'd kidnapped Nick, the Road Runners had easily captured the frequency of the forty-year-old garage door system and programmed a remote to match it. It was easy because there were fifty-seven videos on YouTube that explained how to do it. There were no videos that explained how to get into the vault and bypass the multiple alarm systems.

Nick and the four men spilled out of the van carrying duffel bags. They ducked under the garage door, and the last one, Zarko, closed it behind them. The van drove off, made a U-turn, and parked half a block down with the headlights off. The driver was sticking around as their lookout.

"They're inside," Kate told her father on her disposable cellphone. She stood in the shadowed alcove of a closed falafel joint on the west side of Lange Herentalsestraat, midway between the garage and the parked van where the driver was watching for signs of trouble. She cupped the phone in her hands so it wouldn't emit any light. "One of the men is definitely Nick."

"It's dark out and you're twenty yards away," Jake said from a car parked up the street, just above the intersection with Schupstraat and the police kiosk. "How can you be sure it's him?"

"I know how he moves."

He moved like a panther. She'd had the crazy urge to run out the instant she saw him, but Kate remained very still. She didn't want to attract the attention of the driver in the parked van.

"Now what?" Jake asked.

It was a good question. She hated the idea of sitting there while one of the biggest heists in history was pulled off right in front of her. But her top priority was Nick. For a moment she considered overpowering the driver in the van and either taking his place or putting a gun to his head to get him to do as she wanted, but there were too many ways that scenario could go wrong.

"We wait," she said.

In the garage, the five thieves put on night vision goggles. Vinko went up to the locked door that led into the building and ran Litija's tenant ID over the scanner. The door unlocked. Vinko bent down, stuck a rubber wedge under the door to keep it open, and the men headed down the main corridor. When they reached the lobby, Borko went off to deactivate the DVR in the control center while Nick and the three other men took the stairs down to the vault.

They walked out of the stairwell into the foyer that faced the imposing vault door. Nick unzipped one of the tote bags he carried and removed a suction cup tool commonly used to carry heavy panes of glass. There was a vacuum-tab suction cup on either end of the horizontal handle. Nick placed one suction cup against the magnetic plate on the vault door, the other on the matching plate beside it, and pulled back the locking tabs. The suction cups held. He used an electric screwdriver to unscrew the magnetic plate from the doorjamb.

Nick pocketed the screws and looked at Zarko, who stood in front of the vault door, bouncing on his heels, anxious to get started. The stitched cuts on Zarko's face were swollen and red. Nick thought he should probably see a doctor about that.

"You can open the vault now," Nick said. "But very slowly."

Zarko entered the combination, turned the three-pronged spindle wheel to retract the locking pins, and pulled the heavy door open. As he did, the magnetic plate on the jamb came away with the door, dragging wires out of the wall socket. Nick stared at the magnetic plate. If it fell, they were finished. But the suction cup device kept the two plates together, maintaining the magnetic field as if the door was still closed.

Nick watched closely to make sure the wires didn't break. He waited until the door was open just wide enough for a man to enter the vault by slipping under the taut wires that were attached to the magnetic plate.

"Stop," he said.

Zarko did. Now the iron gate was all that separated them from a bank of safe-deposit boxes filled with millions in diamonds.

Zarko bounced on his feet again and tipped his head toward the gate. "How do we open it?"

The other three Road Runners looked at Nick too, eager to see what he'd do next.

"With a paper clip," Nick said.

Nick reached into his pocket. He held up a paper clip between his index finger and thumb for them to admire. The four men stared blankly at him.

"Trust me," Nick said. "Best tool ever designed by man."

Nick unbent the paper clip into a straight wire, went to the supply closet door, and effortlessly picked the deadbolt lock.

He opened the door, reached inside the closet, and came out holding a bizarre four-sided key that looked both ancient and magical. The thieves stared, astounded.

"How did you know it would be in there?" Dusko asked.

"Human nature." Nick slipped past the open vault door to get to the gate. "There's only one key and the guards don't want to lose it. They also want it handy if something ever goes wrong with the remote locking mechanism. So they hung the key in the closet. I'm sure it wasn't kept here to start with, but it's probably been there for at least a decade or two."

"Morons," Zarko said.

Nick slid the key into the gate's lock. "That's what happens when the same security people do a job for forty years without any incidents. They get lazy."

He opened the gate and slipped the key into his pocket as a souvenir. He reached up and stuck a piece of black electrical tape over the light sensor on the ceiling. He pulled off his night vision goggles.

"You can turn on the lights now," Nick said.

Zarko hit him from behind with a lead sap, once to get him down, and once more to keep him there.

Kate was still standing in the dark alcove, leaning her back against the front door of the falafel joint, when she saw the garage door roll open at the Executive Merchants Building and the van begin to slowly drive up the street.

She called her father. "They're coming out."

Jake started his car but kept his headlights off. "I'm ready."

When the van passed Kate's hiding place, she bolted across the street and ducked behind a car that was parked close to the garage. The van stopped in front of the open garage. Four men carrying heavy duffel bags dashed out of the garage and jumped into the van. Nick wasn't one of them.

Damn!

"Follow the van," Kate said into her phone. "Don't lose those men and the diamonds. Ram them and call the police if you have to."

"Where are you going?"

"To find Nick. He didn't come out."

She stuck the phone into her pocket and got ready to move. The van drove off. The garage door started to come down. Kate raced for the garage, dove to the ground, and rolled under the descending door an instant before it closed.

And this is why I don't spend a lot of time ironing my clothes, she thought, getting to her feet, noticing that the knee was ripped out on her jeans.

The door to the building was wedged open. Kate ran inside to the lobby, went straight for the stairs, and took them down to the bottom floor. The vault door was open, with some kind of suction tool stuck to the front and wires dangling from the wall. She ducked under the wires and into the vault. Nick was on the floor sprawled motionless among hundreds of mangled safe-deposit boxes, loose cash and papers, assorted jewelry, gold bars, silver coins, and scattered diamonds.

Kate dropped to her knees beside him and quickly scanned his body for injuries. Blood matted the side of his head, but he was breathing, and his eyes were fluttering open.

"Nick? It's Kate. Can you hear me? Nick!"

He winced as he regained consciousness. "Crashing headache," he said. "Blurred vision. Think I see an angel." He managed a small smile. "You found me."

"I swore to you a long time ago that I'd never let you get away."

"I didn't think I'd ever be thankful for that," he said.

Kate helped Nick up, sitting him against the wall for support. "You have a concussion. We should take this slowly. I don't think the police know about what just went down yet."

She surveyed the pile in the center of the vault. "There's got to be millions of dollars' worth of jewelry, diamonds, and cash that they left behind."

"It was an embarrassment of riches. They only took the very best and left when they had as much as they could carry. Not that I saw what happened. They took me out before the action started."

"You're lucky they didn't kill you."

Nick blinked hard, trying to focus his vision. "I'm no good to them dead. They wanted me to get caught to distract the police and buy them time to get away."

"They weren't afraid you'd talk?"

"What could I possibly tell the police that they don't already know?"

Kate gestured to the bank of safe-deposit boxes. Most of the slots had been forced open, but there were still at least a third of them that hadn't been touched. "How did they decide which boxes to break open?"

Nick's head was starting to clear a bit. "No idea. I wasn't involved in that part of the planning stage."

Kate's phone vibrated in her pocket. She retrieved her phone and answered it. "Where are you, Dad?"

"Still parked on the street."

Nick squinted at her. "You brought your dad?"

"I told you to follow the thieves!" Kate said to Jake.

"I don't care about them or the diamonds," Jake said. "I care about you. You have two minutes, maybe less. The police are swarming the place. I bet now you wish I'd gotten that rocket launcher."

"Get out of here and burn your phone."

She split open her own phone, removed the micro SIM card, and swallowed it.

Nick stared at her in disbelief. "Did you just eat your SIM card?"

"I don't want anyone finding it. The phone is a disposable, and to my knowledge I didn't make any traceable calls, but better safe than sorry." She dropped the phone onto the floor, smashed it under her foot, and kicked the debris away. "The police are coming. Something must have triggered the alarm."

Nick had a sinking realization. He moved aside and glanced with dread behind him. He'd been leaning against the heat and motion sensor and had wiped the hairspray off it with his back.

"You have to arrest me," he said to Kate.

"Think again. Get up, we'll find a way out." She reached for him but he resisted, grabbing her wrists to get her attention.

"There's only one way out of this vault," Nick said.

"You'll find another," she said. "You're Nick Fox. That's what you do."

"Not this time. You have to arrest me. If you don't, we'll both go to prison. You need to get in touch with Jessup. Find out what was in this vault. I'm thinking it might have contained more than diamonds."

They could hear a rumbling upstairs, like a herd of cattle running through the halls. The police were in the building. They had only a few seconds left.

Kate took out her gun and tossed it onto the pile of stuff the thieves had left behind. "Lie facedown on the floor."

"You're so hot when you take charge," Nick said.

Nick lay facedown on the floor, and Kate straddled him. She pinned one of his arms behind him, reached into her coat pocket with her free hand, and whipped out her badge just as a half dozen police officers spilled into the vault, their guns drawn.

"I'm Special Agent Kate O'Hare, Federal Bureau of Investigation," she said. "This man is mine."

5

Kate sat in an interrogation room that was just like every other one she'd ever been in. It had the same cinder block walls, the same piss-yellow fluorescent light, and the same dirty mirror that hid whoever was watching. The only difference was that this time she was the suspect being questioned.

Chief Inspector Amelie Janssen sat across the table from her with notepad and pen. The detective's shoulder-length hair had a just-got-out-of-bed wave to it. Probably because she'd just gotten out of bed. It was 4 A.M.

"I can't count all the laws that you've broken," Janssen said. "If it were up to me, you'd be in handcuffs and ankle chains like any other common crook. But it's not my decision. It's up to the general commissioner, and she's waiting to hear from the prime minister's office, which is demanding an explanation from the U.S. ambassador in Brussels."

"I captured an international fugitive who is wanted in a dozen countries, including this one," Kate said. "So instead of complaining, you should be congratulating me."

"You're right. Where are my manners?" Janssen said. "Congratulations on helping the Road Runners pull off the biggest diamond heist in the history of Belgium."

"I had nothing to do with that."

"You certainly didn't do anything to stop it. As far as I'm concerned, you're an accessory after the fact."

"I apprehended the man responsible for the crime," Kate said. "Or have you forgotten that?"

"While the rest of the Road Runners got away with the diamonds," Janssen said. "If you'd told us you were here and what you were doing, we could have staked out the building and captured them all in the act."

"I didn't know there was going to be a robbery."

"Okay." Janssen leaned back in her seat again. "So explain to me how you ended up in the vault with Nicolas Fox."

Kate had learned from Nick that the best lies were the ones that stuck as close to the truth as possible. So she followed his advice.

"There were rumors for months that Fox had joined the Road Runners. So when I heard that Dragan Kovic and several members of his gang were spotted last week in Honolulu, I got on the first flight out there to see if they'd left any tracks,"

Kate said. "They did. I found out where Dragan went to rent a car, then used the GPS records for the vehicle to retrace his movements for the few hours that he was on the island. That led me to the store where his gang bought their disposable phones, which have unique identifying numbers. With that information, and some help from a friend at the NSA, I was able to pull the call records. There was only one call off the island."

"To the Executive Merchants Building," Janssen said.

"You got it."

"You should have notified us at that point."

"I didn't have anything," Kate said.

"You had enough to go on to fly here and watch the building, hoping you'd spot Fox or a Road Runner who could lead you to him."

"Yes, but it was an outrageous long shot. I didn't even tell my bosses what I was doing. I just cashed in some vacation time and booked a flight."

Janssen sighed and made a note to herself on the pad. Kate tried to read it upside-down, but it was in Flemish. "What happened next?"

"Jet lag," Kate said.

"I don't understand."

"I was sitting in a dark alcove across the street from the building and I fell asleep."

"You're kidding me."

"I wish I was, because it's humiliating. But I'd barely slept for the last week and I'd been watching the building all day. I was exhausted. When I woke up, a van was pulling away and the garage door was closing. It didn't feel right so I made a run for it."

"You could have gone to the police instead. They were right up the street."

"I am the police," Kate said.

"Not here."

"It's who I am everywhere, and since I only had a split second to act, my reflexes took over. I managed to roll under the garage door right before it closed," Kate said. "I took the stairs down to the vault and discovered that the three-ton door was wide open. I was sure that the vault had been emptied, that the thieves were long gone, and that I'd slept through the heist. I lowered my guard, which is how Fox got the jump on me when I went into the vault. We fought and I won."

Janssen stopped taking notes and set her pen down. "What was Fox doing there?"

"I assume that he was double-crossed and left behind," Kate said. "Maybe we'll find out, and get a lead on the missing diamonds, when you stop wasting valuable time questioning me and we begin interrogating him."

"You aren't getting near him," Janssen said. "You're out of this."

"He's my prisoner."

"You have no authority here to arrest anybody. You can

stand in line to extradite him with all of the law enforcement agencies in Europe. That is, after he's released from our prison, in thirty years."

There was a knock on the other side of the mirror. Janssen threw a glance at the mirror and saw her own irritated expression reflected back at her.

"Stay here." Janssen gathered up her notebook and pen and left the room.

Kate thought she'd given a good performance. Her story unfolded like a farce but it would be very hard for Janssen to prove it wasn't the truth. However, it was just the beginning. The U.S. State Department, Justice Department, and the FBI would demand answers too, and probably her badge, if not her head.

Janssen came back in and held the door open. "You can go, but you can't leave Antwerp. We're holding on to your passport and your badge until we decide what to do with you."

Kate stood up. "What about Nicolas Fox?"

"He's not your problem anymore."

Kate stepped out of the monolithic police station into the Saturday morning sun. She walked up the street, past coffeehouses and upscale clothing shops, with no particular destination in mind.

She was emotionally numb. She'd come to Antwerp to save Nick, and instead she'd put him in prison. There was a time, not so long ago, when she would have celebrated his capture. Instead, she was already thinking about how she was going to manage to get Nick free.

She caught a glimpse of a familiar figure reflected in a shop window. It was Jake. She didn't turn to acknowledge him. He'd approach her when he was certain nobody else was on her tail. She wanted to be sure too. So now her wandering had intent.

She crossed the Groenplaats, a large plaza ringed by cafés and bars, and headed for the Cathedral of Our Lady, a Gothic monument to failed dreams that had taken two hundred years to build and yet was still incomplete. The cathedral was supposed to have had two matching four-hundred-foot towers. But in the 495 years since the church opened its doors, only one tower had been finished, and could be seen all over the city, while the other tower remained uncompleted and half as tall.

To reach the cathedral's entrance, Kate had to go down a narrow cobblestone street, a bottleneck of restaurants, coffeehouses, and Leonidas chocolate shops, all crammed tightly together and stuck to the side of the church like barnacles. At the base of the cathedral's unfinished tower was a sculpture of four stonemasons at work. She stopped to look at the sculpture, not to wonder if it was a critical statement about the glacial pace of construction, but to see if the bottleneck had revealed anyone shadowing her. It hadn't. Her father walked past her and went inside the church.

Kate followed him and discovered that the church charged admission. Her father hadn't lost any of his edge, she thought.

Paying for a ticket and going through the turnstile presented an obstacle that would flush out anybody following them. She paid her six euros, walked through the turnstile, and entered the vast nave with its impressive vaulted ceiling.

At the base of each pillar holding up the church were altars to the various craft and professional guilds that had been leaders of the community in ancient times. The altarpieces were large paintings by Flemish masters. The paintings depicted guild members demonstrating their particular trades.

She stood in front of the altarpiece for the fencing guild, which had once served as Antwerp's de facto police force. It was a painting of Saint Michael, the guardian of paradise, and his army of angels battling a seven-headed dragon and a legion of naked man-beasts with what looked like monster masks over their crotches.

"Those are some nasty codpieces," Kate said in a voice slightly louder than a whisper.

Her father pretended to take pictures of the nave with his cellphone. "They sure are. Codpieces are uncomfortable enough to wear without fangs and horns on 'em."

"I'm not going to ask how you know that," she said.

"What happened in the vault?" Jake asked.

"I was caught in the act of arresting Nick. I told the police that I'd tracked him here from Hawaii and stumbled into the heist."

"I'm glad you were able to smooth-talk your way out of jail. I was already making plans to help you."

"What did you have in mind?"

"I was going to do what any sensible father would in a situation like this," Jake said.

"You started looking for a good criminal lawyer?"

"I ordered explosives from my buddy in Amsterdam."

She looked at him. "*That's* what you consider the sensible thing? Blowing a hole in the police station and mounting a jailbreak?"

"Of course not. That would be insane."

"Then what were the explosives for?"

"I was going to ambush the armored police van carrying you to court on Monday morning and blast open the doors to set you free."

"At least that won't be necessary now." Kate took a seat in the row of pews behind him and lowered her head.

"The plan is still on," Jake said, snapping some more photos. "Now we can use them to bust Nick out. We've got forty-eight hours to work on the details and steal the necessary vehicles. A garbage truck and two motorcycles should do it."

Good grief, Kate thought. I'm going to steal two motorcycles and a garbage truck! As if she hadn't already broken enough laws. She pressed her lips together and made the sign of the cross.

"What are you doing?" Jake asked. "We're Presbyterian."

"The agreement Nick had with the FBI was that if he was ever caught by the police, anywhere in the world, our operation was over and he'd be on his own."

"I didn't agree to that," Jake said. "Besides, he's my friend and you love him. That's more than enough for me."

Love him, she thought. Jeez Louise. That's wrong on so many levels.

"I don't . . . you know," she said to her dad.

"What?"

"The *L* word."

"Love?"

"Yes. The *L* word and *Nicolas Fox* shouldn't be said in the same sentence. Especially not out loud."

Jake gave his head a small shake. "How would you describe your relationship with him?"

"Reluctant partners," Kate said.

"Okay, I'll buy that. What else?"

"I guess I think he's hot."

"Too much information," Jake said. He got up with his back to her, and left a disposable phone behind on the pew. "Get some rest. Call me when you're ready."

6

Kate walked back to her hotel. She needed some sleep to clear her head. She needed to make sure that whatever the plan, her dad wouldn't end up in a Belgian jail too.

She went to her room, found her iPhone, and left her boss, Carl Jessup, a voicemail that said only "What was in the vault?"

Kate flopped facedown on the bed fully clothed and fell asleep almost instantly. It felt like she'd closed her eyes for only a second when she was awakened by the electronic trill of her iPhone. The time on the clock radio, next to her phone, was 3 P.M., and the caller ID on her phone read "Jessup."

Kate grabbed the phone. "O'Hare," she said.

"How much of the story that you told the Belgian police is true?" her boss asked. His Kentucky drawl was disarmingly low-key. It was as if he was casually asking about the weather, or the price of turnips, and not about an international incident that was likely to end Kate's career with the FBI.

"Ninety percent," she said. "What I left out was that Nick was kidnapped by the Road Runners to pull off the heist and that I came here to rescue him."

"Then you did the right thing going to Antwerp without telling me," Jessup said. "You gave us plausible deniability."

"That was the idea."

"I sincerely doubt that."

"How much trouble am I in?" she asked.

"That depends on if you get caught," Jessup said.

"I think they bought my story."

"I'm not talking about that," Jessup said. "I'm talking about you breaking Nicolas Fox out of jail."

"Excuse me?" Kate could feel beads of panicked sweat appearing on her upper lip. How did Jessup know she was planning a jailbreak?

"I'm expecting the Belgians to throw you out of the country within forty-eight hours, so you don't have much time to free Nick, and you need to do it without hurting anyone. If you get caught, we'll say it was a desperate act by a crazy FBI agent who fell in love with the man she was chasing."

It wasn't that far from the truth, but even if Jessup knew it he wouldn't sanction a jailbreak for it. There had to be another reason.

"I can't believe you're asking me to do this, sir. I expected you to tear my head off and order me to forget about Nick."

"I would have, and I'd still like to, but we believe one of the safe-deposit boxes in that vault contained a vial of smallpox," Jessup said. "Now the Road Runners have it. The smallpox was probably their target all along."

"How is that possible? Smallpox was eradicated decades ago, and the only samples that exist are at the CDC in Atlanta and a lab in Russia."

"Yes, that's been the general assumption."

"'Assumption'?"

"Well, it's not like somebody went around to every lab in the world and verified that each smallpox sample ever collected was destroyed. However, since nobody has been infected in forty years, the accepted belief is that the virus was wiped out and the only samples of the virus are secured."

"You're telling me that isn't true."

"In the early 1990s, a Soviet defector revealed to MI5 that the Russians were secretly developing a super-virulent strain of smallpox, in blatant violation of international agreements, through a civilian drug company called Biopreparat. After that came out, the U.S. and NATO threatened an all-out bioweapons arms race, so the Soviets caved, ended the program, and destroyed the smallpox."

"But not all of it," Kate said.

"They were in the midst of complying with international demands when the Soviet Union collapsed and descended into chaos. One of the bioweapons scientists, Sergei Andropov, fled Moscow with a vial of smallpox in his pocket to sell to the highest bidder. Sergei settled in Antwerp, where his cousin Yuri Baskin was a diamond merchant. But before Sergei could make a deal with anyone, he was killed in a car accident. The vial was never found."

"But you think Sergei gave it to Yuri," Kate said, "who stashed it in his safe-deposit box in the Executive Merchants Building vault and was afraid to touch it after his cousin's suspicious death."

"It was only a theory before, but now we're certain that's what happened," Jessup said. "The Belgian police found some of Sergei's research notes from Biopreparat on the floor of the vault along with a cigar-sized metal container that could be used to store a vial."

"How could the smallpox virus still be alive after all these years?" Kate asked, though she wasn't sure *alive* was the right word.

"The temperature in the vault was kept at a constant sixty degrees," Jessup said. "Even if the temperature wasn't controlled, we know the virus could still survive. A forty-five-year-old vial of smallpox was found two years ago in Washington, D.C., by a custodian. It was in a cardboard box in an unlocked closet at the National Institutes of Health. Testing of the sample at the CDC revealed it was still viable."

Kate was wide awake now. "That's frightening."

"Not as much as Dragan Kovic selling smallpox to ISIS or some rogue nation and what they might do with it. Smallpox is the deadliest virus humanity has ever known. It killed three hundred million people in the twentieth century alone. All you have to do is inhale one microscopic particle and you're infected. You become a walking chemical weapon that infects everyone within a ten-foot radius."

"Nobody is vaccinated for smallpox anymore," Kate said. "Most of the population has no immunity. The virus could spread at light-speed through a major city."

"That's the nightmare scenario," Jessup said. "You need to break Nick out of custody. Then the two of you have to retrieve that vial, find out what it was going to be used for, and stop the plot, whatever the hell it is."

"Yes, sir."

"And stop threatening to kill Cosmo."

Kate disconnected and set her iPhone on the bedside table. She reached down to her purse on the floor, dug around for the new disposable phone that her father had given her in the church, and hit the preprogrammed key that dialed his cell. He answered on the first ring.

"Jake O'Hare, Man of Action."

"I'm ready," Kate said.

Early Sunday morning, Kate put on her sweats and jogged into Stadspark, which had once been the site of a Spanish fort. She dashed across the footbridge, over a duck pond that had been part of the fort's moat, and then followed a paved trail as it snaked into a canopy of trees and bushes. She stopped at a stack of stones that appeared to have once been a man-made waterfall but that was dry and weedy now.

She made sure she was alone before retrieving blasting caps and a small brick of C4 plastic explosive that had been hidden there the night before by her father's buddy the arms dealer. She stuffed the goodies into her hidden running belt, jogged out of the park, and went shopping for duct tape, a razor blade, paper clips, and another disposable phone. The Meir, Antwerp's main shopping street, was lined with renovated medieval buildings shoulder to shoulder with modern re-creations. Every two feet there seemed be another Leonidas chocolate café, the Starbucks of Belgium. The Leonidas cafés were inescapable, so she surrendered and got herself a hot chocolate.

Kate was halfway across her hotel lobby when she was stopped by a paunchy forty-something man in a rumpled business suit. He had the bloated belly and pained expression of a man who'd been constipated for days, perhaps even months.

"Miss O'Hare?" the man asked, sizing Kate up from a computer-generated picture of her that he held in his hand.

Career bureaucrat, Kate thought, smiling politely. American. No doubt clogged up with schnitzel.

"Conrad Plitt," he said. "I'm attached to the U.S. embassy in Brussels."

"I was expecting to see an FBI legat," Kate said, referring

to the FBI legal attachés at U.S. embassies who worked with local law enforcement agencies on cases involving American interests.

"Sorry to dash your hopes, but sending an FBI agent here to deal with this muck-up would only worsen an already terrible situation," Plitt said. "It would imply to the Belgians that the FBI had prior knowledge of your actions or that they tacitly approve of your conduct. We can't have that. Besides, the FBI has notoriously poor diplomatic skills, which you've profoundly demonstrated already."

She might have been offended by his comment if it hadn't been totally true. Not to mention she was standing there holding the makings of a bomb in a grocery bag.

"What happens now?" she asked.

"My job is to convince the Belgians that despite your unorthodox and inappropriate conduct you're a hero and that the apprehension of Nicolas Fox is a win for everybody. If I can do that, I deserve the Nobel Peace Prize. The first step is for you to offer the Belgian authorities your total and unconditional cooperation with their investigation."

"I'd be glad to do that, but they've made it clear they don't want me involved."

"They still don't," Plitt said. "But Nicolas Fox does. He refuses to talk to anybody but you."

"He's playing with us," Chief Inspector Amelie Janssen said, clearly not pleased with the way things were proceeding.

"Of course he is," Kate said. "What did you expect?"

Kate was standing in an observation room, looking out at Nicolas Fox. He was sitting at an interrogation table, and he was wearing an orange jumpsuit, his wrists in handcuffs and his ankles in chains. And yet, he not only appeared relaxed and content, but somehow managed with his posture to make the hard, stiff chair seem incredibly comfortable. There was a time when his cool attitude would have irritated Kate as much as it obviously irked Janssen. Now Kate found it reassuring to see him in control of himself and his environment.

She hoped she appeared equally in control. If she did appear equally in control she thought it would be an acting miracle because she didn't *feel* in control. What she felt was *sick*. Not exactly on the verge of throwing up but moving in that direction. She was making a maximum effort to put up a hard-ass front. She'd decided on a role. She'd rehearsed her lines. She'd put some Imodium in her purse just in case.

Jeez Louise, she thought. This isn't my *thing*. I'm good at enforcing the law, not breaking the law. How did I get into this *mess*? She narrowed her eyes at Fox. It's *him*, she thought. It's my stupid obsession with Nicolas Fox.

"Are you okay?" Janssen asked Kate. "Your face is flushed."

"I'm fine," Kate said. "I'm just *angry*. I *hate* this guy."

Not far from the truth. She hated him. She liked him. She hated him. She liked him. And she especially hated him because he looked so damn good in his jumpsuit. It was just wrong, wrong, wrong.

Kate flipped through several pages of inventory itemizing everything that was stolen from the vault, with the notable exception of the vial of smallpox.

"He's a con man," Kate said. "Manipulating people is what he does for fun and profit."

"That's why it was a huge mistake for my bosses to give in to his demand that we bring you in. I warned them not to do it, but although they have badges, they are politicians, not police."

"Were you getting anywhere with him?"

"No, but now that you're here, it completely undercuts my authority in the interrogation. He'll think that he's the one in charge now. It won't be easy getting back the upper hand."

Kate put a paper clip on the papers. "If you want him to give you information, you're going to have to play his game."

Kate walked out of the observation room and into the hallway, where a uniformed guard stood outside the interrogation room door. Janssen nodded her approval at the officer, and he opened the door for Kate.

She strode into the interrogation room, sat down at the table, slipped the paper clip off the papers, and made a show of examining them. Everything Kate and Nick were about to say and do was for Janssen's benefit. But Kate also had a message to convey to Nick and a delivery to make.

"You're looking good," Kate said.

"Orange is my color."

"I'm referring to the handcuffs," Kate said. "You were born to wear them."

"They're a bit snug."

She looked up from her papers. "You're facing a long prison stretch, and once you get out there are a dozen countries lined up to lock you away again."

"I've always been a popular guy."

"It seems you weren't that popular with the Road Runners. They double-crossed you and got away with hundreds of millions in diamonds. That's got to hurt."

"I pulled off the biggest heist in Belgian history," Nick said. "Making history is not a bad way to end a career."

"You can thank your so-called friends for your grand finale. Tell me where they are and what they're doing with the diamonds. Maybe you can do a little less time. Where do we find Dragan Kovic?"

"Haven't you heard about honor among thieves?"

"They betrayed you."

Nick shrugged. "Not all thieves have honor."

Kate leaned forward. "I'm offering you your only chance for vengeance against the people who put you here."

"You put me here. Not talking is how I get my revenge." Nick leaned forward too. "Your screwups led to the success of the biggest diamond heist in Belgian history. You'll probably lose your badge."

Kate gathered up her papers, leaned back in her seat, and shook her head in disappointment.

"My job is done anyway. I vowed that I'd never let you get away, and I meant it." She got up and went to the door, pausing for a moment to take one more look at him before leaving. "Remember that on Monday morning when you're on your way to prison."

She walked out, satisfied that she'd delivered her message to Nick and more. Now Nick knew that she'd be making her move on Monday morning and, while they were nearly nose to nose over the table, he'd taken the paper clip she'd brought for him.

Janssen met Kate in the hall. "That was a waste of time."

"I wouldn't say that. I got him talking."

"But he didn't say anything," Janssen said.

"The man loves to hear his own voice. He'll give me something next time, and then something more after that, just to keep the conversation going. Before it's over, he'll give up the gang."

"There won't be another meeting." Janssen held out a plane ticket. "You're on the eleven A.M. flight Monday to Heathrow with a connecting flight to Los Angeles."

Kate didn't take the ticket. "I'm the only one he'll talk to and the only one with a shot at breaking him."

"While you are somewhere over the Atlantic, there will be a press conference here announcing the arrest by Belgian police of international fugitive Nicolas Fox, the mastermind behind the vault robbery. We'll thank the FBI for providing crucial resources, and that will be the end of U.S. involvement in our ongoing investigation and manhunt."

Plitt had done his job with surprising speed, Kate thought. Maybe he deserved a Nobel Prize after all. She took the ticket from Janssen.

"This is a mistake."

"Bon voyage, Agent O'Hare," Janssen said. "A police officer will be waiting at your hotel at nine A.M. to escort you to the airport."

With those words, Amelie Janssen officially set the timer ticking on Nicolas Fox's escape.

7

At 6:45 A.M. on Monday, Kate left her hotel for her morning run in a tank top, jogging shorts, and a running belt full of explosives.

She jogged a block west into Stadspark and quickly veered off the paved trails into a thicket of bushes where her father had stashed a gym bag that contained a loose black sweat suit, a black balaclava, and gloves. She pulled the clothes on over her own. The size and dark color of the sweats had been chosen to obscure her figure and allow her to pass for a man. Kate put the balaclava on her head, rolled up the face mask to form a rim across her brow, then dashed back out onto the path and out of the park.

Kate jogged up Bourlastraat and slowed to a walk as she approached Leopoldplaats, where four streets intersected around a statue of King Leopold on horseback. There was a lattice of electric cables overhead that powered the trams that crisscrossed the plaza every few minutes. She stopped and pressed her back against the wall of the 150-year-old three-story stone building that occupied the corner. The building had a tower with a dome shaped like a wizard's hat and topped with a spire that looked to her like a boa constrictor that had swallowed a basketball. It was why Kate had picked that spot to wait. Nobody glancing in her direction would notice her with all of that Gothic gaudiness screaming for attention.

She surveyed the scene. Most of the cafés and shops that ringed the plaza hadn't yet opened. The vehicle traffic was light in all directions, and only a few people were on the streets. On the south side of the plaza, a huge garbage truck idled at the corner of a side street, facing the plaza and alongside a parking area for bikes, scooters, and motorcycles. An especially observant passerby might have noticed that two of the motorcycles, parked side-by-side, had keys in their ignitions.

The trap was set. Now all they needed was the mouse.

At that moment, a handcuffed and ankle-chained Nicolas Fox was led out of the back door of the police station by two uniformed police officers and guided into the back of a paddy wagon. Nick climbed up into the van and sat on one of the two metal benches. The only window was the mesh-covered porthole into the front crew cab. One of the officers secured

Nick with a seatbelt and shut the thick rear door, locking it from the outside.

The two officers climbed into the front, which had special windows designed to withstand the impact of rocks and other hard objects typically thrown at cops in riot situations. But they weren't heading into a riot. This was just a routine prisoner transport, one of many they did each day, and they had no reason for concern. So after they drove off, neither one of the officers glanced over their shoulders into the porthole to see what Nick was up to. If they had, they might have seen him spit a paper clip into his hands.

Nick figured the trip to the new Palace of Justice near the banks of the Schelde River would take twenty minutes at most. They would travel east on a street that changed names four times, then southwest on a wide tree-lined boulevard that changed its name five times and then followed the path of the walls that once ringed the ancient city. The Palace of Justice's distinctive roofline, evoking the masts and sails of the ships that once traveled the river, made it look like the police were delivering prisoners for a cruise instead of a jail sentence. But Nick knew the van wouldn't be reaching its destination this morning and, being an experienced criminal, he had a pretty good idea where Kate would be making her move.

He easily unlocked his handcuffs and chains with the paper clip and braced himself for action as the van rolled into Leopoldplaats.

. . .

Kate pulled the balaclava's mask down over her face as the paddy wagon entered the plaza from the west. The garbage truck charged out of the northbound street like a freight train, T-boned the paddy wagon on the passenger side, and bulldozed it into the wide stone base of the King Leopold statue.

The two dazed but uninjured police officers were trapped in the crew cab. The driver's side door was pinned against the statue while the passenger side was smashed against the huge grill of the garbage truck, which was driven by Jake, his face hidden behind a balaclava.

Kate ran to the back of the paddy wagon and took the explosive out of her belt. The bomb looked like a cellphone and spark plugs wrapped in white Silly Putty. She hammered the door with her fist, then stuck the bomb to the door, right on top of the locking mechanism.

"Cover your ears and hit the floor," she said in her most manly impersonation. "And pray we didn't use too much C4."

Nick immediately flattened himself facedown between the benches and pressed his hands against his ears. He hoped any shrapnel from the door would pass over his head.

The two officers heard the warning too, and kicked at the windshield with their feet, but it was futile. The glass was designed to withstand much worse abuse. Jake ducked down under the dashboard of his truck.

Kate ran back the way she came, and as she did, she hit

a key on the cellphone in her pocket that auto-dialed the phone that was wrapped in the C4. The bomb exploded like a thunderclap, the sound echoing off the buildings in the plaza.

Nick sat up, his ears ringing, and saw daylight through the jagged, smoking hole in the steel door where the locking mechanism had been. He pushed the door open and jumped into the street. He saw a figure in black running away, assumed it was Kate, and was about to follow her when someone grabbed his arm and he heard a familiar voice.

"Your ride is this way," Jake said, gesturing to the two motorcycles parked across the street.

"Thanks for coming," Nick said.

"My pleasure. Nothing beats a jailbreak for fun and wholesome father-daughter bonding." Jake glanced back at the two furious officers. One of them was already on the radio, calling for backup. "We've got to go."

They dashed across the street and jumped onto the motorcycles. Jake took off first across the plaza and Nick followed his lead just as a tram passed behind them, blocking the officers from seeing which way they went.

Nick looked for Kate as they sped away, but she was gone.

Kate didn't have a lot of time. The police were coming to the hotel in less than an hour to escort her to the airport. She ran back to the park and into some bushes, removed her black clothes, covered them with dirt and leaves, and dashed out onto the trail again in her original jogging attire.

She returned to the hotel at 8:15 covered in sweat. She smiled politely at the man at the front desk as she caught her breath at the elevator.

Jake led Nick into an underground garage a few blocks away from Leopoldplaats. They rode their motorcycles down two levels to a stolen Renault that Jake had parked there. There was a set of clothes for Nick folded neatly on the backseat. He quickly changed out of his orange jumpsuit into a polo shirt, jeans, and running shoes. Jake handed him the car keys, five hundred euros, a disposable phone, and a pair of Ray-Ban sunglasses.

"Is there anything else you need?" Jake asked, pulling off his balaclava.

"This is more than enough. In fact, it's too much." Nick tossed the car keys back to Jake. "I can find my own way out of the city."

"Are you sure?" Jake said.

"Evading capture isn't much of a challenge now that Europe has open borders," Nick said. "The only way a fugitive can get caught these days is if he gives himself up."

Nick shook Jake's hand, slipped the Ray-Bans onto his face, and sauntered casually to the stairwell.

Kate showered, changed into a T-shirt and jeans, grabbed her go bag, and got down to the lobby promptly at nine. No airport escort in sight. She heard sirens and honking horns coming from the street and the rumble of helicopters flying low overhead. Nick's explosive escape and the police response had created a traffic nightmare throughout the city.

She found a couch that had a view of the door and the street beyond, picked up a day-old issue of *USA Today* from the coffee table, and flipped through it while she waited patiently for her escort to arrive.

Her iPhone rang at 10 A.M.

"Hey, Katie Bug," Cosmo said. "Where are you? I bet you're out of country, right? That's so cool. You're like James Bond only you're a girl. Did you see him in *Spectre*? Man, I loved when he blew up that building in the beginning. And then did you see the part where he kicked the guy out of the helicopter? I want to kick a guy out of a helicopter someday. That would be so cool, right? Did you ever kick someone out of a helicopter?"

"I'm kind of busy right now, Cosmo."

"I know. I know. I hate to bother you, but Jessup needs your form HB7757Q."

"I thought you needed SQ009?"

"That one too. HB7757Q is for hotel rooms exceeding your allowed per diem. You probably don't have anything to put on that one, right? I mean, how much could you spend on a room? I stayed at a Hampton Inn once and I got free breakfast. It was awesome. I could fill these out for you if you want. You could just give me the info and I could fill out the forms. I could go to wherever you are or you could come here. If it's after hours you could come to my house. I know how to make Swedish meatballs in a toaster oven and I have some apricot schnapps."

"Yeah, that sounds good, but I don't think I can do any of that right now."

"Or we could just have mixed nuts. I get them in bulk at Costco."

Kate disconnected. She felt very righteous because she hadn't threatened to shoot him.

A white Opel Astra pulled up in front of the hotel, and Amelie Janssen emerged. The chief inspector had a grim expression on her face and walked into the lobby like someone facing a triple root canal followed by a colonoscopy. Kate stood up, grabbed her bag, and met Janssen at the door.

"This is a surprise," Kate said. "I was expecting a rookie cop and a ride to the airport in the backseat of a filthy patrol car."

"That was the plan," Janssen said, "but there was an incident this morning and I wanted you to hear about it from me personally."

"What kind of incident?"

Janssen put her hands on her hips, instinctively staking her position and bracing herself for the unpleasant experience to come. "Fox escaped."

Kate swore, turned her back to Janssen, and took a few steps away, putting some distance between her and the chief inspector while presumably getting a grip on her anger. The truth was that Kate didn't have much faith in her acting skills and was afraid her performance would ring false eye to eye.

The truth was, she was struggling not to smile. Kate took a deep breath and faced Janssen again. Now if Kate wasn't showing her rage, Janssen would chalk it up to admirable self-control.

"How did it happen?" Kate asked, her words clipped, her voice flat.

"The prisoner transport vehicle carrying Fox to court was rammed by a garbage truck. Two assailants blasted open the transport with explosives. Fox and the assailants escaped on motorcycles. Nobody was hurt, and the whole thing was over in two minutes. It was a professional job, crude in its simplicity, but executed with precision."

"Another Road Runner smash-and-grab, only this time they took Fox instead of diamonds," Kate said, stepping up to Janssen again. "It's right out of their playbook."

"So it is, and that means they've already split up and will be out of the country within a few hours, if they aren't already. But we'll launch an intense manhunt for Fox anyway and notify international authorities to be on high alert."

"That explains why Fox wouldn't give me anything on the Road Runners," Kate said. "It wasn't about honor. He knew they'd be coming back for him."

8

The most wanted man in Belgium wasn't thinking about who might be pursuing him. He was enjoying a croissant, a selection of fresh fruit, a yogurt, and a hot cup of coffee in his leather seat in the first-class compartment of the Thalys high-speed train to Paris. He'd arrive at Gare du Nord station in forty minutes. This, Nicolas Fox thought, was the civilized way to break out of jail.

He wasn't worried about being spotted by any police officers that might be waiting to greet the train. The authorities were frantically searching for a fugitive, and he didn't look like one. A person's appearance, Nick had learned, was as much about attitude as facial features and build. The Ray-Bans and the relaxed, unhurried gait of a man preoccupied by the email on his phone were all he'd need to become essentially invisible. He would blend into the crowd on the train platform and let the stream of humanity carry him out into the city.

Nick sipped his coffee, settled back in his seat, and fantasized about what his reunion with Kate O'Hare would be like. He wouldn't mind if they were both naked.

Kate flew to Heathrow Airport in London but intentionally missed her connecting flight to Los Angeles. She wasn't going to leave Europe until Dragan Kovic was out of business, and she and Nick had recovered the smallpox.

She hadn't heard from Nick yet, but before she'd left Antwerp, she received a text from her father in Amsterdam. He was boarding a flight to Los Angeles. His successful escape gave Kate some peace of mind and some assurance that Nick had also got out of Belgium safely.

Kate's idea of airport shopping was Sunglass Hut and See's Candy, so she was surprised to discover Caviar House & Prunier as she walked through the terminal. She was wondering how many people cracked open a $400 tin of fish eggs for an in-flight snack, when her cellphone vibrated, announcing the receipt of a text message. It was a street address in Bois-le-Roi, France, from "Dr. Richard Kimble," the hero of the classic TV series *The Fugitive*. Nick was safe and waiting for her.

She looked up the address on Google Maps and booked the first available flight to Paris. Ninety minutes later, she arrived at Charles de Gaulle Airport, where she rented a compact

Citroën with a stick shift and drove the seventy-five kilometers south to Bois-le-Roi.

It was nightfall by the time she reached the tiny village, located where the dense Fontainebleau forest met a bend in the Seine. The streets were narrow, potholed, and uneven. Her car bumped along past old homes made of stone, their windows bordered with heavy shutters that had protected the inhabitants over the centuries against harsh weather and even harsher invaders.

Kate passed through the village and continued down a road that was little more than a rutted path. It ended at a property ringed by a low, rough wall cobbled together out of sharp jutting rocks and bricks and mortar. She drove through the open gate, her tires crunching on the loose gravel, and gaped at the house in front of her. Low-slung and sprawling, it was mostly stone with a leaf-strewn, sagging tiled roof. Smoke curled out of the two lopsided chimneys, and flickering candlelight glowed behind the windows.

Kate thought the picture would be complete if the Seven Dwarfs were standing in front of the house singing "Heigh-ho, heigh-ho!" It was a house that belonged in a children's storybook. It was cozy and warm and inviting.

The front door opened and Nick stepped out. He was casually dressed in a cable-knit sweater and khaki slacks. Classic attire for the country gentleman welcoming a visitor to his bucolic home.

Kate got out of the car and walked toward him. The

fairy-tale image of the Seven Dwarfs faded and was replaced with the Big Bad Wolf luring Little Red Riding Hood into his lair.

"You're the woman of my dreams," Nick said.

"I bet you say that to every woman who breaks you out of jail."

"Only the FBI agents."

"I feel like I've given myself completely to the dark side."

"Not completely," he said, "but I have plans to finish the process."

"Do those plans involve a glass of wine?" Kate asked.

"I have an excellent burgundy."

Kate shucked her jacket and took the glass of wine from Nick. "I hadn't expected to find you in a country cottage. I've always thought of you as more black glass and chrome."

Nick looked around. "It's a pleasant refuge. It's actually one of my favorite places."

Kate tasted the wine. "Is this home?"

He settled his hands at her waist and pulled her close. "Home is an elusive concept for me." He took her glass, set it on an end table, and kissed her. The first kiss was feather light. The second lingered. The third kiss was full-on passion. When they broke from the third kiss, Kate was unbuttoned and missing her underwear.

"So soft," Nick murmured, his hand on her breast.

Not so much him, Kate thought. He was the opposite of soft. He was . . . holy moly.

. . .

Kate had no idea what time it was when she awoke next to Nick in the huge four-poster bed, only that it was a new day. A gentle breeze drifted through the half-open windows, rustling the curtains and carrying with it the woodsy scent of the forest.

She sat up and looked at the white plastered walls, the hardwood floors, the thick, rough-hewn wood beams across the ceiling, and the collection of meticulously detailed ships in bottles displayed on shelves around the room.

"What is this place?" she asked.

"Just one of my little European hideaways."

"How many do you have?"

"I try not to keep much cash in banks. I know how easily they can be broken into. So I put most of my money into real estate. It's hard to steal a house, though I've done it."

"I'm sure there's nothing you haven't stolen." She picked up a ship in a bottle off the nightstand and examined the elaborate galleon. "Did you steal this as well?"

"My neighbor's hobby is making those, and he can't stop. His home is full of them so he gives them away to everybody in town. The rest end up here. I don't mind. He looks after the house and the Jag for me while I'm away."

She put the bottle back on the nightstand. "'The Jag'?"

"I've got a restored 1966 Jaguar E-Type convertible in the barn."

"Of course you do."

"If you're nice to me I'll take you for a ride."

73

"I have to be nice *again*?"

He kissed her bare shoulder. "If you want to go for a ride."

Being *nice* to Nick was now at the top of Kate's list of favorite things. It was even ahead of parachuting out of a plane. Being *nice* to him had rewards for her that could only be described in terms of volcanic eruptions.

"Okay," Kate said, "but we have to speed it up. We have work to do."

"Honey, you can't put a time limit on perfection. And it's too late to recover the diamonds, if that's what you're thinking. The loot was split up immediately after the heist, and the diamonds are being recut, so they'll be unidentifiable. Most of them will end up back in Antwerp soon, bartered and sold by the same merchants that they were stolen from."

"It's not about the diamonds," Kate said. "You were right. That wasn't what Dragan was really after. It was a vial of smallpox. We have orders from Jessup to find Dragan Kovic, recover the smallpox, and discover what he's plotting."

"That's serious," Nick said, taking a lingering look under the bed linens at Kate. "Give me ten minutes, tops."

"Deal."

Kate dug into her breakfast of hot chocolate, fresh croissants, and cheese. "That ran longer than ten minutes."

"Not my bad," Nick said. "I could have been done in *three* minutes."

"I had a concentration problem. My mind kept wandering back to how we're going to find Dragan."

"Finding Dragan is going to be easy. After a job, most of his gang goes back to their home turf in Serbia, and he hides out in Italy. That's where he does all his business and where the corrupt authorities, under the finger of the Naples and Turin mafia, protect him. I know that he's somewhere on the Amalfi Coast, so that's where we'll go and make ourselves obvious."

"What will you do when you meet him?"

"Offer to join the Road Runners, of course," Nick said. "Working on the inside is the only way we'll find out what happened to the smallpox and why he wanted it."

"What makes you think he'll take you back?"

"It's either that or he'll kill me."

"And if *that's* what he decides to do?"

"You'll stop him," Nick said. "That's your role in this charade. You'll be my bodyguard, partner in thieving, and sex therapist."

"Works for me," Kate said.

Nick and Kate arrived in Sorrento, Italy, that night. It had been a five-hour journey to get there. It took one hour to drive by limousine from Bois-le-Roi to the airport, two hours to fly by private jet to Naples, and finally forty minutes by yacht to cross Naples Bay. The yacht was graciously provided by the Hotel Vittorio Sorrentum, the world-class five-star resort where Nick had booked a suite with bay views.

Sorrento was an ancient resort town perched high atop the peninsula's sheer cliffs and squeezed between craggy mountains and a deep gorge. The temperate Mediterranean climate, combined with a unique location that was easy to defend and hard to attack, made Sorrento the perfect getaway for the wealthy, the powerful, and the detested of ancient Greece and the Roman Empire. It was a place where they could sip *limoncello,* gorge on pasta, and engage in their favorite debaucheries without worrying too much about their own safety. Dragan Kovic's presence here proved that was still the case.

The Hotel Vittorio Sorrentum, where Nick and Kate were staying, was two hundred years old and built atop the ruins of a Roman emperor's villa. The hotel was perched on the edge of a high cliff overlooking Naples Bay, the yacht harbor, and the swimming docks below. Their suite had elaborate frescoes on the ceiling, was furnished with antiques, and had a long veranda facing the moonlit sea. Two shot glasses filled with ice-cold *limoncello,* Sorrento's famous lemon liqueur, were waiting for them on a silver tray on the dining table when they came in.

"Criminy," Kate said. "What did this cost? Couldn't you have just gotten a room? Did we really need a suite with a view? How am I going to explain this to Jessup? What am I going to do about form HB7757Q?"

"Tell Jessup the suite came with complimentary *limoncello*."

Kate knocked back her *limoncello*. "The Hampton Inn gives you free breakfast."

"I don't think there's a Hampton Inn in Sorrento."

"Just saying."

Kate looked out the window at Mount Vesuvius in the distance. "Do you think Dragan has heard you're here?"

"He knew before we arrived. I registered in the hotel under my last alias, Nick Sweet, the one Dragan used to find me in Hawaii."

"Then he'll know that you want to be found."

"We're playing a game. The next move is his. Let's stretch our legs and take a walk through town."

"Let me get my tourist essentials and we'll go."

Kate removed a Glock and a combat knife from her suitcase. Nick had acquired them for her from his disreputable sources before they left France.

She put the wrinkled blue blazer on over her blouse to hide her gun and slipped the knife into an ankle sheath.

Nick was wearing a perfectly ironed white linen shirt and tan slacks.

"Nice shirt," Kate said.

He tugged on one of his sleeves. "Handmade by Jean Philippe, Singapore."

Kate tugged on her blazer sleeve. "T.J.Maxx, Tarzana."

They took the elevator down to the lobby, walked through the lush flower garden, and emerged onto Piazza Tasso, the town square that spanned the deep gorge that for centuries cleaved Sorrento in half. The plaza was defined by a bright yellow baroque church, cafés, and bars with crowded outdoor seating. Corso Italia, Sorrento's central thoroughfare, was closed off to vehicle traffic at nightfall and was jam-packed with people out for a stroll.

Nick and Kate slipped into the flow of people moving down the brightly lit street past clothing stores, gelato shops, and the occasional British pub catering to the annual contingent of rowdy U.K. tourists. There was a party atmosphere on the boulevard but, as exuberant and alcohol-fueled as it was, it felt to Kate more like a kid's birthday celebration at Chuck E. Cheese's than Mardi Gras in New Orleans. The only danger she sensed came from two men who'd been following them since they'd left the hotel.

"Let me show you the old town," Nick said, making an abrupt turn down an alley, not much wider than a footpath. The alley led to Via San Cesareo, a pedestrian-only street that was barely wide enough for two lines of people walking single file in each direction.

Kate could smell garlic, lemon, fish, cooking fat, and leather as they passed the open restaurants and shops. The scent of sweat, tobacco, sunscreen, and perfume came off the crush of people.

"This was the site of the original walled city, built by the Greeks centuries before the birth of Christ," Nick said. "The buildings are tall and the streets are intentionally narrow to keep people in the shadows and cool in the heat."

Everywhere she looked, there was someone selling fresh *limoncello* and countless other lemon-infused products, from candy and soap to candles and lipstick. There were also shops selling tiles, sandals, paintings, leather bags, pottery, and other handmade goods. All produced by tired artisans who were right there, hunched over their worktables, as if to prove everything was locally made.

Some people a few steps ahead stopped to sample the *limoncello* being offered by two rival shopkeepers on opposite sides of the street, causing a foot traffic jam that pushed Kate up against Nick's back for a moment.

"It's a pickpocket's dream here," Kate said.

"Not a bad place for an ambush or a stabbing, either."

"You saw the men behind us," she said.

"There were two more walking toward us before we came down here," Nick said. "They are probably waiting in one of the alleys coming up."

"You led us into a trap."

"I thought I was leading *them* into one." Nick looked over his shoulder at her. "Or was I mistaken?"

She smiled at him. "You're not. Go into that leather store on your left and head to the back."

They passed the warring *limoncello* merchants and entered a tiny shop stuffed with handmade leather goods. Hundreds of purses, handbags, belts, and satchels hung from the ceiling and walls. In the back of the store, surrounded by scraps of leather, an old man was sewing a handbag.

Kate backed into a cranny beside the door while Nick moved further into the store, pretending to admire a messenger bag. She took a belt off the wall, looped it through its buckle to create a choke collar, and waited.

A moment later, one of their pursuers stepped in. She dropped the belt loop over his head, cinched it tight around his neck, and yanked him back against her. He began to struggle, but abruptly stopped when he felt the sharp tip of her knife against his spine.

"If I jam my knife between these vertebrae, I'll cut the nerves that control your lungs. You'll suffocate from a stab wound," she whispered into his ear. "At least I think so. I've never had a chance to try it. But I'm eager to see if it works."

Hard to tell if the man understood English. Good to see that he understood the seriousness of the knife at his back.

Nick stepped up, removed the gun that the man had half-tucked into his pants, and aimed it at the doorway as the second man came inside.

"Good evening," Nick said. "Come in and join us."

The second man saw the situation his partner was in, and the gun aimed at his own gut, and raised his hands.

"Drop your gun in a handbag," Nick said. The man did as he was told, dropping the gun into the nearest open purse. "Now, gentlemen, do you speak English?"

They nodded yes.

"What was the plan this evening?" Nick asked them.

"We were told to bring you to see Mr. Kovic," the man in

the doorway said, speaking with a thick Serbian accent. "For a friendly talk."

Kate tugged on the belt, tightening it around her prisoner's neck. "What about the two men waiting up ahead? What were they going to do?"

"Box you in so we could take you down to the car on Via Accademia. That's all. Nobody was supposed to get hurt."

"Tell Dragan I'd be glad to talk with him," Nick said. "He's warmly invited for breakfast tomorrow on the terrace of my hotel. Say around eight?"

"He won't like this," the man in the doorway said.

"Tell him the lemon tarts are excellent," Nick said.

Kate removed the belt and stepped back.

Nick kept his gun on the men as they left, then he dropped it into the purse with the second man's gun. Kate slipped her knife back into her ankle sheath, and Nick carried the purse up to the old man, who was still working on his bag. The old man was unperturbed, as if incidents like this happened in his store every day.

"We'd like this purse, please," Nick said.

"That will be a hundred euros," the old man said.

"The price tag says fifty," Nick said.

"That's the price of a purse," the old man said. "Gun totes are more expensive."

Nick paid him the hundred euros and they left the store.

9

Nick and Kate had dinner in their suite. Smoked red sea bream with a salty cinnamon brioche as an appetizer, followed by seaweed pasta with Venus clams, sea urchins, and chives as their entrée, and warm lemon cake with a lemon sorbet for dessert. They finished their meal with the obligatory icy shots of *limoncello*.

"The seaweed and sea urchins were okay," Kate said, "but they're never going to replace mac and cheese."

Nick sat back and watched Kate. "No matter where you go, you are who you are. You're willing to try new things but more often than not you return to your cultural roots. I like that about you."

"And you're the opposite," Kate said. "You embrace your

environment. You're a human chameleon. It's impressive, but sometimes I wonder if you've lost yourself. When you're playing a role, are you standing on the outside looking in, or have you become that person and kicked Nick to the curb?"

"Some of both," Nick said. "When I'm in a con I'm outside, looking in. When I'm in my French country house I'm enjoying that part of me."

"And which one is the seaweed and sea urchin Nick?"

"I like them. I have an adventuresome palate."

Kate thought his adventuresome palate was at least partly responsible for their new sexual relationship. Like seaweed and sea urchin, he would continue to enjoy her when their paths crossed, but she couldn't see him settling for the monotony of monogamy. And she couldn't see herself justifying the relationship once this assignment was completed. She had serious feelings for Nick, but in the end he was a felon and she was the FBI.

In the morning they showered, dressed, and went down to the lobby restaurant for breakfast on the wide terrace that jutted out over the cliff. The low stone wall along the edge of the terrace was adorned every few feet with marble busts of ripped men and voluptuous women. Perhaps the busts were an incentive, Kate thought, to encourage guests to take it easy at the buffet.

Nick selected a table facing west, giving them a view

across the gorge to Sorrento, the bay, and the villas along the mountainous peninsula. Kate, being Nick's bodyguard, sat with her back to the view, preferring to keep her eye on the hotel and anybody who came out to the terrace. She was the first to see Litija stroll toward them like she was on a fashion show runway. Litija was wearing a wide-brimmed red sun hat, enormous round sunglasses, a white skintight dress with bracelet sleeves and a very short skirt that Kate thought could use a couple more inches of material.

Litija came up behind Nick and bent down to kiss his cheek. "Nick, you devil. Who let you out?"

"She did." Nick tipped his head to Kate and stood up to pull out a chair for Litija. "I'd be under lock and key if it wasn't for Kate."

"Proving once again that behind every great man is a resourceful woman," Litija said, offering her hand to Kate as she sat down. "I am Litija."

Kate shook her hand. "So, does this mean Dragan has you to thank for his success?"

"I wouldn't be that presumptuous." Litija smiled, plucked a grape from the fruit bowl, and popped it into her mouth. "He has lots of women. I'm just here having a little vacation after spending months in dreary Antwerp."

"Will he be joining us?" Nick asked.

"Don't be ridiculous," Litija said. "He can't take the risk of being seen in public with you. You're a wanted man."

"So is he," Nick said.

"But he didn't just escape from Belgian police custody. You're the most wanted man in Europe right now."

"He put me in that situation."

Litija took another grape. "That's something you two can discuss at his villa. It's beautiful, right on the coast. His boat is waiting to take us there."

"I don't think that's a wise idea, based on the welcome we got last night," Nick said.

"That was an unfortunate misunderstanding. Dragan is a careful man and all he wanted to do was invite you over for a drink," Litija said. "His overly cautious approach can sometimes come across as unintentionally rude."

"At least it was more polite than kidnapping Nick at gunpoint and shipping him overseas in a coffin," Kate said.

"That's true!" Litija laughed and wagged a finger at Kate. "I like the way you think. But I wouldn't talk to Dragan like that. He doesn't have a great sense of humor."

"I'd really like to avoid another journey in a coffin, especially one that lasts an eternity," Nick said. "That's why I'd prefer meeting him in daylight in a public place."

"You won't be in any danger at Dragan's villa," Litija said. "If you're worried, bring your weapons. You can have a gun in each hand and a knife in your teeth if that makes you feel better. Nobody will take them away from you."

"I can guarantee that," Kate said.

"That's what I've heard," Litija said, then turned back to Nick. "So, really, Dragan is the one who should be concerned about his safety, not you. What possible reason can you have for not accepting his invitation now?"

"None at all," Nick said. "Shall we go?"

"He can wait." Litija reached for a croissant. "I haven't had breakfast and I love the *sfogliatelle* here. Have you ordered a bottle of champagne yet?"

"Coming right up," Nick said, and waved to the waiter.

Kate didn't know what the heck a *sfogliatelle* was but she suspected it would be expensive. And champagne. *Ka-ching!* She hoped there was a lot of space for itemizing on form HB7757Q.

Dragan's fifty-foot open-air yacht was classically Italian in its styling, rich in polished mahogany and supple leather, with the sculpted lines of a sports car and the iconic aura of a movie star. The pilot and deckhand, nautically dressed in jaunty blue sailor caps and white Paul & Shark polos and shorts, were the two men that Nick and Kate had confronted the previous night. If the men held a grudge, they didn't show it, though they definitely seemed uncomfortable in their uniforms.

Kate thought they looked like they were auditioning for jobs at Disney World, all suited up in Mr. Smee outfits.

The men seated Nick, Kate, and Litija on board, untethered the lines from the dock, and steered the boat out of the marina.

They maneuvered past the anchored yachts and around the coming-and-going ferries that served Naples, Capri, and the resort towns further south along the Amalfi Coast.

"This is the scenic route to Dragan's villa," Litija said as they cruised past Marina Grande, a fishing village nestled in a cove below Sorrento. "It's also the most direct. For centuries, the only way to get to his villa was by foot or by donkey. Can you see me on a donkey?"

They headed south on the choppy turquoise sea with the high jagged cliffs and rocky coves of the Sorrento peninsula on their left and the mountainous island of Capri on their right. The edge of the peninsula was largely undeveloped, covered in chestnut trees and scrub, too steep and rough in most places for anything but the occasional stone watchtower, a vestige of the time when pirates and invaders were a constant threat, and observers sent out smoke signals to warn of imminent attacks.

There was no doubt in Kate's mind that one or two of the towers were still manned. Dragan's men would be watching, sending back the modern-day version of a smoke signal alerting Dragan of anyone venturing into his territory.

The boat veered toward a sharp gorge. As they got closer, she could see that the gorge created a small cove hidden behind two tall rock formations that looked like stone fists rising up from the sea.

The water inside the cove was calm and lapped on a

pebbled beach that gave way to a stacked rock sea wall and wooden dock. The ruins of an old village built in the bedrock reminded Kate of caves, and she was fascinated with the elaborate Moorish façades.

Above the village, she could see terraces and tunnels cut into the cliff face. Steep, winding steps led up to a large stone building on a craggy point. The building was an architectural Frankenstein that combined the ruins of a church, a fortress, and a villa with a long sea-facing terrace and battlements along the precipice. It would be a long walk up, and Kate was looking forward to seeing Litija attempt it in her five-inch stiletto heels.

Nick looked at the cliff face. "Chairlift?" he asked.

"Better than that," Litija said. "There's an elevator."

She led them along the sea wall to one of the buildings embedded in the hillside. They took a few steps inside, where an elevator was cut into the rock. Litija pressed the call button, and the door slid open.

"This shaft has been here for centuries," Litija said. "I can't remember what for. There are all kinds of passages and shafts here. But Dragan stuck an elevator in this one, which is a good thing, because with these heels, I'd never be able to climb a thousand limestone steps."

Damn, Kate thought. She'd been ready to race the bitch.

The three of them stepped into the elevator, which was large enough for six, and Kate thought it went up faster and smoother than the one in the Federal Building in Los Angeles.

Apparently, international diamond thieves could afford better contractors than the U.S. government.

Kate brushed her jacket back and put her hand on her gun just in case there was an unwelcoming welcome committee. Litija noticed and smiled.

"A Glock 27. Nice. I prefer the Sig Sauer P239," Litija said. "But there's nowhere to hide it on this dress."

"You could put it under your hat," Kate said.

"That's where I keep my garrote," she said.

The elevator stopped and the doors opened onto the terrace. Kate was expecting a militaristic vibe, something in keeping with a fugitive criminal's stronghold. What she saw instead could have been a five-star resort. There were a dozen chaise lounges facing the sea. A deep blue lap pool hugged the hillside and was fed by a little waterfall. A long arched colonnade draped in blooming bougainvillea led to the villa. Dragan Kovic, dressed in all black, looked out of place in his colorful surroundings.

Dragan stood at the edge of the terrace beside a mounted telescope aimed at Capri. He wore a linen Nehru jacket open over a silk T-shirt, skinny jeans, and loafers.

"Nick, it's so good to see you," Dragan said. "Congratulations on your remarkable escape, though I think you owe your inspiration to us."

"If not my inspiration," Nick said, "certainly my motivation."

"Did you come here to kill me?"

"I'm not a killer," Nick said.

Dragan looked over at Kate. "No, but I suspect she is."

Kate had her eyes on the man beside Dragan. He looked like he'd shaved his face with an outboard motor and was regarding her as if she were livestock on an auction block.

"I can be," Kate said. "If I'm provoked."

Dragan followed her gaze. "Zarko and I will be on our best behavior."

"I wish that had been your attitude on the diamond heist," Nick said. "Instead, you double-crossed me, cheated me out of my share, and left me to take the fall."

"I heard that you put yourself in that position," Dragan said.

"How could I have possibly done that?"

"Zarko told me that you tried to escape with some diamonds while the men were preoccupied breaking open the safe-deposit boxes."

"That's what he did." Zarko looked Nick in the eye as he lied. "So I put him down. He may have just been sneaking off, but I think it was more than that. He wanted payback for snatching him in Hawaii. He was going to slip away with some diamonds and trip a silent alarm so we'd get caught. If I hadn't stopped him, your best men would be in jail and you'd be the humiliated victim of one of his famous cons."

"Turning my own heist against me and walking away richer for it," Dragan said. "That sounds like a trademark Nick Fox con to me."

"I admit I wasn't thrilled about being kidnapped, but I have too much pride in my work to sabotage a chance to pull off the biggest heist in Belgian history," Nick said. "By breaking into that vault, I did something everybody thought was impossible. Having that feather in my cap is worth more to me than a pocket full of diamonds. More important, I would never double-cross my crew, even one that kidnapped me. I have my reputation to consider."

Dragan glanced at Zarko. "He makes a good point."

"Of course he does, he's a con man," Zarko said. "He'll turn any situation to his advantage with fast talk. Look how he went from being your hostage to being a partner in the heist."

Litija laughed and stretched out on a chaise lounge. "He's got you there, Nick. That was slick."

"There's a lot to think about," Dragan said. "But we'll sort it out to everyone's satisfaction before the day is done, I promise you. In the meantime, I hope you'll make yourselves at home here at Villa Spintria."

"Is this a brothel?" Nick asked.

Dragan cocked his head, clearly amused. "Why would you say a thing like that?"

"Because *spintriae* were ancient Roman coins that depicted an astonishing variety of sex acts and were used to pay prostitutes."

"I'm impressed, though I suppose when it comes to money, even coinage as rare as *spintriae,* you would know about it," Dragan said. "This place has been many things, including a monastery and a fortress. During the restoration of the property, barn, and orchards, we unearthed some *spintriae*. Perhaps they spilled from the pocket of a soldier or were a prized possession of a lecherous monk. We'll never know."

"They're adorable," Litija said, pulling a necklace from under her collar. There was a spintria coin dangling from the gold chain.

Adorable was not the adjective Kate would have used to describe the position, or the sex act, that the woman and two men were demonstrating on the coin.

Nick leaned down to Litija's chest for a closer look at the coin. "If the U.S. Treasury put that on coins instead of dead presidents, coin collecting would become every boy's favorite hobby."

"What you may not know is that *spintriae* is also what Roman emperor Tiberius called the men and women he brought to his villa on Capri to pleasure him," Dragan said. "Those who didn't please him got tossed off a three-hundred-meter cliff to the sea. That spot became known as the Salto di Tiberio, the Tiberius Drop. You can see it from here. Come take a look."

He patted the telescope, which was beside a squared opening in the low wall where a cannon once stood. The opening made Kate nervous, given the topic of Dragan's little speech. But if Nick was concerned, he didn't act that way. He walked up to the telescope and peered through it. Kate kept her hand on her gun, ready to shoot Dragan if he made a move on Nick.

"There's not much to see," Nick said. "Just some crumbling walls."

"It was magnificent in its day," Dragan said. "I wanted to re-create the splendor of his villa and his pursuit of pleasure, without the debauchery."

Zarko snorted. "Where's the fun in that?"

Dragan shoved Zarko over the wall.

The sudden, violent action took them all by surprise. One second Zarko was standing there, and the next he was gone. Litija bolted up from her chaise lounge in shock. Kate drew her gun out of reflex. Nick took a slight step back from the wall, but otherwise kept his calm.

No one was more surprised than Zarko, who was so astonished to be plunging to certain death that he didn't start screaming until an instant before hitting the rocks below.

"But I did like the Tiberius Drop," Dragan said in a matter-of-fact way. "So all of that considered, Villa Spintria seemed like a fitting name for this place. I hope that answers your question, Nick, and resolves some of our issues."

Nick peeked over the edge at the rocks below. "It's a step in the right direction."

"I'm glad to hear it," Dragan said. He walked over to Litija, took her trembling hand in his own, then turned to Nick and Kate with a gracious smile. "Come with us. I'll show you around."

Dragan ignored Kate's gun and strolled toward the

flower-draped colonnade. Nick joined Kate and tapped her right arm.

"I think you can put that away now," he whispered. "It's impolite."

Kate holstered the gun but kept her hand near it. "He just murdered a man in cold blood."

"It's a good sign," Nick said.

"Because it wasn't you?"

"It means he needs me more than he needed Zarko."

"So we're in," Kate said. "But in for what?"

10

Dragan led them around to the east side of the villa to show them the view of his acres of lemon trees. A centuries-old stone farmhouse, serving as his processing plant, was located in the middle of the orchard.

"Villa Spintria is not just my vacation getaway," Dragan said. "It's a business. We make *limoncello* here that's sold throughout Italy. It has a unique flavor that comes only from our lemons thanks to the enchanted spot where they are grown."

There wasn't anything enchanting about the spot where Zarko had stood, Kate thought, or where he'd landed.

"The business is a legitimate front for laundering your money," Nick said.

"It's more than that. I like to see the trees on the hillside, to smell the lemony scent sweetening the sea breeze, and to enjoy a *limoncello* after my meals. It makes Italy a totally immersive experience for me. But the business also explains what we're doing out here if anyone is curious."

"And it explains why you have armed guards walking the property," Kate said. She couldn't see the boundaries of his land, but she did notice the sentries in the turrets atop the villa.

"We don't want anyone stealing our lemons," Dragan said.

"You can't be too careful," Nick said. "There are thieves everywhere."

Dragan led them to the villa, and they entered a large room with a barrel dome ceiling painted in gold leaf. Kate thought the room might have been the refectory of the former monastery. There were open windows facing the hills to the east and the sea to the west. It created a pleasant cross breeze that carried the sweet, salty scent that Dragan liked so much. Kate liked it, too. There was something naturally relaxing about it, offsetting the fact that a man had just died.

Dragan motioned for them to sit on one of the two couches on either side of a table where a pitcher of chilled lemonade and several glasses had been set out on a silver platter.

"I assume you didn't just come here to settle a dispute," Dragan said. "You would like to collect your share of the Antwerp heist, which I'm glad to give you. But what if I could offer you that and so much more?"

"I'm listening," Nick said, taking a seat on a couch facing the sea.

Kate sat beside Nick, and Litija poured lemonade into the glasses. Kate noticed Litija's hand was still trembling. Obviously the lemony sea breeze wasn't doing much for her.

"You can let your money ride, so to speak, and add it to your share of the biggest robbery we've ever attempted," Dragan said, sitting on the couch facing them and the lemon groves beyond. "Perhaps the biggest ever attempted by anyone."

"That's quite a boast," Nick said, taking a sip of lemonade. "But you'll have to be more specific."

Dragan glanced at Kate, then back at Nick. "I'd like to be, but first I have to know that I can trust you, that I have your complete loyalty."

"Shouldn't I be the one concerned about that after what happened to me in Hawaii and Belgium?"

"That's what I mean," Dragan said. "I need to know if that lingering resentment is something I should be worried about before I bring you into the big caper."

"And before I get involved with you again," Nick said, "I need to know that I won't be double-crossed."

"I have a solution that should reassure both of us," Dragan said. "I have a diamond heist planned for tomorrow afternoon in Paris. It's a modest job that has been in the works for months. Zarko was going to be the lead man. But now that he's unexpectedly dropped out, I find myself a man short. I'd like you to take his place. If the job goes well, then I'll bring you into the big caper."

"And if I'm not interested in either one?" Nick asked.

"I'll give you your share of the Antwerp heist now, and you'll go on your merry way," Dragan said.

Nick took another sip of lemonade while he pretended to contemplate his options. But Kate knew there was nothing to think about. He had to say yes if they were going to infiltrate Dragan's organization and find out what had happened to the smallpox vial.

"You wouldn't be offering me 'the big caper' unless you desperately needed my unique expertise to pull it off. So I'll do this job tomorrow on two conditions," Nick said. "First, I get Zarko's share of the Paris heist on top of what you already owe me, regardless of whether I decide to stick around afterward."

"Agreed," Dragan said.

"Second, Kate comes along, too," Nick said. "I need someone in the crew I can trust to watch my back."

Dragan studied Kate. "How do I know she's up to the task?"

"I broke Nick out of police custody," Kate said. "I planned it and executed it within forty-eight hours of his arrest. I think that speaks for itself about my capabilities and experience."

"I only work with the best," Nick said to Dragan. "In fact, as far as I'm concerned, this job tomorrow is *your* audition. I expect to see precision and professionalism at every level, or I'm out."

"There he goes," Litija said. "Turning it around on you again, Dragan. I've never met anyone so slick."

"Neither have I," Dragan said. "Nick is one of a kind, and he continues to prove it, which is as irritating as it is impressive."

He shifted his gaze to Kate. "You're in, but your share will come out of Nick's pocket."

"I don't care whose pocket it comes from as long as it ends up in mine," Kate said.

"Then it's settled. You'll both be staying here tonight and traveling with us to Paris by private plane tomorrow morning," Dragan said. "I've already taken the liberty of checking you out of the hotel and having your things brought here."

"You were pretty sure of yourself," Nick said.

"I'm a hard man to say no to," Dragan said.

Kate was hoping that if Dragan had checked them out he also took care of the bill. God knows what the champagne and *sfogliatelle* cost.

Dragan left Litija behind in the refectory and took Nick and Kate into a windowless room decorated with framed antique maps on the walls and an antique floor globe in one corner.

"This is a remnant of the old fortress and served as the commander's map room. It's where he planned tactics and strategy," Dragan said. "I use it for the same purpose. I stare at the ceiling and hope for inspiration."

Kate looked up. The ceiling was covered with a fresco of the heavens and the Greek gods that commanded them. She was about to look away when something caught her eye, and she did a double take. The illustration of Zeus, the god of gods, had Dragan's face, pockmarks and all. What a lunatic, she thought.

He walked over to an architect's model of a building that was displayed on a table in the center of the room. "Do you recognize this?"

It was an octagonal building with an open square in the middle. A street ran through the middle of the square, and there was a tall, slender box standing upright in the center. The box had a drawing of a column that had a statue of a Roman Caesar on top. There was another box that had been cut to fit over a portion of the building on one corner of the model.

Nick bent down and studied the model. "Place Vendôme."

"You know Paris," Dragan said.

"I know where the best jewelry stores in the world are," Nick said. "You aren't seriously considering hitting them?"

"Why not? It's a great score, and the location is perfect. There's only one way in and out." Dragan pointed to the street that ran through the middle of the octagon. "Rue de la Paix. The buildings on either side of the square are continuous and essentially form two walls. That makes it easy for us to control the flow of traffic."

"It also makes it easy for the police to box you in," Kate said.

"That's not going to happen," Dragan said in a dismissive tone that did not invite argument.

"Is this going to be another smash-and-grab?" Nick asked.

"You make it sound so crude," Dragan said. "But yes, it is."

"I see two problems. The biggest one is right here, next door to the Ritz hotel." Nick pointed to the building next to the one covered with the box. "That's the Ministry of Justice, which runs the nation's courts and prison system. There are police officers armed with automatic weapons inside and outside the building at all times. They can show up at any of the jewelry stores within the plaza in seconds."

"Set that quibble aside for now," Dragan said. "What's the other problem?"

"After your smash-and-grab on the Champs-Élysées, the city installed solid steel pillars a couple feet apart to prevent cars from leaving the street and smashing through the storefronts. They run all along the inner circumference of the octagon."

"Ordinarily, those pillars would be an impediment, but not now. We have a once-in-a-lifetime window of opportunity. The Colonne Vendôme and the Ritz are currently being renovated. They are entirely covered in scaffolding and hidden behind decorative shrouds." Dragan tapped the slender box in the center of the square and then the one covering the building in the corner. "Usually, it's an open square, but now there are plywood fencing and trucks around the base of the *colonne* and construction workers everywhere."

Nick smiled. "And you've had your men working among the construction crew for months."

"Indeed I have. At four o'clock tomorrow, several of our construction workers will place the ends of two parallel scaffold platforms on two of the steel pillars in front of Boucheron jewelers at the northeast corner of place Vendôme and rue de la Paix."

Nick nodded, getting the picture. "Transforming the pillars from obstacles into an inclined ramp for a speeding Audi."

"*Your* speeding Audi," Dragan said. "You and Kate will go airborne and crash through the front window of the store. You will get out, smash the display cases with hammers, steal the jewels, and exit on foot to rue de la Paix, where two motorcycles will be waiting for you both to make your escape. While you are doing all of that, the same sequence of events will be happening at the opposite end of the square, at the Bulgari store on the western corner of place Vendôme and rue de la Paix, with another set of thieves."

"Two robberies at once?" Nick said. "Isn't that pushing your luck?"

"We'll never get an opportunity like this again to strike place Vendôme," Dragan said. "We'd be fools not to take full advantage of it."

Nick tapped the Ministry of Justice building. "And what about this building full of police? You haven't explained how you are going to deal with that quibble."

"No, I haven't. It's not necessary for you to know those details. It's a separate operation. But let me give you some peace of mind. There are construction office trailers, stacked on top of each other, that have created a temporary four-story building in front of the Ritz that significantly blocks the view of Boucheron from the police officers stationed at the front door of the Ministry of Justice," Dragan said. "The scaffolding, scrim, and plywood fencing around the Colonne Vendôme blocks their view of Bulgari, too, not that you should be concerned about what is happening there, either."

"The police may not see the robberies go down, but they are certainly going to hear them," Kate said. "They can get across the square while we're still smashing display cases and seal up the two ends of the street, boxing us in. It will be like shooting fish in a barrel. How are you going to stop that?"

"All you need to know is that we will," Dragan said. His voice was sharp. It was clear he didn't like the questioning. "There is no point in cluttering your head with irrelevant information. I want you concentrating on your jobs. I don't want you distracted thinking about what someone else is supposed to do. That would jeopardize the entire operation. You have enough to think about as it is and a strict timetable to follow."

"He's right, Kate," Nick said. "We'll do our parts and trust that everyone else is doing theirs."

"So you're in?" Dragan asked.

Nick smiled. "Like you said, it's a once-in-a-lifetime opportunity."

More diamond robberies, Kate thought. I'm going to spend the rest of my life in jail and then I'm going to burn in hell.

They spent the next hour going over the exact details and timing of the robbery, their escape, and their rendezvous afterward with Dragan, who would not be participating in the crime. The fact that he'd be sitting it out really bothered Kate. It meant that Dragan would be avoiding all the risk and, if things went bad, he'd be able to walk away and go right back to business.

"Now that we have the details straight, you are free to enjoy my property," Dragan said. "A light lunch will be set on the patio. You can help yourself to refreshments. Your guest suite is just down the hall."

11

ragan left Kate and Nick and was on his way to his first-floor office when he ran across Litija sitting on a couch, drinking *limoncello* from the bottle.

"I don't understand you, Dragan," she said in their native Serbian.

"Good. If I was easily understood, I'd also be predictable. I'd be imprisoned or dead by now."

"*You* told Zarko to leave Nick behind in the vault. You wanted Nick to become the focus of the police investigation and distract them from you. When you lied about it to Nick today, Zarko backed up your story with more lies." She took a swig from the half-empty bottle. "You rewarded Zarko by pushing him off a cliff to protect your lie from ever being revealed."

Dragan pitied her. She was a versatile operative, able to go undercover to lay the groundwork for a heist, or use her body to seduce a useful person of either sex, or participate as a pinch hitter in any aspect of the robbery itself. But as effective as she was, she lacked imagination, a chess player's ability to see several moves ahead. She would never become more than she was today, a pawn in someone else's game. *His game.* He didn't like explaining himself to anyone, but he saw it would be necessary if he wanted to keep her.

"You are mistaken, Litija, about why I did it. I made a strategic decision to achieve our objectives. I hadn't counted on Nick escaping, but since fate stepped in and brought him to me I decided he would be an asset. Zarko and Nick would never have worked well together, and I needed the skills that Nick has more than those that Zarko possessed. The only asset Zarko retained was the benefit I could derive from his death. It sent a message to Nick that I was clearing the path for him to join us. So I sacrificed Zarko for the mission."

This was all true. But Dragan had also been eager to try out his Tiberius Drop. Zarko happened to be standing in the right spot, and Dragan had almost no impulse control. He didn't see the need to share any of that with Litija.

"You see no value in loyalty," Litija said. "Everyone is expendable to you. You sacrificed Zarko, a fellow Serbian, a man who had loyally served you for years. You have no heart."

It was a good thing they weren't outside standing on the terrace when she'd said that, or she would have experienced the Tiberius Drop herself. Dragan had zero tolerance for criticism. He supposed he could break her neck, but that would require more effort than he was willing to expend right now. And finding her replacement would be tedious. It would take weeks of interviews, watching candidates demonstrate weapons skills, watching them in hand-to-hand combat with his men, watching them fuck his entire staff, including ugly old toothless Maria, who tended the garden and smelled like dead fish. A shiver of revulsion ripped through him at the memory of Litija with Maria. He had to give it to her. The girl had stamina. And as if all that wasn't exhausting enough, he would have to personally test out the few women who survived. He didn't have the time right now to go through that, so he ignored the insult and answered the underlying question.

"Nick is brilliant, but he doesn't always work alone," Dragan said. "He often assembles a highly skilled crew for his jobs, and individually they're nearly as good as he is. Until his escape, I didn't know that his crew had any lasting allegiance to him. Now we not only get Nick, but his people, too, to help us on the next phase of our plan, assuming that he passes the place Vendôme test first. We'll be able to accomplish our near-term and long-term objectives much sooner, and with a greater chance of success, than we could have without him."

Nick and Kate left the house and walked to the far edge of the pool to stand by the waterfall where they couldn't be overheard.

"Airborne?" Kate said. "Are you kidding me? We're going airborne and then we're going to crash through a storefront and smash jewelry cases with a hammer. What is this, Hollywood? That stuff only happens in movies. They use stunt drivers and fake storefronts. People don't actually do this stuff. It isn't done!"

"I think I can do it," Nick said.

"Think? That indicates doubt. That's right next to I *don't* think I can do it. I want no part of this ridiculous scheme. I'm not robbing a jewelry store in place Vendôme."

"It could be fun," Nick said, grinning at Kate. "Flying through the air, smashing into stuff."

"Seriously?"

Nick shook his head. "No. When I pull a heist I make sure there's no danger to innocent bystanders, and for the most part I only con people who deserve it. This is not something I would ever choose to do. I'm participating in this because there's a lot at stake. We've been tasked to get the smallpox vial, and that's what we're going to do."

"If we get caught, it will create an international scandal, and we'll lose our best chance at stopping Dragan. He'll go underground. We won't know what he's done with the smallpox until people somewhere start dying horrible deaths."

"We won't get caught," Nick said.

"How do you know?"

"Because Dragan and his crew are great at this."

"You say that like you admire him."

"I appreciate his skills," Nick said. "He's a criminal mastermind."

"He's a homicidal psychopath."

"That's definitely a character flaw, but he's exceptionally good at what he does. His robberies look like quickly improvised smash-and-grabs. But the truth is they are the result of careful preparation, undercover work, and split-second timing. Dragan has the patience to play the long game. There aren't many people in this business who do."

"You're willing to play the long game," Kate said. "On the surface you seem like a spontaneous kind of guy, but you actually have a lot of patience."

"You noticed."

"Hard not to."

"You're referring to my expertise as a master criminal, right?"

"Of course."

Nick grinned and Kate grinned back.

"There are other times when patience comes in handy," Nick said.

"Are you bragging?" Kate asked.

"Just saying."

Place Vendôme, originally called place Louis le Grand, was built in 1699 as a luxury townhouse development for the rich. That's what it was until one day in 1792, during the French Revolution, when nine aristocrats got their heads cut off and stuck on spikes in the middle of the square. Overnight the neighborhood became place des Piques (Place of Spikes) and a popular setting for public executions. It took another hundred years before the square got its new name and once again became an enclave for the rich, not only as a place to live, but more important for the job at hand, to spend outrageous amounts of money on precious jewels.

At exactly 3:57 P.M. on Thursday Nicolas Fox drove a black Audi A4 into place Vendôme. Kate O'Hare sat in the passenger seat thinking about all of those heads on spikes and how hers could soon be on one, too, figuratively speaking. The Boucheron jewelry store was directly ahead. The Ministry of Justice was to their left, and there were four police officers armed with M16s standing outside and even more of them inside. This was an extremely dangerous heist, and they were entrusting their escape, and possibly their lives, to the Road Runners and their ability to stop the police from responding. Kate didn't like putting her safety into anyone's hands but her own.

At the same moment that Nick drove into place Vendôme, an identical Audi with two Road Runners inside entered the square from the opposite end of rue de la Paix and headed in their direction. The two cars passed without seeing each other because the sheathed scaffolding and plywood fencing around the 144-foot-tall Colonne Vendôme in the center of the plaza blocked opposing traffic from view.

"I ambushed a police transport on Monday to rescue a

crook and here I am on Thursday, robbing a jewelry store," Kate said. She and Nick were buckled tight into their seats and wore matching crash helmets with tinted visors that obscured their faces. "They didn't train us for this at Quantico."

"That's why the FBI needs me to catch people like me. Sometimes you have to commit crimes to prevent bigger crimes," Nick said. "The curriculum at Quantico needs to be changed. They should invite us in to teach."

The very thought gave Kate a queasy stomach.

Ahead of them, four construction workers emerged from behind the *colonne*'s fence, crossed the street, and laid the ends of two scaffold platforms down on the small steel pillars that stuck out from the sidewalk in front of Boucheron.

"I'll be sure to mention the change in curriculum when I testify in my defense," Kate said. "Maybe I can get the charges against me reduced."

"Keep that positive attitude," Nick said. He floored the gas pedal and pressed the horn to warn anyone in the store about what was coming.

The four construction workers scrambled out of the way an instant before the Audi hit the improvised ramp.

Kate's heart stuttered as the car went airborne and headed straight for the elegant limestone façade of the jewelry store, with its large windows and ornamental columns. The building looked monumental and foreboding, daring them to do what the centuries, revolutions, and wars seemingly could not—break down the walls.

Even though she knew the front end of the car had been structurally reinforced for the collision, all of her instincts told her that driving into anything at high speed was suicide. It didn't help that she also knew that the Audi's air bags were disabled. She placed her gloved hands flat on the dashboard and braced for impact.

The Audi blasted through the window in an explosion of glass, plaster, and limestone, smashed through a display case in a spray of diamonds and splintered wood, and came to a stop in the center of the store.

Kate opened her eyes, relieved that she was conscious and in one piece. The windshield was shattered. She could hear alarms ringing. She drew her gun, unbuckled her seatbelt, and got out of the car. Dust was settling like snow. Four store employees were backed up against the far wall in terror. The guard, dressed in a suit like a secret service agent, was rising from the floor near the door and reaching for the gun in his shoulder holster in the same motion.

"Don't do it," Kate said, aiming her gun at his forehead. "Drop the gun and kick it under the car." He did as he was told and she gestured to him to join the others against the wall.

Nick smashed display cases with a pickax, scooped up the diamonds, and dumped them into an open backpack that he wore on his chest instead of his back. Kate kept the five employees covered and glanced at the watch on her wrist.

By her estimate, unless something incredible was done,

they had less than thirty seconds before the police officers from the Ministry of Justice took them down.

A few moments before the two Audis crashed into the two jewelry stores, two large dump trucks full of rubble that had been parked beside the *colonne* simultaneously pulled out into the rue de la Paix and turned across it, blocking the street and sealing off the plaza from traffic. The drivers leaped out of their trucks and ran away as their vehicles emptied their loads into the street.

At that same instant, a dozen police officers poured out from the Ministry of Justice and ran across the plaza toward the jewelry stores on the two ends of rue de la Paix. That was when a series of carefully timed small explosions started going off like a sequence of fireworks. The blasts released the massive scaffolding around the *colonne,* which unpeeled itself like a giant banana. The poles and scrim tumbled to the plaza and forced the police officers to scramble back to avoid being crushed.

It was in the midst of that smoke, chaos, and destruction that Nick and Kate ran out of the jewelry store, jumped onto two motorcycles parked on rue de la Paix, and sped northwest toward place de l'Opéra, one of the busiest and most crowded intersections in Paris. Seven streets branched off the plaza outside of the grand gilded Paris opera house, creating an enormous churn of man and machine.

They snaked through the traffic, making a hard right onto

rue du Quatre-Septembre, then a sharp left onto a narrow one-way street. They came to a sudden stop at the intersection with the broad boulevard des Italiens, where there was a long line of motorcycles parked on the sidewalk in front of the Gaumont Opéra multiplex movie theater. Nick and Kate parked their motorcycles with the others, left their keys in the ignitions to encourage theft, and went to the ticket window. They were ten minutes early for the 4:15 showing of the latest *Mission Impossible* movie.

Nick removed his helmet, holding it at an angle that obscured the view of the ticket window security camera. Kate took her helmet off as well, her back to another camera pointed at the entrance to the theater.

"Deux billets pour Mission Impossible, *s'il vous plaît,"* Nick said, passing some euros through the slot to the female cashier. She passed back two tickets. Nick and Kate entered the theater and immediately split up to go to the restrooms.

As Kate went into the women's room, Litija emerged from one of the four stalls, leaving a large Galeries Lafayette shopping bag and a purse behind. Kate went into that stall and closed the door while Litija washed her hands at the sink.

She set her helmet on the floor, unzipped her jumpsuit, and opened the shopping bag, which held a sundress and flip-flops. She quickly changed into the new clothes and stuffed her helmet, gloves, and jumpsuit into the bag. Kate dropped the Glock in the purse, hung the strap on her shoulder, and walked out.

Litija took the shopping bag and left without saying a word. Kate approached the mirror and checked to see if, in her professional opinion as an FBI agent, she looked like someone who'd just robbed a jewelry store.

The dress and the flip-flops said *no*. The expression of horror said *yes*. She forced herself to relax and smile. For the greater good, she thought, checking her watch. It was 4:09. In one minute, the sold-out 2 P.M. showing of *La Dernière Vie*, a World War I epic and the most popular movie of the week in France, would be letting out.

She knew that Nick was in the men's room changing his clothes and handing off the diamonds to the Road Runner who'd been waiting for him just like Litija had been waiting for her. Those two Road Runners would dispose of the two thieves' jumpsuits and helmets and then transport the diamonds to the next person in the relay race to get the loot out of the country as fast as possible.

Kate took a pair of large sunglasses out of the purse, put them on, and walked out of the bathroom just as the audience for *La Dernière Vie* spilled out of one of the auditoriums. She slipped into the middle of the exiting crowd and so did Nick, who now wore a lightweight gray hoodie, jeans, and tennis shoes. He came up beside Kate and put on a pair of Ray-Bans as he stepped into the sunshine outside.

"*Formidable,*" Nick said, referring to the film they'd supposedly just seen. "*Marion Cotillard était incroyable.*"

"*Oui,*" Kate said. That was the extent of her French, and she had no idea who Marion Cotillard was. Inspector Clouseau was the only French character she knew, and a Brit had played him.

Nick took her hand and together they turned right on boulevard des Italiens toward place de l'Opéra. Traffic was gridlocked. The air was alive with the sound of sirens and horns. There was a palpable, urgent energy on the streets. Something had happened. Kate picked up a word here and there from the people they passed.

"Diamants!" "Voleurs!" "Place Vendôme!"

When they reached place de l'Opéra, everyone was looking down rue de la Paix toward the helicopters and smoke in the sky over place Vendôme. Nobody had any reason at all to notice Nick and Kate, who darted across the street and took the stairs down to the metro station.

There was a southbound train arriving as they reached the tracks, and they took it. They didn't care which line it was. The more transfers they had to make between metro lines to their destination, the better it was. It would be harder to follow their tracks. Nick and Kate settled into a seat. It wasn't until that moment that Kate felt that they'd made their escape.

"It's a shame we couldn't stay for *Mission Impossible*," Nick said. "We probably missed an exciting heist."

12

After two metro transfers, Nick and Kate got off at the Mouton-Duvernet station and climbed the stairs to the street. They emerged on avenue du Général Leclerc beneath a distinctive green cast-iron archway and a *Métropolitain* sign written in a florid art nouveau script that screamed "You're in Paris!"

They were in the heart of the fourteenth arrondissement, a neighborhood known primarily for the massive Montparnasse Cemetery crammed with ornate tombs and for the fifty-nine-story office tower that rose over it like an enormous black headstone.

Nick and Kate walked a half block south on avenue du Général Leclerc, then turned right on rue Brézin, a one-lane street that ran only a single block from east to west. They were just another anonymous, unremarkable couple out for an evening stroll on a street lined with apartment buildings and a wide assortment of shops. Nick gestured across the street to Picard, a store with a giant snowflake in the window.

"That's a grocery store made just for you," Nick said. "All it sells is frozen food."

"You say that like it's a bad thing," Kate said. "I'm too busy chasing bad guys to cook."

"That's why restaurants were created," Nick said.

"I go to restaurants."

"I'm talking about the kind without a drive-through window."

"They're too slow and overpriced," Kate said. "Speaking of food, should we pick up something at Picard's to heat up for dinner?"

"I'd rather turn myself in to the police and eat whatever the jail is serving."

"You're too snooty about food," Kate said.

Nick smiled. "I can see this is going to be a major stumbling block in our relationship."

"We have a relationship?"

"You haven't noticed?" Nick asked.

"I hadn't given it a name."

"*Relationship* is a broad term. It can mean most anything."

"What does it mean to you?"

"In our case? Partner, lover, pain in the ass."

Kate nodded in agreement. "That covers it."

They took rue Brézin to its end at a T-intersection with avenue du Maine. It was just a half block shy of the spot where five other streets hit the wide tree-lined boulevard from various angles, creating a whirlpool of traffic.

Nick and Kate's destination was a six-story apartment building directly across from rue Brézin on the wedge-shaped corner of avenue du Maine and rue Severo. The building looked like the bow of a ship, heading due north through a sea of cars to the Montparnasse office tower. On the ground floor, there was a pharmacy and a business that sold coffins and headstones. Kate pointed to the plush coffin in the window as they approached the door to the apartment building.

"I wonder if Dragan gets a discount on those," Kate said.

Nick waved a digital key over the scanner beside the door, unlocking it. "He probably owns the shop."

They entered a lobby facing another locked door, this one made of glass, allowing them to see the spiral staircase in the foyer that led up to the apartments. Nick waved his key over the scanner beside the list of apartment buzzers, and they heard the telltale click of the second door unlocking.

The building was hundreds of years old and was in relatively good shape, but the spiral staircase that led up to the apartments was too tightly wound to fit even a tiny elevator. So they climbed the stairs to the sixth-floor apartment where they were meeting Dragan Kovic. It was a long climb up on wooden steps bowed from centuries of use. Kate couldn't imagine living there and having to lug groceries, or anything else, up those stairs every day. But then maybe this was how French women stayed thin. That and smoking instead of eating.

The creaking steps announced their arrival long before they got to the sixth floor. The door to the apartment was partly open. They stepped inside a large room that was unfurnished and painted bright white. The ceilings were trimmed with elaborate crown moldings, cornices, and rosettes, the walls with half-height wainscoting. Against all that whiteness, black-clad Dragan Kovic stood out dramatically, as if he were illuminated from every angle. He sat in one of three folding chairs in the center of the living room, a bay window behind him overlooking the busy street below.

"Did we pass the audition?" Dragan asked.

"You did," Nick said, closing the door behind them. "Your team was precise, disciplined, and professional. I'm very impressed."

"Likewise," Dragan said. "You were briefed on the plan only last night and yet, without any prior location scouting or dry runs, you performed flawlessly. I commend you."

"I take it the other team got away safely," Kate said.

"They did. And the ten million dollars in diamonds we acquired from the two robberies are already being dispersed for cutting and resale," Dragan said. He then shifted his attention to Nick. "So now you are at a crossroads. You are free to leave with your share of this robbery and the one in Antwerp. You are also welcome to join us in our biggest endeavor. But if you agree to participate, there is no backing out. I need your decision now."

"The way I see it, you and I are the best at what we do, but together, we could reach heights neither one of us could on our own," Nick said. "So yes, I'm in, for the challenge as much as the profits."

Dragan shifted his gaze to Kate. "And you?"

"I go where he goes," Kate said. "I'm good, but I need direction."

"I admire a person who has an objective view of their own skills," Dragan said, "as well as their limitations."

"There's one more thing we have to settle," Nick said. "I won't go into another heist blind, like the Antwerp job. Before I sign on, I need to know what the objectives really are."

"I don't understand what you mean," Dragan said.

Nick sighed with disappointment. "Our partnership hasn't even started yet and already you're lying to me. I know about the vial of smallpox."

Dragan jerked at the mention of the deadly virus. It was as if he'd been given a small electric shock.

"How did you know about the vial?" Dragan asked.

"Because I am very, very good at what I do," Nick said.

"That's not an acceptable answer."

The two men were staring at each other eye to eye, so neither of them noticed Kate slip her hand into her purse and grab her gun. She'd be ready if things quickly went bad.

"I've had my eye on that vault for years and I've tried to

learn as much as I could about what was in those safe-deposit boxes," Nick said. "Before the police grabbed me in the vault, I noticed that box number 773 was open and on the floor next to me. That box belongs to diamond merchant Yuri Baskin. His cousin was Soviet bioweapons expert Sergei Andropov, who died in Antwerp before he could sell a vial of smallpox he'd smuggled out of Russia. The vial was never found. It's been assumed for decades that the vial was in Yuri's box. If it was, I've got to ask myself, 'What does a diamond thief want with one of the most lethal viruses on earth?'"

Dragan continued to stare at Nick for a long moment before coming to a decision. "If I tell you, and then you decide to walk away from this, I'll have to kill you."

Nick laughed. "You'll kill me *now* if I walk away, so what have you got to lose? I was a dead man the moment I admitted that I knew about the smallpox."

Dragan flicked his gaze toward Kate for a moment. Long enough to notice the Glock pointed at him. Then focused back on Nick and smiled. "I'm not so sure about that. You like to take big risks with your life."

"That's what makes life fun," he said.

"Please sit down," Dragan said. "I have a story to tell you."

Dragan took a cigar out of his pocket and lit it with a match.

"Does it have a happy ending?" Nick asked as he took a seat on a folding chair.

Kate remained standing, only slightly more relaxed, gun still in hand. She was dealing with a guy who'd had someone paint him as Zeus on the ceiling of his office. She thought either he had a sense of humor or else he was majorly nuts. She was going with the latter.

"That will be up to you," Dragan said and blew a puff of smoke in his direction.

"In February 1972, a Yugoslavian went on a pilgrimage to Mecca and came back to Kosovo infected with smallpox. He had no idea that he was infected, of course, and since he'd recently been vaccinated, he only developed a slight rash and therefore didn't see a doctor for treatment. He infected eleven people, just by being near them," Dragan said. "One was a teacher who spread the virus to thirty-eight more people, mostly the doctors, nurses, and patients in the three hospitals in three different cities where he was treated and misdiagnosed. In his final days, the teacher's eyes turned black. His skin broke out in blood blisters and split open. His internal organs disintegrated and blood poured out from every orifice in his body. That's because smallpox destroys the membranes that hold the body together, inside and out. It's like decomposing alive. A horrible, agonizing way to die."

Dragan spoke in a detached way, a distant observer of a long-ago event. But as the story got bloodier, he leaned forward, his arms on his knees, bringing himself closer to his guests as he became more engaged. He flicked some ashes on the floor and continued.

"It takes two weeks after someone is exposed to smallpox before doctors can detect it or someone shows symptoms. But by then, it's too late. The sick are already highly infectious, spreading the virus to anyone within ten feet," Dragan said. "So the epidemic moves in waves, with the number of sick growing exponentially. The only way to stop it is to quarantine the sick and vaccinate everyone else. So that is what the government did. The army sealed off entire towns. Public gatherings were banned across the nation. Ten thousand people suspected of being infected were herded up and quarantined in apartment buildings encircled by barbed wire and armed soldiers. Eighteen million people were vaccinated. The epidemic was over in eight weeks. In the end, only about two hundred people were infected and thirty-five died. It could have been much worse."

"Were you in Yugoslavia at the time?" Nick asked.

"I was nine years old." Dragan pointed to his pockmarked face with his cigar. "That is how I got my lovely complexion. The lasting, parting kiss of smallpox to those it has abandoned. Ever since then, I've been enchanted by that demon."

"I'd think after what you've been through, you wouldn't want anything to do with smallpox," Kate said.

"I'm immune now to her charms, but I remain in awe of her deadly power. I've finally found a way to harness that power for myself," Dragan said. "I think that's always been my destiny."

"I'm a thief and a con man," Nick said. "Not a salesman. If that's what you are hoping to get from me, I'm afraid I wouldn't know where to even begin looking for a smallpox buyer."

"I have no intention of selling smallpox to anyone. I used half of the money that we've earned from our heists, prior to the Antwerp job, to recruit scientists and build a state-of-the-art weapons lab to develop my own cache of weaponized smallpox. What I was lacking until now was a start-up sample to work from."

"If you don't intend to sell the smallpox," Kate said, "why build a lab to create more of it?"

"Because I want to unleash smallpox on an American city."

"What will you gain?" Nick asked.

"I want to cash in on the massive drop in the stock market that is sure to follow the 'terrorist attack.'"

"That's where the rest of your money is going," Nick said. "You're going to invest two hundred million dollars on Wall Street betting against the market. It's a safe bet, because you'll know exactly when the market is going to plunge."

"That's right," Dragan said.

Nick let out a slow whistle of admiration. "You'll make *billions*."

"*We* will." Dragan stood up, excited, practically evangelizing now. "It will be the greatest score of our lives, perhaps the greatest in the history of crime. The riches we will reap almost defy imagination."

But that financial windfall would be earned on the deaths of thousands of people, Kate thought. Nobody in the United States is vaccinated for smallpox anymore and, as a result, there weren't tens of millions of vaccines on hand to inoculate the population of a major city. The epidemic would rage a lot longer, and claim more lives, than it had in Yugoslavia more than forty years ago. It would be a catastrophe of epic proportions.

She was tempted to shoot Dragan right now, or at the very least arrest him, and bring the plot to an end before it could get started. But that wouldn't get the smallpox sample back or prevent others in his organization from moving forward with his plans without him.

"It's a brilliant scheme," Nick said. "But I still don't see why you need me."

"As it turns out, the smallpox sample we acquired from Antwerp is small. My scientists are working with it even as we speak but it will take time to get the quantity I need. If I had a second sample the process would go much more quickly."

"I have no idea where to find that," Nick said.

"I do," Dragan said. "Everyone thinks that only two samples exist, one in America and one in Russia. The truth is, there are many unrecorded samples that were collected back when smallpox was widespread. Those samples are secretly stored and studied in government, institutional, and private high-security biolabs located in several countries. One of them happens to be a mile from this apartment."

"You want me to steal it for you," Nick said.

"Or I'll kill you."

Dragan made it sound like a joke, but they all knew that it wasn't. He appeared to be alone but there were almost certainly armed men inside and outside the building awaiting his word on whether to let Nick and Kate leave alive.

"Well, that makes it an easy decision," Nick said. "I'll steal the smallpox, but I want forty percent of the profits from the stock market gamble."

Dragan laughed. "You're a very amusing man. I'll give you your share of the Antwerp and Paris heists and you can bet that against the market yourself. You'll do extremely well."

"I'll definitely be doing that," Nick said. "In addition to my forty percent."

"You're being ridiculous. You don't deserve forty percent."

"I deserve more, but I'm being generous. Without me, you won't have the smallpox you need to make the investment pay off. This isn't a heist you can accomplish with one of your glorified smash-and-grabs."

"So I'll kill you and find someone else with the expertise to steal the smallpox for me."

Kate's grip tightened on her gun, and she steeled herself for action. Dragan didn't appear to be armed. Nick didn't look worried at all.

"You wouldn't have kidnapped me for the Antwerp job if there was somebody else," Nick said. "But let's say that there is someone out there. How many years will it take to find him? And what if you're wrong, and he's not another Nicolas Fox? You could lose the millions you've sunk into the scheme already. Are you really willing to take that gamble?"

Dragan pondered his cigar for a moment, took a long drag,

savoring it, then blew out the smoke. "What makes you so sure that you'll be able to break into the lab and steal the smallpox?"

"Because I'm the best," Nick said. "We both know it."

"Fine," Dragan said. "You can have ten percent."

"Forty," Nick said.

"Fifteen."

"Forty."

"Fifteen," Dragan said. "And that's my final offer."

"If I am going to do this, we're going to be partners."

"If you don't do this, you're going to be dead."

Nick waved off the comment as if it was meaningless and not the genuine threat that Kate knew it was.

"I'm showing you my respect, and acknowledging the considerable investment you've already made, by giving you sixty percent instead of insisting on fifty-fifty," Nick said. "I get forty percent. Or you can execute us now."

Kate raised her gun and pointed it at Dragan's head. "He can try."

That's when she noticed the red dot of a sniper's targeting laser on Nick's forehead and another on her chest. There were snipers on the building across the street. Nick was aware of the targeting dots, too, but he ignored them.

"Make up your mind," Nick said. "I'm hungry. Robbing jewelry stores gives me an appetite."

Dragan sat down, perhaps to give his snipers a clean shot,

or to rest while he considered the offer. After a minute that felt to Kate like forever, he finally smiled, leaned forward, and offered his hand to Nick.

"Sixty-forty," Dragan said.

"You have yourself a deal," Nick said and they shook hands.

"The lab is within the sprawling Institut National pour la Recherche sur les Maladies Infectieuses complex on rue Denfert-Rochereau," Dragan said. "Walking distance from this apartment, which you will be using as your base of operations. The challenge isn't just breaking into the lab, but safely acquiring the sample and transporting it," Dragan said. "One mistake and lots of people will die."

"Don't tell me you're worried about the loss of human life," Kate said.

"Of course not. I'm worried about it occurring before I place my bets on the table," Dragan said. "Not only wouldn't I profit from the accident, but a smallpox epidemic in Paris would put authorities worldwide on heightened alert. It might even prompt mass vaccinations, which would severely dilute the impact of a future attack."

"I value my life and my future earning potential too highly to allow that to happen," Nick said. "We'll take all of the necessary precautions."

"I'll give you all of the manpower, cash, and resources that you need to do this right," Dragan said. "Just give me a shopping list."

"I'll do that," Nick said. "But I'll also have to bring in people of my own who have specialized skills and who I can depend upon."

"Can you trust them not to talk?" Dragan said.

"As much as you trust your people," Nick said. "But they'll be freelancers and they won't know the big picture, only the immediate objective, so you won't have to kill them afterward."

"You're beginning to understand me," Dragan said.

"I know you can play the long game, but I'll say this anyway so there's no misunderstanding," Nick said. "You need to be patient. It's going to take me some time to case the institute, come up with a plan, recruit my people, and set the stage for the robbery."

"Are we talking weeks or months?"

"I won't know until I have a plan," Nick said. "But I get bored easily, so figure on weeks."

"Litija will move you into the apartment tonight." Dragan passed a card to Nick. "You can reach her at this number. She can reach me."

Once again, Kate noted, Dragan was keeping a safe distance from the operation. Nick pocketed the card and stood up.

"Send my share of the two robberies to my Cayman Island account," Nick said. "I'll give you the number. I won't do anything for you until I see those dollars in my account."

"Where are you going?" Dragan asked.

"I thought I'd take a stroll to place Denfert-Rochereau," Nick said. "And see the lay of the land."

"I'll send your money, but don't think about running out on me," Dragan said. "Or I'll torture and kill both of you."

Nick shook his head. "You can't go ten minutes without making a threat, can you?"

"It's called leadership," Dragan said. "Stay in touch."

13

Nick and Kate walked back across avenue du Maine and along rue Brézin. Kate didn't speak until they were heading up toward the Mouton-Duvernet metro station.

"What possessed you to tell Dragan that you knew about the smallpox?" Kate asked.

"I wanted to hurry things along."

"You could have hurried us into graves."

"It worked, didn't it? He told us his whole, twisted plan."

"I wanted to shoot him in the head."

"Has anyone ever talked with you about anger management?"

"Yes," she said. "That's why I *didn't* shoot him. But he still has to be stopped."

"He will be," Nick said.

"I could alert Jessup right now so he can organize a multi-agency raid on Dragan's place in Sorrento."

"Wouldn't do us any good," Nick said. "We don't know where he's going from here. Even if he does go back to Sorrento, you don't know if his lab is there, and his sources in Italian law enforcement will tip him off about the raid. He'll escape, you'll confiscate a bunch of lemons, and lose your best chance to stop his scheme."

"So what do you suggest we do?"

"We steal the smallpox for him," Nick said. "Or at least make him believe that we have."

"I get it," she said. "You're going to switch the real smallpox with a harmless vial of something else."

"I don't know what I am going to do. But you've heard the phrase *Follow the money,* right?"

"It's a tried-and-true method of investigation. It almost always leads to the heart of any criminal conspiracy."

"We're going to use the same approach. Only we're going to 'Follow the pox' to find his lab and the virus that he's already got."

They walked past the Mouton-Duvernet station and up to place Denfert-Rochereau. Here seven streets converged in a plaza around a bronze sculpture of a proud lion the size of a bus.

"That's the Lion of Belfort, a bronze replica by Frédéric-Auguste Bartholdi of his monumental sandstone sculpture

133

in the hills above Belfort, a village near the German border," Nick said. "Bartholdi is perhaps best known for the Statue of Liberty. The lion honors French Colonel Denfert-Rochereau, who defended Belfort 'like a lion' against a Prussian siege for a hundred days in 1870 even though he was vastly outnumbered."

"Why do you know so much about some random sculpture?"

"I've thought about stealing it," Nick said.

"Why would you want to do that?" Kate said. "It's huge, it weighs tons, and it's right in the middle of a busy intersection. It's impossible to steal."

"That's why I want to," Nick said. "Maybe we can do it at the same time that we steal the smallpox."

"Steal the lion another day," Kate said. "Let's keep this simple. Relatively speaking."

Nick's cellphone chirped. He took it out of his pocket and glanced at it. "Our millions have arrived. Dragan may be a homicidal lunatic, but he pays his bills promptly."

"That's his one virtue," Kate said.

"He also produces an excellent *limoncello.*"

They crossed the plaza, where avenue du Général Leclerc became the tree-lined place Denfert-Rochereau, and continued walking up the west side of the street.

There was a florist on the corner, and then a nail salon, a furniture store, and an empty storefront, boarded up and available for rent. Beyond that was a block of beautifully renovated four-story buildings. It took a moment for Kate to realize they weren't individual buildings nor were they old. It was actually a recently constructed, single structure more than a half block long with multiple old-style façades that gave the impression of being several different buildings. But even that view was deceptive. It was actually a long wall with offices on top. The windows on the ground floor were barred and there were no doors to the street, just a guard-gated archway midway down the block leading to a motor court and more buildings beyond. There was a plaque written in French on the wall. Nick read it and gave Kate a translated summary.

"This was the site of the Saint Vincent de Paul Hospital for Children, the Home for Young Blind Girls, and other medical institutions. The original chapel is still here, but the rest has become the National Research Institute for Infectious Diseases." Nick stepped back from the wall and gave it, and the gate, a quick once-over. "It can't be any harder to break into than the Antwerp diamond vault."

"Perhaps," Kate said. "But diamonds can't kill you."

Nick and Kate took the metro from the place Denfert-Rochereau to Gare de Lyon train station, and from there they took a commuter train for the half-hour journey to Bois-le-Roi. They walked the two miles from the train station to Nick's house in silence, lost in their own thoughts.

Kate trudged through the door, slumped against the wall, and closed her eyes. "Stick a fork in me."

Nick leaned into her. His hands were at her hips and his lips skimmed across hers. "I'm feeling romantic."

"Ommigod," Kate said, more groan than spoken word. "What are you, Superman? How can you possibly be feeling romantic? I'm so tired I can't feel my fingertips."

"No problem. I'll help you get to the bedroom, and then all you have to do is lay there."

"Fine," Kate said. "Don't wake me when it's over."

"Okay, but you'll be sorry if you sleep through this. I have some new moves."

"Maybe I just need coffee."

"Good idea," Nick said. "You get comfortable and I'll whip up a double espresso."

Kate opened her eyes and stretched. She was alone. A shaft of light peeked from between the drapes and spotlighted the pillow where Nick should have been. She touched his side of the bed. It was cold. He hadn't been in bed for hours . . . if at all. She checked her iPhone on the nightstand for the time. It was a little after 6 A.M. Kate slipped out from under the heavy comforter and padded barefoot into the living room.

Nick was working at his laptop and making notes by hand on a yellow legal pad. There was an open Paris map, a half-empty pot of coffee, and a crinkled-up Toblerone wrapper beside the laptop.

"What are you doing?" Kate asked.

"Plotting a crime."

"You never came to bed."

"No. You instantly fell asleep so I drank the coffee and

came in here to work. I couldn't stop thinking about stealing the smallpox. There was too much I didn't know. So I started doing some research. The institute comprises half a dozen buildings. They are patrolled 24/7 by armed security guards and covered by hundreds of cameras, inside and out. Every door is locked, and they require a card key to open, even the broom closets and bathrooms."

"That's not surprising." Kate went into the kitchen to make fresh coffee. The kitchen had a cast-iron stove, a farmhouse sink, butcher-block countertops, and a coffee maker so elaborate that Kate thought it might be capable of cold fusion. It was too daunting to even think about using it. What was the point of having a rustic old kitchen if he was going to put that appliance on the counter?

"There's more," Nick said. "To get to the biocontainment labs, you not only need a card key, but you have to pass a fingerprint scan and retina scan at every stage. There are at least eight doors to pass through before you finally get to a seat in front of a microscope."

"Do you have any instant coffee?" Kate asked.

"I have rat poison," he said. "It's probably tastier. I'll make you an espresso in a minute."

Kate opened the refrigerator and surveyed the contents while Nick continued his briefing.

"The labs are also under constant video surveillance and are protected by an array of high-tech gizmos, including motion detectors and infrared sensors," Nick said. "I was wrong. A biocontainment lab is even better protected than a diamond vault."

"You like a challenge," Kate said.

The refrigerator was filled with various cheeses, several paper-wrapped packages of butcher-sliced meat, a packet of smoked salmon, and some eggs. There were grapes, mushrooms, carrots, asparagus, and green peppers in the drawers. It all looked like too much work for breakfast. She'd have traded it all for Folgers crystals and Cocoa Krispies.

"But I've got some good news," Nick said.

She closed the refrigerator and looked back at him. "You have Cap'n Crunch?"

"The labs have independent air flow and exhaust systems separate from the rest of the building to keep any viruses from escaping. As an extra precaution, the labs are all underground and practically encased in concrete."

She gave up on food and drink, took a seat in a chair beside him. "Why is that good news?"

"Because the metro, the sewer, the city aqueduct, and the catacombs all run under the place Denfert-Rochereau."

"The 'catacombs'?"

"Abandoned limestone quarries under the city that are filled with the bones of millions of dead Parisians that were unearthed from cemeteries over the centuries," Nick said. "Part of it is a popular tourist attraction."

"My God."

"They used to give boat tours of the sewers, too."

"Makes me wonder what Paris Disneyland is like."

"The point is, the ground underneath the institute is a maze of tunnels. We can dig our way into the lab."

"Do you know where to find the lab and the smallpox?"

"Nope, that's top secret. The institute isn't supposed to have smallpox. We'll never find out where it is."

"I'm sure you'll come up with a way to find it," Kate said. "In the meantime, I'll run into town and get us some Pop-Tarts."

"They don't have Pop-Tarts here," Nick said. "They have fresh croissants and baguettes."

"You really are out in the boonies. It's a good thing Paris is only a thirty-minute train ride away."

"I thought you were giving up the microwave for me."

"I never said that and, besides, you don't microwave Pop-Tarts," Kate said. "How can you be a criminal mastermind and not know that? They are a tasty toaster treat."

"Forget about Pop-Tarts," Nick said. "I've got the plot all worked out. It doesn't matter where the lab is, or where they keep the smallpox, because we don't need to know any of that to pull off this heist."

"Maybe I'm tired, and in desperate need of caffeine and sugar, but I think I'm missing something," Kate said. "How can we break into a lab and steal the smallpox if we don't know where the lab or the smallpox are?"

"Because we're not tunneling into the lab." Nick pulled over his Paris map and circled a building next door to the institute on avenue Denfert-Rochereau. "We're going to tunnel in here."

Kate looked at the map. The building wasn't labeled. "What's in there?"

"It was a terrible Indian restaurant for a while," Nick said. "Before that it was a travel agency. Now it's vacant and available for rent. But soon there's going to be a world-class level-four biocontainment lab in the basement."

Now it was all becoming clear to Kate, and she couldn't help smiling at the beauty of the con. "We're going to break into a fake lab and steal fake smallpox."

"That's the idea," he said.

"It's so wonderfully simple." How did he come up with that so fast? It was one of the things about him that used to aggravate the hell out of her when she was trying to arrest him.

"It's not quite as simple as it sounds," he said. "To succeed, we have to pull off a dangerous balancing act that could go wrong in a thousand different ways."

"Creating the fake lab is the kind of thing we've done before," Kate said. "We've got a crew we know can do it."

"The trick isn't building the set, it's making the Road Runners, a group of very smart professional thieves, believe that they're tunneling into the real lab and that the smallpox is genuine," Nick said. "The heist needs to feel completely authentic in every way. Not just the work itself, but the palpable risk, the ever-present sense of danger. We have to create a totally immersive physical and emotional experience. One false note and it's over."

"So where do we start?"

"With omelets and espresso."

14

Uber driver Gaëlle Rochon was on her way to pick up a couple at the Parc des Buttes-Chaumont. She thought this was a charming name for what was once an abandoned limestone quarry used as a garbage dump and a pit for dead horses. In 1867, the putrid site was transformed into a popular Paris park, a romantic landscape painting come to life with a faux Roman temple atop a lushly landscaped, dramatic peak on a mountain in the center of an artificial lake. When Gaëlle looked at that lake, she imagined the dead horses floating just below the surface.

Of course, she'd always been more interested in what lay beneath Paris, and in the city's past rather than its present. It was her father's fault. The widower had spent his life as an *égoutier,* a worker in the sewers, pushing muck along the channels with his ever-present *rabot,* a pole with an angled paddle at the end. On nights and weekends, he and his beloved precocious daughter explored the secret world of the catacombs. When her father died five years ago, she followed his final wishes and scattered his ashes in the ossuary beneath place Denfert-Rochereau. Now, when she wasn't driving the streets of Paris, she spent every free moment wandering the two hundred miles of forbidden catacombs beneath them, the sewers, subways, canals, quarries, and crypts that made up the underworld. She was twenty-seven years old, five foot three, blond, and slim. Maintaining her weight was important for crawling through some of the tight tunnels between chambers without getting stuck.

She knew her way around Paris much better from below than she did from above, except when it came to the nineteenth arrondissement, where Parc des Buttes-Chaumont was located. This was her neighborhood, and this Uber pickup was her first of the day. She pulled up to the park's entry gate at place Armand Carrel in her rented Peugeot 508 sedan and got out to greet her clients.

Gaëlle wore a gray pantsuit and an open-collared white shirt so that she looked more like a personal chauffeur than a taxi driver.

The stylish young couple, obviously Americans, immediately double-checked her identity from her photo and the make of the car that popped up on the Uber app on the man's iPhone. She opened the back door of the Peugeot for them in the meantime.

"Good afternoon," she said. "Where can I take you?"

"Au Vieux Campeur, 48 rue des Écoles, s'il vous plait," the man said.

"Oui, monsieur." He got extra points from Gaëlle for having a perfect French accent.

She knew Au Vieux Campeur well. It was a sporting goods shop that sold a lot of the equipment that *cataphiles* like her needed to explore the underground. The store was in the heart of Saint-Germain on the Left Bank, which was great news, because getting there would take the couple past a lot of Paris highlights, like the Pompidou Centre and Notre Dame, and that usually led to a more generous tip. She got behind the wheel and headed west on rue Armand Carrel.

"My name is Nick, and this is Kate," the man said in English.

"Nice to meet you," Gaëlle said.

"We're thrilled to meet you, too, Gaëlle," Kate said. "We're looking forward to you showing us around after we do some shopping."

"Are you interested in a city tour?" Gaëlle asked them.

"Definitely," Kate said.

"I can show you the sites, but I have to warn you, I'm not a tour guide," Gaëlle said. "You'll get better details from your guidebook."

"Not for the catacombs," Nick said. "We'd like to see what lies beneath Paris."

She eyed him suspiciously in her rearview mirror. Who were these two? How did they know she was a *cataphile*?

"There's a tour of *les catacombes* ossuary at place Denfert-Rochereau," she said. "I can drop you off out front. Tickets are twelve euro. I can pick you up at the exit on rue Rémy Dumoncel when your tour is over."

"We want to see more than the bones," Kate said. "We'd like to get a feel for the catacombs as a whole, the entire network of subways, sewers, quarry galleries, and access tunnels under Denfert-Rochereau."

"What makes you think I know anything about that?" Gaëlle asked.

"Because you were practically raised down there, and the sewer workers are like your family," Kate said. "That's why the police and the agents of the Inspection Générale des Carrières turn a blind eye to your trespassing. Anybody else who spent as much time down there as you do would have been put in jail or bankrupted with fines by now."

It was obvious to Gaëlle now that it was no coincidence they'd ordered an Uber pickup at Buttes-Chaumont Park. They knew she'd be the closest Uber car because they knew that's where she lived. *They were waiting for her.* That creeped her out big-time.

"How do you know who I am?" she asked. "Who are you?"

"Two fun-loving, adventurous people who are very curious about the underground," Nick said. "And who have the resources to find the best person in Paris to be our guide."

"We're sorry if you feel we've invaded your privacy," Kate said. "We meant no offense or harm. We'll make up for it by paying you your day fare plus a thousand euros to take us on a guided tour of the underground."

The money was definitely enticing, but she couldn't shake the uncomfortable feeling that came from these two Americans knowing so much about her.

"I don't have the gear for it, and neither do you," Gaëlle said.

"That's why we're heading to Au Vieux Campeur," Nick said. "We'll buy whatever is needed for ourselves and for you. So you'll also be getting brand-new spelunking gear out of this on top of what we're paying you."

The deal was getting better every minute, but even so, it felt wrong, like she was betraying something sacred. The catacombs were her sanctuary.

"If you're looking for a place to take that unique Paris selfie that nobody else has to show off to your Facebook friends, then forget it," Gaëlle said. "The real catacombs, not the cleaned-up, well-lit portion that's open to the public, are not a tourist attraction. It is a very special place that needs to be respected."

"We'll treat it like a church," Nick said.

"It's also rough and dangerous down there. There are no

bathrooms, drinking fountains, or places to get a latte. The air can be dusty and foul. You'll have to crawl through some tight spaces, wade through raw sewage, and walk through unstable caverns that could collapse at any time. If you're the slightest bit claustrophobic, you will be entering hell," Gaëlle said. "It's a rugged wilderness. It's not a walk in the park."

"We can handle ourselves," Kate said.

Gaëlle glanced back at Kate and Nick and appraised them. They were fit, and there was a steely confidence in Kate's eyes. Gaëlle believed they could take care of themselves. Even so, she didn't like it.

"The spiders down there are as big as your hand and have a nasty bite," Gaëlle said. "The rats aren't afraid of people and will attack if they feel cornered. There's rat feces and urine everywhere and, if it gets in an open wound, it can kill you."

"And yet, you love it underground," Kate said.

"The catacombs are left over from underground quarrying for limestone that began in the thirteenth century and didn't end until 1860. For centuries, people have worked or sought refuge in the catacombs. There's sketches, murals, carvings, and graffiti from the Prussian war, the storming of the Bastille, the German occupation during World War II, the riots of the 1960s, every historical event you can think of and some you never heard about."

"It's a natural museum," Nick said.

"It's much more than that," Gaëlle said. "There's also the bones of six million Parisians down there, nearly three times the living population of Paris. Maybe their ghosts are there too, and that's what makes the silence so profound. It's an escape from everything, true peace. There are places so quiet, it feels as if you've escaped from your body and merged with the earth and everybody who has ever walked on it. The past is alive down there in ways no museum could ever be."

"Now you know why we picked you as our guide," Nick said. "Do we have a deal?"

"If I see you take a single selfie," Gaëlle said, "I'll smash your phone with a rock."

15

After a shopping spree at Au Vieux Campeur, where Gaëlle had them buy enough equipment to scale Mount Everest, she drove them south through place Denfert-Rochereau. She parked on avenue Jean Moulin, where the street passed over railroad tracks. Both sides of the embankment were lined with cyclone fencing.

The three of them got out wearing blue coveralls and calf-high steel-toed rubber boots. In their heavy-duty nylon backpacks, they had helmets with headlamps, kneepads and elbow pads, industrial rubber gloves, plastic goggles, dust masks, reflective flagging tape, canteens, flashlights, and first-aid kits. Gaëlle also made them throw in ropes, chest and waist harnesses, ascender clamps and descender clamps, caving hammers, and carabiners just in case they wanted to rappel down to the center of the earth.

"This is the Petite Ceinture, the 'little belt,' a rail line built by Napoleon the Third. It followed the walls that once encircled Paris," Gaëlle said, leading them over a bridge. "It was basically abandoned in 1934, but the tunnels, stations, and tracks all still exist."

On the other end of the bridge, the cyclone fencing had been cut, creating a flap that could be pushed open. Gaëlle crouched down and climbed through. Kate and Nick followed. Gaëlle led them down the chipped concrete steps that ran alongside the graffiti-covered footings of the bridge to the tracks below.

"There are many levels to the underground," Gaëlle said as they walked along the tracks. "The sewers, aqueducts, and metro lines are closest to the surface at thirty to fifty feet below. There are some church crypts, utility tunnels, and underground garages that go just as deep. The limestone quarries and ossuaries are fifty to ninety feet below the streets and are interconnected by Inspection Générale des Carrières, or IGC, access tunnels. The IGC monitors the below-ground quarries for public hazards like extraordinary contamination or possible collapse."

The embankment seemed to get deeper as they walked, and the streets above began to fade away in the upper periphery of Kate's vision. The weedy, rusty tracks and the overgrown plants on either side of her made it easy to imagine they were in a postapocalyptic world where nature had taken back everything that man had built. As they neared the mouth of a railway tunnel, Kate realized that there were no longer any buildings around, only trees and dense shrubs, and that the street noise was nearly gone.

"Where are we?" she asked.

"Parc Montsouris," Gaëlle said and stopped in front of the railroad tunnel. "Time to suit up."

She unzipped her backpack and put on her gloves, helmet, and kneepads. Nick and Kate did the same.

Gaëlle flicked her helmet light on and walked into the dark tunnel. The walls were covered with graffiti, and the air was heavy with the stench of urine and stale beer. The floor of the tunnel was littered with mattresses and discarded cans and bottles. Midway down the tunnel, Gaëlle stopped in front of a piece of plywood wedged up against the wall near her feet.

"There are many ways into the catacombs. You can get in through basements, parking garages, metro tunnels, sewer lines, and manholes. We are already forty feet below street level here, so this saved us a descent." She slid the plywood aside to reveal a jagged hole cut into the stone, barely large enough for a person to fit through. "Go in feetfirst and drag your pack in behind you. Watch your head when you get up."

She took a rag from her pocket and tied it in a knot around her neck.

"What's that for?" Kate asked.

"Habit and tradition," Gaëlle said. "The sewer men began wearing these knotted rags centuries ago to protect themselves from the biting spiders that can drop on them. But mostly I do it because I'd feel naked without it under there."

Terrific, Kate thought. Biting spiders. How fun was that?

Gaëlle climbed in, followed by Nick and then Kate. It was a tight fit, opening to a passage that was barely three feet high. They walked in a crouch for about twenty yards, their helmets scraping against the stones sticking out of the ceiling, before they reached an intersection with another corridor where they could stand upright. The walls in this corridor were a mix of carved rock and stacked stone reinforcement.

Gaëlle stopped and pointed to an engraved plate in the wall that read *Avenue d'Orleans.* "In many places, the names of the streets above are engraved in the walls."

"By whom?" Nick asked.

"Miners, sewer workers, smugglers, resistance fighters, the IGC doing inspections, or just somebody handy with a hammer and pick," Gaëlle said. "You'll find signs here going back centuries. This is an old one. Avenue d'Orleans was changed in 1948 to avenue du Général Leclerc. It's easy to find your way around in the sewers. For every street in Paris, there is a matching sewer underneath, right down to the street signs on the corners."

They entered a corridor with knee-high water and sloshed through it for a while until they reached some dry tunnels that spilled out into a series of larger caverns, all covered with artwork. Sculpted gargoyles peered out at them from one cavern. In another, limestone pillars sculpted to look like people holding up the earth.

"How often do the police patrol down here?" Nick asked.

"Police patrols are limited," Gaëlle said. "And there's a lot of ground to cover. Since the Paris terrorist attacks, the police are less interested in writing tickets for trespassing than making sure nobody puts a bomb under the Louvre. So they tend to patrol under important buildings now."

"Can we turn off the lights?" Kate asked. "I'd like to see the darkness and hear the silence."

They turned their helmet lights off and then the lanterns. The blackness that came was the most complete Kate had ever experienced. The only sound she heard was their breathing.

They turned their lights back on and Gaëlle led them out of the cavern, down a long, low corridor, and across another gallery and into one of the many tunnels. She stopped in front of a chest-high hole cut in the wall. The hole was about the size of a doggy door. When they emerged on the other side of the hole they were standing in a river of dry human bones that rose as high as Kate's ankle. The floor of the entire corridor, as far as their headlamps could reveal, was covered with bones.

"You get used to it," Gaëlle said, heading on down the tunnel. "After a while, you forget they are bones."

Kate and Nick followed Gaëlle out of the ossuary, up a ladder of iron rungs embedded in the wall, to another level. This was a more modern passage, finished in smooth

153

concrete and lined with all kinds of pipes, wires, and electrical conduits.

"This is a telecom and utility corridor," Gaëlle said. "Built about thirty years ago, but workmen are always down here, adding new lines for cable television, high-speed Internet, whatever. You'll also find cables like these running through some of the ossuaries."

"In case the dead want to check their email," Nick said. "Or binge on *The Walking Dead*."

"I've done both," Gaëlle said.

"I thought you came down here for the solitude," Kate said.

"Not always," Gaëlle said. "Sometimes I just want to relax, watch a movie, and really crank up the sound, so I bring down my laptop and hijack a movie off one of the cables. The acoustics down here are great."

"You're not worried about anyone hearing you?" Nick asked.

"We're under thirty feet or more of limestone. You could bring a band down here for a concert and nobody will hear a thing."

They went down several intersecting utility corridors, some of them lit by lights on the walls, until they came to a door that looked like a watertight hatch from a submarine. Gaëlle spun the wheel, opened the heavy door, and they stepped into a wide, arched chamber with a river of sewage running down the center. The smell wasn't as a bad as Kate had expected. It wasn't much worse than a men's locker room. A blue plaque with white letters on the wall read *Boulevard Saint-Jacques*.

"This is one of the sewer lines," Gaëlle said. "The sewer men walk along the side paths with paddle tools to move the muck along. Or a bunch of men will drag a sluice boat through the center channel with ropes to do the job. The work hasn't really changed in centuries."

They walked along the concrete banks, which were dimly lit every few feet by industrial lights on the wall. Gaëlle pointed out the huge pipes above them that carried freshwater and a series of tubes that used to be part of the post office's vast abandoned pneumatic network for delivering letters to buildings by compressed air.

They crossed a bridge over the sewer channel to a ladder built into the wall that went up about twenty feet into a circular shaft. Kate looked up and saw a pinhole of sunlight streaming through a manhole cover.

Gaëlle climbed up the shaft, moved the manhole cover aside, and they were bathed with sunlight and blasted with noise. Kate and Nick followed Gaëlle up and found themselves standing on the sidewalk of boulevard Saint-Jacques, facing place Denfert-Rochereau and the Lion of Belfort. Kate had to squint and hold a hand up to shade her eyes. The sunlight seemed unusually harsh after the pitch-darkness of the underground.

"I brought you up here because this spot is unique," Gaëlle said and pointed to the train station across the street. "That's the regional rapid transit system line, the RER. There's also a metro station here, a subway line, the sewers, an aqueduct, utility corridors, and, below it all, the catacombs. All the levels of the underground world come together here. It also used to be the entrance to Paris. It's a short walk back to the car from here, or we can go through the sewer instead."

Kate wanted the fresh air but the sewer would give them more privacy for the conversation they still needed to have. "Let's take the sewer."

Gaëlle seemed surprised by the answer, but shrugged and headed back into the manhole. "As you wish."

Kate followed her down, and Nick brought up the rear, sliding the manhole cover back into place behind them. They walked alongside Gaëlle on the concrete banks to the sewer underneath place Denfert-Rochereau, then crossed a metal bridge to follow the line that ran under avenue du Général Leclerc.

"We didn't ask you to show us the underground out of idle curiosity or for the unusual experience," Kate said.

"I assumed there was more to it," Gaëlle said.

"Nick and I are operatives for an international private security company, and we've been hired to prevent a biological attack on the United States. The group that's planning this attack intends to steal the killer virus for their weapon from a basement lab at the Institut National pour la Recherche sur les Maladies Infectieuses."

"On Denfert-Rochereau," Gaëlle said, putting the pieces together. "They're going to dig their way in."

"They are and they aren't," Nick said. "We've infiltrated the group to trick them into breaking into a fake lab in the basement of another building on the same street. We need you to help us fool them."

"What could I do?" she asked.

"You'd be their guide. You'd lead them to the dig site by a different route each day, supposedly to avoid attracting attention, but really just to confuse them," Nick said. "We could also switch out some of the street signs underground to add to their confusion."

"After what we've experienced today," Kate said, "I don't think confusing them is going to be that hard."

"If what you are saying is true," Gaëlle said, "why is a private security firm stopping this terrorist attack and not the police? Who hired you?"

"We can't tell you who our client is," Kate said. "But I can say that we're often hired because we can ignore laws, jurisdictions, and national borders that restrict the ability of law enforcement agencies and governments to do their jobs."

"We aren't accountable to taxpayers, either, and have very deep pockets," Nick said. "We'll pay you a hundred thousand euros to help us."

Gaëlle stopped and stared at him. "How much?"

"One hundred thousand euros."

She kept staring at him. *"Mon Dieu. Vraiment?"*

"*Oui,*" Nick replied.

"Before you get seduced by the money," Kate said, "you need to know that what we are asking you to do is extremely dangerous. You'll be undercover among killers. We'll be there with you, and we'll do our best to protect you, but we can't guarantee your safety."

Gaëlle narrowed her eyes. "How do I know you're who you say you are?"

"You don't," Kate said. "You'd have to trust us."

"Two complete strangers that I just met," Gaëlle said. "Telling a pretty fantastical story."

"That's right," Kate said.

"But once you're involved, you'll see the inner workings of the con and the time, effort, and expense that's going into it," Nick said. "It will be immediately clear to you that we couldn't be doing anything else except what we say we are."

"There will also be nothing stopping you at any time from walking away or going to the police or telling the bad guys who we are," Kate said. "So the trust works both ways. We'll be trusting you with our lives and those of our team."

"You have other people involved in this?" Gaëlle said.

"People we've recruited for their special skills," Kate said. "Just like you."

Gaëlle thought about it for a long moment. "I haven't done much with my life. I just drive people around and wander through dark tunnels, lost in the past or myself. What good has it been? What have I achieved? If I can use that experience to save lives, then everything I've done up until now has actually meant something. So yes, I'll help you, and I'll take your money, too."

Nick shook her hand. "Welcome to the team."

16

Chez Schwartz Charcuterie Hebraique de Montreal opened in 1928 on boulevard Saint-Laurent. It was in an area smack between Montreal's English-speaking population to the west, the French-speaking to the east, and the immigrant, ethnic mix that populated the strip in between. While that area transformed over time from an ethnic ghetto into the hip, artsy heart of the city, Schwartz's remained essentially unchanged and became famous for its "smoked meat," a fatter, spicier, Canadian version of pastrami. There was always a line out the door for a seat at one of Schwartz's communal tables because only sixty customers at a time could fit inside. Even so, Huck Moseby had a table completely to himself to enjoy his "extra fat" smoked meat sandwich, French fries, and Cott Black Cherry soda.

It wasn't because he was wealthy, powerful, or someone so outwardly repulsive or frightening that others steered clear of him. Huck was an average-looking forty-four-year-old man, slightly pudgy and perhaps a little too pale, wearing a ragged Musée de Florentiny T-shirt with a faded picture of Rembrandt's *Old Man Eating Bread by Candlelight* on the back. So he fit right in. The place was full of hipsters in fashionably vintage clothes and stylishly torn jeans.

After twelve years employed as a sewer engineer for Hydro-Québec, Huck had acquired a faint, but persistent, *l'air du poop* that wouldn't go away, no matter how much he showered nor how many gallons of Old Spice that he put on. It was also why he hadn't been laid in six years, except for a merciful prostitute who'd had a raging head cold.

It was a sad, pitiful situation that would have destroyed the self-respect of most men. But Huck Moseby wasn't most men. He took strength from the secret knowledge that he was a criminal genius. A few years ago, he'd committed the biggest robbery in Canadian history, tunneling into the Musée de Florentiny from the sewer to steal their entire collection of masterworks. Problem was there were two other robbers, a man and woman in ski masks, who coincidentally were already in the museum stealing the Rembrandts. The couple wouldn't let him have a Rembrandt or anything else, sending him back into his hole at gunpoint with only a Musée de Florentiny T-shirt to show for his brilliance and months of toil. The other thieves got the paintings, the glory, and even the credit for tunneling in, though he had no idea how they'd actually entered the museum. The paintings were recovered, but the two thieves were never caught.

It was because of that life-defining event that he wore the T-shirt almost constantly and wouldn't buy a new one even though they were still sold, in a variety of sizes and colors, at the Musée de Florentiny gift shop. The T-shirt was his armor against the indignities he had to endure each day.

He was taking a bite out of his thick sandwich when an attractive couple in their thirties sat down across from him at the table. He chewed and silently counted off the five seconds it usually took for his scent to travel across a tabletop and for the couple to awkwardly depart. Ten seconds passed, and they were still sitting there, perusing their menus while presumably awash in his *odor d'égout*.

"I've never seen a Jewish deli with a menu in French," the man said.

"I guess you aren't as worldly as you think you are," the woman said.

Huck felt a strange chill. There was something both sexy and familiar about her voice.

"We never got around to visiting this place on our last trip to Montreal," the man said.

"We were in a bit of a hurry," the woman said, and abruptly met Huck's gaze, startling him.

He'd never seen her face, but he was certain that he'd looked into those striking blue eyes before.

"Please tell me you've washed that shirt since we gave it to you," Kate said to Huck.

Huck dropped his sandwich on his plate and felt his heart drop along with it. *It was them.* The thieves who'd robbed the museum of their Rembrandts and him of his glory.

"It's you," Huck said, knowing the words were lame the moment he'd said them. "The two thieves who stole those paintings from me."

"They weren't yours," Kate said, "though they might have been if you'd got the drop on us instead of us getting the drop on you."

"It just wasn't your lucky day," Nick said.

"It wasn't fair," Huck said. "You got the Rembrandts. You could have let me take a Matisse or a Renoir. You were leaving them behind anyway."

"We were on our way out and wanted to make a clean getaway," Kate said. "We couldn't take the risk that you'd accidentally activate an alarm or otherwise alert the authorities."

"But you're right," Nick said. "It wasn't very gracious of us. We've been troubled by it ever since."

"Really?" Huck said.

He was flattered that they'd given him any thought at all. Somehow, it made him seem part of the fraternity of master thieves. But then he reminded himself of how they'd humiliated him and quickly changed his tone and demeanor.

"Troubled?" Huck said. "Is that how you felt rolling in your millions while I slept in this crummy T-shirt?"

Kate's eyebrows inched up. "You sleep in that shirt?"

"Figuratively speaking. The point is, I thought there was supposed to be honor among thieves, and you two showed none."

"You're right," Nick said. "We disrespected you. That's why we're here, to make amends."

"Are you going to give me a million or two?" Huck asked and picked up his pickle. "If not, you can shove this pickle up your ass and leave."

"We want to make it up to you by bringing you in on a heist that requires your unique expertise," Nick said.

The man who'd stolen the Rembrandts from the Musée de Florentiny was coming to Huck Moseby for his expertise. That was even better than a million dollars. It confirmed everything Huck believed about himself and that had sustained him for so long. He really was a criminal genius.

Huck leaned forward and whispered, "What's the caper?"

Kate leaned toward him and instantly thought better of it. He really did smell bad. "Are you familiar with the Road Runners?"

Of course he was. "They are international diamond thieves, maybe the best in the world."

"We're working with them, but we're going after something more valuable than diamonds," Kate said. "We're stealing a biological agent from a high-security research lab in central Paris. We're tunneling into the lab through the sewers. It's extremely dangerous and if we're caught, we'll be spending our lives in a French prison."

"That's why we need Huck Moseby," Nick said. "You're a professional sewer engineer, an experienced excavator, a world-class thief, and you can pass as French. You were born for this job."

Huck was still reeling from being called a world-class thief. He went deaf and numb for a moment. He didn't listen to what else Nick had said, but after that clear acknowledgment of his talent, he was on board for anything.

"What is it you need me to do?" Huck asked.

"Lead the excavation team and get us inside the lab," Nick said. "You're the best sewer man in the game."

He had a reputation? He was in the game? He was THE BEST? Why hadn't anyone told him? That knowledge, that recognition, would have made the last few years so much different. Somebody should have sent him a certificate or something.

Huck leaned even closer, almost upending the table. He wanted to be sure he was hearing this right and not having a delusional episode. "Let me get this straight. You want me to go to Paris and lead the Road Runners in a dig through the sewers into a high-security laboratory."

"That's right," Nick said, leaning back. "And we'll pay you a hundred thousand dollars to do it."

Huck took a deep swig of his cherry soda, wishing that

it was something stronger, even though alcohol gave him tremendous gas.

He couldn't believe what he'd just heard. The people who'd pulled off the biggest robbery in Canadian history wanted to pay him $100,000 to lead the best thieves on earth in a subterranean heist in the most magnificent sewer in the world. It was all he could do not to cry with joy. But that wouldn't be fitting behavior for a world-class thief. So instead he cleared his throat, sat back, and pondered his soft drink can as if he were actually struggling with the decision.

"Who will I be working for?" Huck asked.

"Me," Nick said.

"Who are you?"

"I'm Nicolas Fox and this is my associate, Kate. You get us inside and we'll do the rest."

Huck's jaw dropped, and he covered up his shock by reaching for his sandwich as if he'd opened his mouth to prepare for a bite. He took a mouthful of smoked meat and used the chewing time to get a grip. Nicolas Fox was a legend. Huck was going to be among the greats.

"You'll be calling the shots underground," Nick said. "You know sewers and excavation and we don't. You'll be working with a local expert on the Paris underground. She will be your number two."

A woman in the sewer. This job was getting better every second. He nodded as he chewed and tried to swallow.

"Your crew will be as many Road Runners as you think are necessary," Nick said. "These are smash-and-grab guys, not diggers, so you'll have to show them the ropes. We'll all be meeting in Paris in seven days for a recon. After that, you'll give me a list of what you need, we'll get it, and then we'll go to work."

"Assuming you're interested, of course," Kate said. "We'd completely understand if you're not. You could die of old age in a French prison that makes Devil's Island look like Club Med."

Huck swallowed, and picked a piece of meat out of his front teeth. He didn't want to appear too eager in front of Nicolas Fox.

"I've got a number of ambitious capers in the cooker here that I can put on hold," Huck said, "but not for a hundred grand."

"How much do you want?"

He was the best sewer man in the game and deserved compensation commensurate with his talent, but he didn't want to let this dream slip through his fingers. "One hundred and twenty-five thousand, all expenses paid, and first-class airfare."

"You drive a hard bargain," Nick said.

"I'm a hard man," Huck said.

He actually was. All this talk of his expertise was better than Viagra, not that he needed it or had any opportunity to put the results to work. But that would change now that he was a master thief. Women would sense his magnificence and flock to him.

Nick glanced at Kate. She gave him a slight nod. Nick smiled and held his hand out to Huck.

"We have a deal," Nick said and got up. "We'll be in touch."

They walked out and Huck was alone again at an empty table, left to wonder if it had all been a figment of his imagination.

"I'm still not comfortable with this," Kate said as they left Huck in Schwartz's and walked down boulevard Saint-Laurent to their rented Porsche Cayenne parked a block away.

"Yes, I know. I noticed how hard you were trying to dissuade him."

"Huck doesn't realize it, but, when we first met him, we saved him from a life of crime and likely imprisonment. Now we've sucked him back into it."

"Not if we don't arrest him," Nick said.

"But we're paying him to commit a crime."

"We're paying everybody in our crew to do that."

"But they are doing it for the right reasons."

"We can't tell Huck that we're conning the Road Runners to prevent a terrorist attack," Nick said. "Huck has to believe in what he's doing to convince the Road Runners that this is real. He's a key part of creating that authenticity I was talking about."

"Is that why you told him who you are?"

"The Road Runners know who I am, that means he has to as well. Besides, it also bolsters our position with Dragan and the Road Runners. He can attest that you and I pulled off the biggest heist in Canadian history."

"We told Gaëlle Rochon about the con."

"Because we need her to confuse the Road Runners underground so they won't figure out they aren't actually digging underneath the institute," Nick said. "She wouldn't have helped if she thought we were real thieves, and Huck won't help us if he knows that we aren't."

"He might have for the money and the thrill."

"Maybe, but it's too risky. It goes back to the authenticity we're trying to create. The Road Runners have to believe that Gaëlle knows her way through the underworld, and that it's as much of a maze as we say it is," Nick said. "That will come through naturally. It doesn't require her to act. Huck can't act. He could barely stop himself from crying when we offered him the job. If Huck knew he wasn't really digging into a real lab, he'd show it. By us not telling Huck, his enthusiasm and determination will be real."

"Okay, but what happens if Huck comes back here after this is over, convinced that he's 'the best sewer man in the game' and starts looking for a museum to rob?"

"He'll be so terrified by the way this heist ultimately turns out that he'll never want to commit a crime again," Nick said. "He'll thank God that he got out alive and with his hundred and twenty-five thousand dollars."

"I hope you're right," Kate said as they reached their car. "Because I don't want his next heist and his eventual imprisonment on my conscience."

"Let's just survive this job first," Nick said, unlocking the car and walking around to the driver's side.

"Good point."

"If I'm wrong about Huck, I promise you that we'll come up with a way to scare him straight."

"You also need to talk to Gaëlle and caution her against talking to Huck."

They got into the car and headed for the airport, where they had a private jet waiting to take them to Los Angeles.

17

Boyd Capwell ran across an open field in Ojai, California. He was being pursued by half a dozen bug-eyed bald women in halter tops and cutoffs. The women were running with their arms outstretched and their gnarled hands clawing at the air in front of them as if it might bring Boyd closer to their drooling, wide-open, shrieking mouths.

He was racing for the forest and freedom when more of the mutant women poured out from between the trees like a tidal wave, screeching their insane, lusty cry as they charged toward him. There was no place for him to go. He was surrounded.

Boyd dropped to his knees, a beaten man, and looked up to the sky. Tears streamed down his chiseled anchorman's face, his fists were balled up with rage.

"Why, God, why? What have I done to deserve your pitiless wrath?"

The sky rumbled, as if God were clearing his throat to speak, and out of the blue heavens came the Hellcopter. An airborne gunship that looked like a flying great white shark sheathed in cannons, machine guns, harpoons, and missiles.

The Hellcopter swooped down low, its machine guns spitting hot death, mowing down the mutant women. Boyd stood up to face the Hellcopter as it landed. The pilot's door opened and out came Willie Owens, boobs first. Her enormous breasts strained against a tight, nearly transparent white T-shirt. Besides the double-D silicone boobs, collagen-plumped lips, and peroxide blond hair, there was nothing mutant about the woman in the Daisy Duke shorts and pumps. She was all woman and proud of it.

Willie strutted up to Boyd, tore open his shirt, buttons flying, and appraised his body, which wasn't bad for a guy in his forties who didn't exercise.

"Finally, a real man," she said.

"Finally, a real woman," he said.

He reached for her breasts, and she kicked him in the knee.

"Cut!" Boyd yelled, clutching his knee.

Nick Fox turned to Chet Kershaw, a big bear of a man in his early forties with a professional makeup bag slung over his shoulder. Nick and Chet were standing together out in a field, under a tent that covered a bank of monitors. The monitors showed various angles on the action. Kate O'Hare and Tom

Underhill, an African American man in his thirties with a tool belt around his waist, were in the tent, too. Tom was holding a remote control joystick to pilot a drone with a tiny GoPro camera attached to it. They were watching the live stream of the GoPro's video on one of the monitors.

"Was that kick in the script?" Nick asked.

"Nope," Chet said.

Chet was the last in a family dynasty of Hollywood makeup artists and special effects masters adept at all the live, "on set" magic in front of the cameras that was now primarily done digitally in postproduction.

"That was my favorite part," Kate said.

"Mine, too," Tom said, landing the drone beside the tent.

Tom's day job was making inventive playhouses, tree houses, and other fanciful structures. He'd retrofitted the old helicopter, which Nick had acquired for a past scam, into a fake Hellcopter combat vehicle for this film.

Willie marched over to them, Boyd trailing after her, limping. She was a fifty-something single Texan with a natural affinity and dangerous zeal for driving or piloting just about anything on land, sea, or air with a motor.

Joe Morey was right behind them, a Steadicam rig strapped to his upper body to hold a digital camera. He was an electronic security and alarm systems expert who excelled in hidden video and audio surveillance.

"Why did you kick me?" Boyd yelled at her. "You killed the emotion of the scene."

"Because you tried to cop a feel," Willie said. "That's not going to happen."

"I wasn't 'copping a feel,'" Boyd said. "My character was reaching out to touch the humanity that he thought he'd lost."

"It was you using this movie as an excuse to feel me up," Willie said. "Something you've wanted to do for years."

"It's acting," Boyd said. "Didn't you read the script?"

"Which you wrote so you could touch my tits."

"Which I wrote to showcase your talent as a pilot, Chet's talent as a makeup and visual effects artist, Tom's talent as an imagineer, Joe's talent with cameras and sound, and my skills as triple-threat multi-hyphenate writer, actor, and director." Boyd looked back at Joe, who seemed startled to be seen. "Why are you still shooting? Didn't you hear me say 'cut'?"

"This is for the behind-the-scenes documentary," Joe said.

"Turn it off," Boyd said, then called back to the two dozen barely dressed, bloodied mutant women in the field. "Take five, but stay where you are. We're going to do a pickup on that last bit of dialogue, and we don't want to screw up the background continuity."

"What are you guys shooting here?" Nick asked.

"A short film we can use as an industry calling card," Chet said. "We'll post it on YouTube, Vimeo, IMDb, places like that. It's what you've got to do to get jobs in Hollywood these days."

"We've all done our best work with you two," Boyd said. "But we can't exactly use you as a reference or show our reel, can we?"

"I see your point," Nick said and turned to Joe. "I didn't know that you had Hollywood aspirations."

"I don't," Joe said. "I'm a single, hot-blooded man and I know my way around cameras and mikes. When Boyd told me he needed a camera and sound guy, and that there'd be a dozen strippers running around half-naked in front of me, how could I say no?"

"I see what you mean," Nick said.

Kate looked out at the women lounging in the field, smoking cigarettes, checking their emails, and snapping selfies. "They're strippers?"

"Who else would play these parts?" Willie said.

"This production must have cost a fortune," Nick said.

"You've paid us a fortune," Boyd said. "Unfortunately, we can't count on you for future employment. Work with you is unpredictable at best, and we've got our muses to serve. So we've reinvested some of our earnings in our own potential."

"I'm surprised you're doing another zombie flick," Nick said to Chet. "I thought you were tired of the genre."

"Those aren't zombies," Chet said.

"They sure look like hungry zombies to me," Kate said.

"It's lust," Chet said. "They don't want to eat Boyd. They want to screw him."

"Good grief," Kate said. "Why would they all want to do that?"

"My character is the last man on earth," Boyd said. "Germ warfare has turned people into sex-crazed mutants. The mutant men are sterile but the women are not. They need me, the last real man, to repopulate our planet and keep our race from going extinct."

"Of course they do," Kate said. "So what's stopping you from giving all those women what they want?"

"They're hideous," Boyd said. "I can't mate with them."

"Because of their appearance?" Kate said.

"Would you want the next evolution of the human race to look like that?" Boyd said. "My character is a reluctant Adam searching for a still human, still hot, postapocalyptic Eve."

Willie raised her hand. "That's me."

"So if you understand that," Boyd said, "why did you ruin the dramatic and emotional payoff to the whole story?"

"You mean the money shot?" Willie said.

"I mean the passionate salvation of the human race."

"Funny you should bring that up," Nick said. "That's kind of why we're here."

"I didn't think this was just a friendly visit," Tom said. "But aren't you being a bit melodramatic?"

"Unfortunately, he's not," Kate said. They were out of earshot of the strippers, but she lowered her voice to a near whisper as an extra precaution. "We need your help to prevent a biological attack on an American city by overseas terrorists."

"Wait a sec," Joe said. "Isn't that a job for Homeland Security, the CIA, or the U.S. military, and not some high-end private security firm?"

Chet laughed at Joe. "You honestly believe that's who they work for? These two go around the world taking down supercriminals. Have you ever thought about the money that they spend on the cons and thefts we've done together? It's millions of dollars. Who could their clients possibly be to pay that bill? That's why I've always figured that they're really working off the books for some U.S. acronym."

"I've never cared," Willie said. "I like the fast cars and the money."

"It doesn't matter to me who they are working for," Tom said. "What matters is that I can trust them, that they're doing the right thing, and that we've put a stop to some very bad people doing very bad things." He turned to Kate. "You can count me in on this."

"I appreciate that," Kate said. "But you don't even know what the assignment is yet, what the risks are, or what we are paying. You have a family to think about."

"That's right, I do," Tom said. "That's why if there's anything I can do to stop that biological attack from happening, I will do it and I won't take a dime for it, either."

"You'll do it for God and country," Boyd said. "That's powerful motivation for a character. I know, because that's my character's motivation today."

"Your motivation today is vanity and booty," Willie said. "You've cast yourself as the last man on earth that every woman wants to screw."

"Who is saving his precious seed for your character out of his profound love for God and country," Boyd said to her, then looked back at Kate. "The point I'm trying to make is that I'm in for whatever part you want me to play in this life-or-death drama. I am an American and this country 'tis of thee."

"I'm in, too," Willie said. "Because I like kicking ass and this sounds like some ass that needs kicking."

Chet raised his hand. "Count me in."

"Me, too," Joe said.

18

An hour later, after the movie was wrapped with Boyd's Adam and Willie's Eve locked in an embrace, they all reconvened in the barn. Boyd, Willie, Chet, Tom, and Joe sat on picnic table benches while Nick and Kate stood in front of them and briefed them on the broad strokes of the new project.

"You and Nick are such complex, conflict-ridden characters," Boyd said. "I've definitely got to play Nick in the movie."

"Wouldn't you rather play yourself?" Nick asked.

"Leonardo DiCaprio will want that part," Boyd said. "So will George Clooney, but I think he's too old to do me justice."

"Sofía Vergara without the accent would do a decent job as me," Willie said. "But she'd need to get a boob job."

"Her boobs are enormous," Chet said.

"Not enough," Willie said.

"I'll settle for any of the Hemsworths," Joe said. "I'm a dead ringer for all three of them."

"Hopefully, there will never be a movie, because if this story ever comes out, we'll all end up in jail," Kate said.

"But the FBI would get us out, right?" Tom said.

Joe gave his head a small shake. "I'm sure it's CIA."

"You're all wrong," Boyd said. "It's the Men in Black."

"No one is going to get us out of jail," Kate said.

She hoped that wasn't true, but there was no guarantee anyone could help them if things went wrong.

"Tell us about this biological attack," Boyd said. "And how my character is going to save a city."

"We've infiltrated a gang of international diamond thieves called the Road Runners," Kate said. "The group is made up almost entirely of ex-Serbian soldiers and led by a lunatic named Dragan Kovic."

"A very smart and cautious lunatic," Nick said. "They've made over four hundred million dollars from their robberies as of this week and have never been caught."

"Now we know what they were doing with all of that money," Kate said. "They've been developing a biological weapon that they will use to attack an American city. They plan to weaponize smallpox."

"My God," Tom said. "That's inhuman."

"They already have a smallpox sample, but it's not quite

good enough for their purposes," Nick said. "So they want Kate and me to steal a smallpox sample for them from a research institute in Paris."

"We need to find Dragan's lab, retrieve the smallpox sample they already have, and stop them from pulling off their attack," Kate said.

"Stealing the smallpox in Paris is how we're going to do it," Nick said. "We're going to use a tracking device to follow the stolen virus back to Dragan's lab and shut them down for good."

"Aren't you taking an enormous risk?" Joe said. "What if you lose track of the smallpox and they get away with it?"

"Eliminating the risk is where the con comes in," Nick said. He looked at Chet and Tom. "You two are going to build a fake biolab in the basement of an empty storefront on the same street as the real lab."

"The Road Runners will break into a fake lab and steal fake smallpox," Kate said. "The vial itself will be the tracking device that leads us to Dragan's lab. Nick and I will be part of the Road Runners crew tunneling into the institute to steal the virus."

"We've also recruited two other people," Nick said. "Gaëlle Rochon, an expert on the Paris underground, who will be aware that it's a con, and Huck Moseby, an experienced sewer worker and tunnel digger, who won't be."

"Gaëlle's job is to lead the Road Runners around in circles

so they don't know they are digging into the wrong building," Kate said. "Huck's job is to supervise the dig into the lab to steal the virus."

"I can get photos and blueprints of a real biolab," Tom said. "Building the fake lab should be easy. The critical issue is how real it has to be, and that depends on whether the Road Runners will be in the room or only seeing it on-screen."

"Same goes for dressing the lab with scientific equipment and props," Chet said. "How much of it has to actually work?"

"I will be the only one entering the lab where the smallpox is supposedly kept," Nick said. "The others won't go any further than the room that leads to it. That's the room we are going to dig into from below. So everything just has to look and sound good."

"Getting the necessary props and equipment, and making them all look like they are working, is not a problem, either," Chet said.

"In that case, if everybody kicks in to help on the construction, I can have the lab set built in a week," Tom said.

"I can dress it up as we go," Chet said.

Joe jerked a thumb at himself. "Where do I fit in?"

Nick turned to him. "We're going to recruit you as part of the Road Runner team to compromise and control the institute's security systems."

"Your cover will be easy to remember," Kate said. "You're going to be you. Not your real name, or your real past, but you'll be demonstrating your real skills."

"I can handle that, but I still don't get what I'll be doing," Joe said. "There is no security system for me to disable because we aren't really breaking into the institute."

"Your job is to create the illusion that we are," Nick said. "Early on in the job, you will tap into the institute's actual video surveillance system and integrate our fake lab's video feed into it for our robbers to see on a monitor that we'll set up underground for them. That will convince them of our make-believe world. On the day we break into the fake lab, you'll put on a convincing show of disabling the nonexistent alarm systems."

"No problemo," Joe said.

"I'm not sure you understand the danger you're going to be in," Kate said, concerned by his enthusiasm. "You're going to be undercover with us among the thieves. You won't be on the dig, you'll be in a van or someplace else nearby. But you will be living and working with the Road Runners while straddling both sides of the operation, the break-in and the con. That's a dangerous balance to maintain. If they catch you, they will kill you."

"I get it, don't worry," Joe said. "I'll create fake software interfaces for my computer screen so even if they have a guy sitting next to me in the van, he won't be clued in to what I am doing."

"Smart move," Nick said. "Because Dragan will probably have someone with you so they can keep an eye on us."

"I only have one question," Joe said. "What are we going to be seeing on the video feed from the fake lab?"

"The scientists at work," Nick said, "and the extraordinary precautions they take as they handle and study the viruses."

"We're going to be those scientists?" Boyd asked.

"You, Willie, Chet, and Tom," Kate said. "Everybody is doing double duty on this job."

"But, Boyd, as the only professional actor among us, this crucial aspect of the con is going to rest on your shoulders," Nick said. "You need to create the world that we're breaking into. We need to feel, through the performances of your cast, how dangerous the job is for these scientists and how seriously they take the risks."

"Who are the characters?" Boyd asked. "What are their backstories? What do they want out of their lives? What personal dramas are playing out through their lab work?"

"We're counting on you to improvise that," Nick said. "It's basically a silent movie, so don't worry about dialogue. But your laboratory technique has to be absolutely accurate. I'll get you training videos. Everything depends on the authenticity of the performances you create on that set."

"It won't be the first time," Boyd said. "I was a background doctor on several episodes of *Grey's Anatomy*. I silently conferred with nurses and other doctors, comforted the loved ones of critically ill patients, and walked urgently down hallways on my way to save lives while Patrick Dempsey and Ellen Pompeo belabored their dialogue in the foreground."

"What am I driving?" Willie asked. "Because you certainly didn't bring me into this for my acting ability."

"Once the fake smallpox is on the move, you'll be driving or piloting whatever vehicles we need to follow it," Nick said. "You'll have cars, a plane, and a boat on tap. Dragan's lab could be anywhere in Europe."

"This is the critical endgame," Kate said. "If we don't find Dragan's lab and retrieve the smallpox, people will die."

Conversation stopped at the sound of a car driving up. The engine cut off. A door slammed shut. Footsteps approached.

Cosmo Uno peered into the barn. "Knock, knock!" he said. "Am I interrupting? What are you doing? Are you making a movie? It looks like you're making a movie. Like you have movie equipment. Is this a wrap party? Am I too late?"

"Ommigod," Kate said.

Nick looked over at Kate. "Do you know him?"

"Cosmo Uno," Kate said. "He works in the cubicle next to me."

"What cubicle would that be?" Willie asked. "Pee-wee's playhouse?"

"Hah, I get that a lot," Cosmo said. "I look like Pee-wee Herman, right? Except he has better clothes. I don't know how he gets his clothes to fit him like that. They're all so tight. Where does he hide his gun, right?"

Nick turned his back to Uno and faced Kate. "If he recognizes me I'll have to kill him."

"If you kill him I'll be your sex slave," Kate said. "I'll do *anything*. I'll learn how to make an omelet, I swear."

"Promises, promises," Nick said. "Get him out of here."

Kate turned Cosmo around and steered him toward the door. "How did you find me?" she asked him.

"I pinged your cellphone and got lucky. I figured it was the perfect time for us to get together and fill out your GS205."

"Are you kidding me? A GS205?"

"I brought an extra pen."

Willie tagged after Kate and Cosmo, draped an arm over Cosmo's shoulders, and pressed her breast into him. "Honey, what's a GS205? Do I need one?"

"It itemizes civilian damages incurred during an active investigation," Cosmo said.

"I don't have any of those," Kate said.

"According to accounting you destroyed multiple cars, a fast food burger joint, a multimillion-dollar high-rise condo in London, a couple boats . . ."

"I have to itemize that?" Kate asked, mentally going through a laundry list that included the jewelry store, armored police van, a couple private residences, some "borrowed" planes, and the DVR that she still hadn't replaced.

"It's all in the manual," Cosmo said. "I have a copy in my briefcase here. Do you know there are a bunch of ladies with bald heads in the parking lot? I think they're smoking dope. One of them said she would give me a tug for five. That's a good price, right? I think she liked me."

"Does our boss know you're here?" Kate asked.

"Maybe not here precisely, but he could find me if he wanted to because I came in a company car and they all have transponders."

"Damn," Kate said. "I was never able to get a company car. How'd *you* get one?"

"I filled out form BBB704ZX," Cosmo said.

"What kind of car is it?" Willie asked.

"It's white," Cosmo said.

Willie looked toward the open barn door. "Can I drive it?"

"No," Cosmo said. "Only people who have filled out the appropriate requisition can drive that car."

Willie leaned in, and Cosmo instinctively looked down at the triple-D nipple that was smashed against his chest.

"I'd really like to see your white car," Willie said. "I'd be *very* grateful."

"We aren't allowed to accept gratuities," Cosmo said, his eyes going a little glazed.

"Just a look," Willie said.

Cosmo was still focused on the nipple. "A look?"

Willie slipped her hand into Cosmo's pants pocket, Cosmo gave a gasp, and Willie pulled out his keys.

"Follow me," Willie said to Cosmo. "I'm going to take us for a ride."

"Maybe a *little* ride," Cosmo said, "but you'll have to fill out pedestrian form WA33."

Willie led Cosmo out of the barn, and there was the sound

of car doors slamming shut. The engine turned over, and Willie spun the tires, sending gravel flying against the barn wall. The car flew past the open barn door like white lightning, and Kate heard Cosmo screaming.

"Eeeeeeeeeeeee!"

"He's from Homeland Security, right?" Chet said.

Kate did a grimace. "Meeting adjourned."

19

Jake O'Hare lived with Kate's younger sister, Megan, her husband, Roger, and their two kids in a hilltop gated community of Spanish Mediterranean–style homes in Calabasas, California. The community was located about an hour south of Ojai on the southwestern edge of the San Fernando Valley.

Megan's house had two detached two-car garages in the front. One of the garages had been converted into a *casita* for Jake with a bedroom, a bathroom, and a living room with a kitchenette.

Kate parked her Crown Vic, a used cop car that she bought at a police auction, behind Megan's new Mercedes C-Class, the Calabasas Corolla. Her arrival excited the family's Jack

Russell terrier, who announced her by barking, jumping, and scratching frantically at the windowed front door.

Megan scooped up the dog and opened the door as Kate approached. "The peripatetic daughter returns."

"'Peripatetic'?" Kate kissed her sister on the cheek, petted the dog's head, and stepped inside the house. "What's that mean?"

"It means you're constantly traveling and rarely around," Megan said, closing the door. She was three years younger than Kate, two inches taller, and a few pounds heavier. She wore a long, loose T-shirt with tight leggings and short Ugg sheepskin boots. "*Peripatetic* is one of Sara's vocabulary words at school this week. We're supposed to amalgamate them into our daily conversation to enrich our family discourse."

Megan's daughter, Sara, was nine years old, and Tyler, her son, was seven. They both went to an elementary school where Megan was president of the PTA.

"Is *amalgamate* also one of this week's words?" Kate asked.

"And also *discourse*. Pretty smooth how I worked them all in, isn't it?" Megan said, leading Kate into the kitchen. "To keep Sara sharp, we're using all of her vocabulary words in regular conversation until her big test at the end of the month."

"You're a very supportive mother," Kate said. "Where are the kids?"

Megan set the dog down. "They're in the backyard, playing with their grandpa before they do their homework. He's

A PRO

Go one-... with a Pro... experience what it's like to be trained by a Professional Athlete.

CITY
SPIN

No traffic to dodge, spin your way through the cardio! Meet all your fitness goals, on the way to the finish line.

TRAIN WITH A PRO

CITY
FIT
HEALTH
HUT

EVERYONE IS WELCOME!

CityCise is more than a gym, we are your local fitness family.

Book your Classes & we will help you get fit.
Our Sessions are suitable for all levels - *including Beginners!*

FREE WiFi | CityFit Health Hut | Coffee | Shakes & Smoothies | Healthy Snacks & Food peripatetic, too. He's always traveling to some reunion for ex-military guys. But I think it's just a cover."

"For what?" Kate asked, trying to sound innocent.

"Mercenary work. He comes home way too happy."

"Maybe he really enjoys reliving old times with his buddies."

"I'm sure he does," Megan said. "By shooting people and blowing things up in some third-world country. And while we're on it, you're looking pretty happy too. Things must be going well with 'Bob.'"

"'Bob'?"

"The forbidden office romance you were contemplating last month. You obviously jumped right into it. You have the skin tone of a woman who is getting laid."

Kate held her arms out in front of her and examined her skin. "There's a skin tone for that?"

Megan held her arm out beside Kate's. "It's this one. Ever since I got my tubes tied, Roger and I can't keep our hands off each other."

"I didn't know you got your tubes tied."

"You would if you followed me on Twitter, friended me on Facebook, or kept up with my Instagram. I tweeted, updated my status, and sent out photos on my way to the operating room."

"That's why I'm not on social media. People are way too open about their private lives. I don't need to see pictures of what somebody had for lunch or hear about how difficult their last bowel movement was or see on a map where they were when either one happened."

"In today's world, if you aren't on social media, you don't exist," Megan said. "You might as well be living in a cave or a monastery."

"I prefer to pick up the phone and talk," Kate said.

"You don't do that, either," Megan said. "Probably because you're too busy with Bob?"

"I should say hello to Dad and the kids," Kate said, heading for the sliding glass door to the backyard.

"You're running away from the subject," Megan said.

"As fast as I can," Kate said and stepped outside.

Megan's backyard overlooked the Calabasas Country Club golf course and the San Fernando Valley. There was a lap pool, a built-in barbecue, and a brown lawn that was slowly dying under the state-mandated water rationing brought on by the drought.

Sara and Tyler were splashing around in the pool, and Jake was watching from a lawn chair.

"Ah," he said. "Here's the peripatetic daughter."

"Sticks and stones," Kate said, pulling a chair up next to Jake. "I could use some help."

"Does it involve a rocket launcher?"

"Possibly."

"I'm there."

Kate gave her father a quick briefing on the con that she and Nick were going to mount in Paris.

"Nick and I will be on the inside with the Road Runners," Kate said. "I need someone on the outside, watching our backs and protecting our crew in case things go wrong."

"I can get some guys for that," Jake said. "I'll need a couple hundred thousand dollars for salaries, weapons, and surveillance equipment."

"It's going to be more than a babysitting job," Kate said. "The tracking device on the stolen vial of fake virus will lead us to Dragan's lair and the real virus. But once we find it, we may not have time to wait for Jessup to organize and deploy a strike team. We might have to take down Dragan and the Road Runners ourselves. That won't be easy. They are Serbian Army Special Forces veterans, and they will be very well-armed."

"I've been up against worse," Jake said. "If you want to make it a challenge, ask me to overthrow a country, too, while we're at it."

"You were younger when you were doing that."

"You think I've lost my edge?"

She shook her head no. "What I'm saying is that you did your time and came out in one piece. Now you're free to play golf, teach hand-to-hand combat to your grandchildren, and help your daughter break a thief out of a foreign prison. It's a dream retirement. You don't have to go up against a small army of trained killers anymore."

"Dragan Kovic intends to attack the United States of America with a biological weapon," Jake said. "I would be honored to die preventing that bastard from succeeding, and so would the guys I'm going to bring in on this. It's a much better way to go than sitting in a recliner watching *Matlock* and waiting for a nurse to change your diaper."

"Is that what you're afraid of?" Kate asked.

"It's one of the few things that truly terrify me."

"What are the others?"

"Outliving you." Jake looked back at Megan, who was wrapping towels around Sara and Tyler. "Or them." He thought for a beat. "And there's a lady handing out samples of cocktail wieners at Costco on Saturdays who scares the bejeezus out of me."

Kate stayed at Megan's for the rest of the afternoon but left before dinner. She drove to West Los Angeles to brief Jessup in his office at the Federal Building. It was a twenty-mile trip that took her over an hour in bumper-to-bumper freeway traffic.

"It's a good thing we broke Nick out of jail again or we never would have known about this," Jessup said after listening to Kate's report.

"Was that decision weighing on you?"

"Like an elephant threw a saddle on me, hopped on my back, and told me to giddyup."

"That's a vivid picture."

"Not as vivid as thousands of people dying of smallpox on the streets of New York City," Jessup said. "That one is going to haunt me. We'll keep an eye out for anyone making significant investments against the market. That way we'll know if an attack is imminent."

"I hope it won't come to that," Kate said.

"Me too. I may have to go to my AA meetings twice a week until this is over to stay sober," Jessup said. "So recover the smallpox fast, get the hell out, and call me when it's done. I'll arrange for the safe pickup or disposal of the virus."

"What about Dragan and the Road Runners?" Kate said. "We need to take them down."

"Not if it's going to jeopardize the mission. The priority is stopping the bioweapon from being made or deployed. Anything else can wait."

"You can apprehend them at the same time the strike team hits the lab," Kate said.

"I can't convince the Justice Department, the Pentagon, or European authorities to authorize a military or law enforcement strike against the lab, in whatever country it ends up being in, without giving them solid evidence to justify the action," Jessup said. "I don't see how I can do that without revealing our covert operation. If I do that, they won't buy the smallpox story anyway, because the FBI will have zero credibility and I'll be in jail. Do you understand what I'm saying to you?"

"The cavalry won't be coming to our rescue."

"I'm sorry, Kate."

"Don't be, sir. I knew before I came here that you'd tell me that," Kate said. "We'll work with what we have."

"I feel like I'm sending you and Nick on a suicide mission."

"Good," Kate said. "Because if I survive, I'm asking for a raise and a company car."

"You'd have to fill out a requisition for the car," Jessup said. "It isn't worth it."

Kate went to the door and peeked outside.

"Is there a problem?" Jessup asked.

"Cosmo Uno."

"He's a good man," Jessup said. "You need him."

"Isn't it bad enough you stuck me with Nick Fox?"

"This is different. This is about paperwork. You aren't filing the necessary reports."

"I always give you a full report."

"About your covert operations with Nick. But you've fallen way behind on your routine paperwork as an FBI special agent and that could start drawing unwanted attention. The last thing we need is anyone in D.C. scrutinizing your activity because you've become sloppy with your paperwork. Be happy you have Cosmo Uno helping you out. It could keep us both out of prison."

"He's in his cubicle, isn't he?" Kate asked.

"Probably."

Kate stepped out of the office and very quietly crept down the hall. She took a circuitous route to the elevator and was almost in the clear when she heard Cosmo calling her.

"Katie! Holy cow, I can't believe it's you. I almost missed you. I bet you came in to see me. Am I right?"

Kate took off at a flat run, bypassed the elevator, and

took the stairs three at a time. Cosmo was a flight of stairs behind her.

"Wait for me!" he yelled. "Did you get an emergency call? Are you gonna use your Kojak light? Do you have one? I can get you one. I can fill out form GS4781 and requisition a light for you."

Kate burst out of the stairwell, sprinted the rest of the way to her car, and took off. She stopped at a light and looked around. No Cosmo. She was in the clear.

I used to be by the book too, she thought. Although she had to admit she was never great with paperwork.

Boyd, Willie, Joe, Chet, and Tom left for Paris with Nick and Kate on a private jet out of LAX early the next morning. The in-flight entertainment was industrial videos of level-four biocontainment labs that played on the cabin's various flat screens.

The first video they watched together was a tour of a lab from the point of view of scientists entering and going to work. The scientists entered the labs through an air lock leading to a locker room, where they undressed. From there they walked naked through another air lock into the dressing room, where they put on cotton scrubs, socks, and surgical gloves. They taped the gloves and socks to their scrubs, then went through another air lock into a room that had a dozen bulky white positive pressure suits hanging from the walls and coiled blue air hoses dangling from the ceiling.

Each positive pressure suit had a huge clear wraparound visor and built-in gloves but otherwise resembled a cross between an astronaut's moonwalk suit and a wetsuit. Air nozzles with a snap coupling at the end hung like tails from each pressure suit. Once the scientists were suited up, they put on rubber boots, grabbed one of the coiled hoses from the ceiling, and snapped them to their air nozzles. The hoses rapidly inflated the suits and puffed them up.

"They look like balloons with people inside," Willie said.

"More like the Stay Puft Marshmallow Man from *Ghostbusters*," Joe said.

"What's the point of inflating the suits like that?" Willie asked.

"If the suit gets punctured," Kate said, "air is forced out instead of sucked in, blowing out the pathogen and buying you some time to get into decontamination before you can get infected."

Kate had some understanding of dealing with deadly viruses. Her military training had prepared her for chemical warfare situations on the battlefield.

"In those suits, it will be difficult to convey our stories through body language," Boyd said. "But thanks to those large visors, we'll be able to express a lot of emotion and narrative with our faces."

"We're going to be silently squirting liquids into pipettes and squinting at viruses through microscopes," Chet said. "Where's the drama in that?"

"Because there's a small tribe in Africa that is going to be wiped out if we can't discover which variation of bird flu jumped from their chickens into their children," Boyd said. "Not just the people but an entire culture are hanging in the balance. So yes, there's drama."

"Can that actually happen?" Tom asked. "Can a chicken sneeze and infect you with something?"

"Do chickens sneeze?" Joe asked.

"Who cares?" Chet said. "We won't be talking and we're going to be in those white suits. Nobody is going to know what's going on."

"They will know the emotion," Boyd said.

Once the suits were inflated, the scientists in the video unhooked the hoses, walked through another air lock, and entered the lab, where they immediately connected their pressure suits again to coiled air hoses that hung from the ceilings.

The lab was filled with workstations, biosafety cabinets, incubators, microscopes, and centrifuges for working with pathogens, freezers for storing the pathogens, and autoclaves for sterilizing equipment. There were also cameras in every corner to allow for constant surveillance.

The scientists filed in one by one, and each went to a workstation. When a scientist walked as far as a hose could go, he unlatched the hose from his suit, set the hose on a hook overhead, then walked to the next station or piece of equipment and attached himself to a new hose there.

There was an adjacent control room, where people could observe the scientists at work and interact with them. It was separated from the lab by a large, super-thick window and an air lock. The observers could see images from the microscopes and the readouts from other devices in the lab on their computer screens.

"The scientists in the lab are isolated physically from everybody else, but they are connected to the outside world electronically," Nick said. "The surveillance footage and the readouts from their equipment can be shared over a secure web connection to scientists within the building and all over the world. They call it the Biosecurity Collaboration Platform."

"I call it an open invitation to hack into the entire system," Joe said. "They might as well have a sign out front that says 'C'mon in, everybody is welcome!'"

"What are those blue suits hanging in the control room?" Chet asked, pointing to suits similar to the pressure suits but not nearly as bulky. "I saw some in the balloon-suit room, too."

"In case the positive pressure suit system fails, or there is some other emergency, those are protective suits with their own battery-operated air-purifying respirators attached," Nick said. "The battery has a four-to-six-hour charge."

"What happens if you're in one of those white balloon suits and have an itch?" Willie said. "Or need to pee?"

"You have to leave the lab and go through decontamination," Kate said. "You're about to see that process now."

To exit the lab, the scientists went through an air lock into a shower room, where their pressure suits were doused for eight minutes with decontamination chemicals. From there, they went through another air lock back into the suit room. They climbed out of the pressure suits, went through an air lock into another changing room, stripped out of their scrubs, gloves, and socks and stuffed everything into a biohazard hamper, and then went naked into another shower room. After showering, they went through an air lock back into the locker room to get dressed in their street clothes.

"How much of that do we need to build?" Tom asked.

"The lab and the control room," Nick said. "We're going to tunnel in through the control room wall. I'll enter the lab through the control room air lock, retrieve the virus from a refrigeration unit in the lab, and off we go."

"You're not going to put on a balloon suit or one of those blue ones?" Willie asked.

"I'm stealing the vial, not opening it," Nick said.

"Be careful," Boyd said. "A horrific lab accident in the Congo left me impotent and destroyed my marriage. Six other colleagues weren't so lucky."

"You know the virus is fake, right?" Kate said. "There is no actual danger."

"That's the careless attitude that gets people killed," Boyd said. "Do you want those deaths, and the shattered lives of their loved ones, on your conscience? I know a man blinded by a deadly lab accident. Now the only thing he sees are the people that he lost."

"Oh God," Willie said. "He's in character already."

"We all need to prepare," Nick said. "The sooner the better. There are more instructional videos on board that you can watch. I've also got books on lab procedure and blueprints of typical biolabs for you to study. Let's get to it. We land in Paris in ten hours . . ."

"That's where Dr. Lyle Fairbanks will find his redemption," Boyd said. "Or lose his soul."

20

Gaëlle Rochon picked them up at the airport the next morning. Introductions were made all around, and she drove them in a rented van to the storefront that Nick had leased on avenue Denfert-Rochereau.

The Indian restaurant that had last occupied the property, and all of its fixtures and furniture, were long gone, but the space still smelled of curry and grease. The windows were covered with cardboard, and there was a thick layer of dust on the hardwood floor.

"There's a large apartment on the second floor," Kate said. "That's where you'll be staying. You'll find cots and furniture up there. While you're out and about on the street, if any neighbors ask what you're doing, tell them we're turning this place into an American-style diner. You're the design team that was brought in from America to do it."

"How do we explain the medical equipment?" Chet asked.

"Say that a clinic of some kind is going in upstairs, but you really don't know much about it," Kate said.

Nick turned to Chet, Tom, and Joe. "Use this floor any way you need to make the set in the basement work."

"Let's take a look downstairs," Tom said.

Nick led the way to the back of the room and a wide flight of stairs to the basement.

"The kitchen was downstairs," he said as they went down the stairs. "So it's a big space with all the utilities you'll need already routed in."

The walls were covered with subway tiles, and the floor was concrete. There were lots of open holes in the walls and floors with pipes sticking out and exposed wiring where kitchen appliances once were.

Tom nodded to himself as he walked the perimeter of the room. "I can work with this. I'll use the existing walls as much as possible and keep demolition to a minimum."

"Give Gaëlle a list of everything you need that can be purchased legally and for cash," Nick said. "I'll get the rest."

"I made up a list on the plane of the laboratory equipment that I need." Chet handed the list to Nick. "Basically it's everything you saw in that lab, along with some compressors and fans to run the air hoses."

Joe tapped the floor with his foot. "I'd like a look

underground. I want to see what cable, telecom, and other utility lines I can tap."

"I'd like to go, too," Chet said. "I need to see the street signs in the sewer and catacombs so I can create convincing fakes."

"I'll be glad to give you both a tour," Gaëlle said. "There are jumpsuits, helmets, and boots upstairs for you. We can go whenever you're ready. One of my favorite manholes is right down the street."

"Welcome to Paris," Willie said.

They spent the next week building the lab, working in shifts under Tom's direction. They also helped Chet with the tedious task of running all the necessary wires, A/V cables, and air supply lines that were needed to operate the lights, positive pressure suit air hoses, surveillance cameras, and scientific equipment. The set was capped with a fake ceiling to hold the lights and the hoses. Two of the actual basement walls were incorporated into the control room, but the rest of the lab was made with fake walls.

The interior walls of the control room and the lab were elaborately tiled, painted, and decorated. But the opposite side, visible only from the outside of the set, were naked plywood and two-by-fours, like the framing of a house without drywall. The fake walls were propped up with wooden braces bolted into the concrete floor. The air lock doors, with the exception of the one between the control room and the lab, opened to the empty basement. The portion of the basement walls visible through the portholes in the lab's air lock doors were painted to imply the room beyond.

"It's as convincing as the hospital set on *Grey's Anatomy*," Boyd declared on the night the set was completed.

The next morning at 9:00, after a last tour of the set, everyone but Nick, Kate, Gaëlle, and Joe got into their positive pressure suits and prepared to do a rehearsal. Joe sat at a console on the first floor and faced two keyboards and four flat-screen monitors aligned in a row.

"There are discreet green lights inside and outside the lab set to let the cast know when the cameras are live," Joe said. "That way they only have to act when we know that someone is watching."

"Let's see the surveillance feed from the real institute," Kate said.

"Breaking into their website was ridiculously easy," Joe said. He tapped a few keys and one of his screens filled with dozens of thumbnail mini-screens showing corridors, labs, parking lots, conference rooms, and offices within the institute. "I'm also hardwired into their surveillance system as a backup. I could probably shut down their alarms and hijack control of their air locks for real if I wanted to."

"It's a good thing we're fake thieves," Kate said. "When this is over, remind me to have a serious talk with their security people."

"Show me our lab," Nick said.

Joe tapped another key, and the empty lab appeared on another screen.

"Can you pull up the surveillance feed from one of their real labs and see how it compares to ours?" Nick asked.

"Sure," Joe said.

An instant later, the image on the screen split, the real lab showing up on the left, their empty set on the right. In the real lab, half a dozen scientists in their white inflated positive pressure suits were diligently at work.

"*Formidable,*" Gaëlle said. "There is no difference."

"Re-creating an empty room is easy," Nick said. "It's the acting that matters. Let's start the show."

Joe hit a button on another console. Suddenly the fans, compressors, and other equipment mounted on the first floor roared loudly to life to pump air into the hoses in the basement set to inflate the positive pressure suits. He pressed a second button that turned on the green light for the actors. That was their call to action.

Boyd, Willie, Chet, and Tom lumbered into the lab one by one, unhooked their air hoses, and moved to their workstations or elsewhere in the room before hooking up to a nearby air hose again. They all seemed to move around the lab with purpose, retrieving samples, putting others away, examining things under microscopes, carefully squirting liquids into pipettes, and putting vials into the centrifuge.

"That's as dull as the real lab work," Gaëlle said. "If there's a story there, I'm missing it."

"That's because we can't see much of their faces from these high angles," Joe said. "Their expressions are lost."

"Don't tell Boyd that," Kate said. "He'll demand close-ups."

"What matters to me is that they are coming across as real lab workers," Nick said. "Let's keep it going for a few more minutes. We don't know how long they will have to perform at any given time. I want to be sure they can sustain it for a while."

On the set, Boyd approached Willie, who was at a microscope, examining a slide. The microscope itself didn't actually work. The magnified image on her monitor was part of a preprogrammed show generated by the computer. He hunched down and looked over her shoulder.

"That's the pathogen that rendered me impotent," he said.

"This is going to be the elbow that renders you impotent if you don't stop crowding me."

"That's not your line," Boyd said. "It's 'You're more of a man now than you ever were, Dr. Fairbanks. You sure as hell aren't impotent when it comes to saving lives.'"

"If I say that, I'll throw up in this suit, which could kill me," Willie said. "I could drown in my own puke."

"The line underscores the sacrifices we make and the ultimate nobility of what we do here," Boyd said. "Do you have a better line that achieves the same thing?"

"Nobody can hear what we say. It's a silent movie."

"Some of the greatest films in the history of cinema were silent," Boyd said. "It's the performance that matters."

"Are you insecure about your virility?"

"That line doesn't work," Boyd said.

"It's a genuine question. You've written two scripts now that are focused on glorifying your tiddlywink. You're obsessed with yourself."

"That's ironic coming from a woman who inflated her breasts like one of these suits."

She tried to elbow him, but couldn't move fast enough with her arm in an inflated sleeve. He easily dodged it.

"Now we have some drama and nobody had to hear a word," Boyd said. "I think I've proved my point."

Proud of himself, Boyd walked away from her toward Chet at another workstation, stretching his air hose taut. He disconnected it but forgot to set it in a hook before letting go. The hose snapped back like a whip, sweeping vials off countertops and whacking Willie out of her seat. A hiss of air came from her suit.

"Congratulations," Chet said. "You've just contaminated the entire lab and probably killed Willie."

"Now I see the story," Gaëlle said. "Willie can't stand him."

"Cut," Nick said with a sigh.

Joe hit the button turning off the green light and shutting down the air system that was inflating their suits.

"Can I talk to them?" Nick asked.

Joe hit a button on a console and pointed to the monitor. "Go ahead, there's a mike embedded in the monitor. They'll all hear you."

"You started off great but then you forgot to follow lab procedure," Nick said. "Trying to elbow a fellow scientist in the groin is a definite no-no in a room full of toxic viruses, Willie. It may not be a written rule, but I think it's generally understood."

"Let's review," Kate said. "Never let go of a taut air hose, Boyd. Always hook it up and make sure it's secure before moving on and connecting to another one. You've seen now what can happen if a hose flies around. A mistake like that could kill people in a real lab but, more important, it will kill me, Nick, and Gaëlle in the real world."

"This was only our first rehearsal," Boyd said. "We are just beginning to find our characters and get comfortable in this space. It's all part of the artistic process."

"You have two days, three at the most, to get it down before showtime," Nick said. "We're picking up Huck Moseby at the airport in two hours."

"That's our checkered flag," Kate said. "The con begins today."

Whenever Huck Moseby dreamed of Paris, it was never about strolling the Champs-Élysées or climbing the Eiffel Tower, or riding an excursion boat along the Seine at sunset, or enjoying a coffee and tart at a sidewalk café. His dream was to visit the sewers, the Shangri-la of waste disposal systems, the inspiration for such literary masterpieces as *The Phantom of the Opera* and *Les Misérables*. There was a time when the Paris sewers were appreciated. In the late 1800s, the rich and powerful would dress up in their finest clothes to tour the sewers on fancy gaslit gondolas to see for themselves the technological and engineering marvel that was the pride of Paris. Far too few people in the world today, in Huck's opinion, realized that the sewers were what truly made Paris the City of Light.

He was thinking about that as he arrived at Charles de Gaulle Airport. Nick, Kate, and a beautiful young blond woman were waiting for him outside customs.

"How was your flight?" Nick asked.

The flight had been seven hours of sheer bliss for Huck. He'd flown Air France first-class, where he was pampered like never before in his life. He was going to forever treasure the faux-leather case of toiletries, the airplane socks, and the eye mask that he'd been given.

"It was great," Huck said. "I'm rested and ready to go."

"I'm glad to hear that," Nick said. "This is Gaëlle Rochon, our guide to the Paris underground. She will be your right-hand man from here on out."

"It's a pleasure to meet you," Gaëlle said to him in French. "I've heard so much about you from Nick."

"Likewise," Huck replied in French. "I am eager to see the sewers."

"I am eager to show them to you," Gaëlle said. "And to learn how they differ from yours in Montreal."

"You've worked in the sewers?"

"No, but my father, my grandfather, and my great-grandfather were all sewer men," Gaëlle said. "The sewer is like my second home. You'll probably find this ridiculous, but sometimes I think I am more comfortable there."

Huck felt color coming into his pale cheeks. He was in love. "I don't think it's ridiculous," he said. "I feel the same way."

"Would you like us to take you to your hotel to rest up?" Kate asked. "Or perhaps get you something to eat?"

"I'm here to work," Huck said. "Show me the blueprints of the lab, a map of the streets, and take me to the sewers."

"It's nice to work with a pro," Nick said.

21

Gaëlle drove them to a side street off avenue du Général Leclerc that was three blocks south of place Denfert-Rochereau. She parked behind a white van with a distinctive SAP logo representing the Section de l'Assainissement de Paris, the city sewer utility. It was a van that Nick had purchased and Chet had painted to look like the real thing.

They got out of the car and got into the van, where Gaëlle presented Huck with a set of genuine SAP overalls, boots, helmet, and the spade-like tool for sluicing sewage. Huck held the tool reverently, as if it were Excalibur.

"This is the Stradivarius of sewer tools," Huck said. "I never thought I'd hold one of these."

"You can have it," Gaëlle said, slowly wrapping a rag around her neck to prepare for her descent.

"It's an honor," Huck said, breathlessly watching her knot her rag as if she were doing a striptease. He pulled a rag of his own out of his pocket and put it around his neck.

"You came prepared," Gaëlle said, watching him tie his knot.

"I'm a sewer man," Huck said. "And a Frenchman."

"*Québécois*," Gaëlle said.

"Are we really so different?"

"I don't know yet," she said. "But I'm looking forward to finding out."

Kate rolled her eyes at Nick, and Nick smiled back.

"I've put the site plan of the Institut National pour la Recherche sur les Maladies Infectieuses and blueprints of the lab building in your bag with your flashlights and other equipment," Nick said to Huck.

Nick had put a lot of effort into having the blueprints forged and the site plans altered to misdirect Huck so he wouldn't know that they would actually be digging into the basement of a building outside of the institute's property. Probably unnecessary, Nick thought. Huck wasn't going to see much past Gaëlle.

"You're not coming with us?" Huck asked, unable to hide his delight that he and Gaëlle would have the sewers to themselves.

"We've been down there already," Kate said. "We know the general spot where we'll be digging. We'd just be in your way while you figure out the technical details."

"Scout the sewer, review the plans at your hotel, then let us know at breakfast tomorrow how long the dig will take, how many men you'll need, and what equipment is required to do the job right," Nick said. "Demand the best tools and don't worry about the cost. Money is no object."

Nick and Kate opened the back of the van, got out, slid the door closed behind them, and headed down the street toward the intersection with avenue du Général Leclerc.

"A match made in heaven," Nick said.

"No kidding. Huck should be paying *us*."

Nick took his phone out of his pocket. "Time to call Litija and get this robbery started."

"Before you call Litija and we end up undercover again with the Road Runners, I'd like to know that Dad and his guys are out there watching. I don't know why we haven't heard from him yet." She took out her own phone and dialed his number.

"Are you sure you want to call now?" Nick said. "It's four in the morning in L.A."

"He's an early riser."

"Howdy-do," Jake said.

"You sound awfully chipper for so early in the morning," Kate said.

"I'm always chipper. Give me a second. I need to flush the *toilette*."

"You're talking to me on the toilet?"

"*In* the *toilette*," Jake said. "I really had to go after all the running around you did this morning. But don't worry, I had eyes on you while I was inside."

"What are you talking about? Where are you?"

Nick tapped her on the shoulder and glanced across the street. She followed his gaze and saw Jake stepping out of a *sanisette,* a cylindrical gray hut on the sidewalk with the word *toilette* written on the side above a map of the neighborhood. There were hundreds of *sanisettes* throughout Paris and they were not only a place to relieve yourself but to find out where you were. The door to the public bathroom slid closed behind Jake like an elevator and the chemical self-cleaning cycle began inside.

Jake strolled down the street, not visually acknowledging her, continuing to talk on the phone.

"We've been here for the last three days," Jake said.

Kate walked with Nick, parallel to Jake, as they all headed toward place Denfert-Rochereau. "Who is 'we'?"

"Walter Wurzel is on the rooftop of the building behind me. He's had you in his scope while I was in the *toilette.* Best sniper there is."

He'd also taught Kate how to shoot a rifle when she was nine and they were all stationed on Guam. But she knew time had taken its toll on him.

"Does he still have cataracts?"

"That was years ago, and even half-blind he can still shoot the ears off a butterfly."

As if to prove it, a laser-targeting dot appeared on Nick's chest.

Nick looked down at the dot. "Friend or foe?" he asked.

Kate smiled. "It's Walter Wurzel saying hello."

Nick had met Walter in Kentucky a few years back on the Carter Grove scam. He'd proven that he was still a good shot on that job, and he'd had one eye patched at the time.

"Who else is on the team?" Kate asked Jake.

"You're being tracked on foot by Antoine Killian, not that you'd ever know it," Jake said. "He's a founding veteran of the Brigade des Forces Spéciales Terre, the French special ops, and he's the living definition of stealth. He's invisible unless he wants to be seen. He blends into the shadows."

Kate was so caught up in talking to her dad that she nearly collided head-on with a morbidly obese man wearing a beret, a tent-sized overcoat, and smoking a huge cigar.

"That was Antoine," Jake said.

Kate glanced over her shoulder to see Antoine tip his hat to her from behind. He took up nearly the whole sidewalk. She looked back at her dad as she spoke into the phone.

"He must be four hundred pounds. How can he possibly disappear into the shadows?"

"Do you see him now?"

Kate whirled around again. Antoine was gone. He must have ducked into a building or a car, but he'd done it with surprising speed and agility, even for someone who didn't measure his weight on an industrial scale.

"Impressive," she said.

"I've brought in Robin Mannering, formerly of the British

Army's Special Reconnaissance Regiment," Jake said. "He's an expert driver, cold-blooded assassin, speaks five languages, and is irresistible to women. We call him the lady killer. He could always seduce a woman close to the enemy into telling us all their secrets. That's him parked in the Alfa Romeo convertible."

The car was at the curb right in front of them. The smiling old man at the wheel had a spray-on tan, capped teeth, and was wearing a toupee. His face was pulled so tight that the double chin above his cravat might once have been his scrotum.

"What's he do these days?" Kate asked.

"Seduces the wives and lovers of heads of state for MI6," Jake said. "The man is a legend."

Nick leaned close to Kate and whispered, "I think the man we just passed is wearing one of William Shatner's old toupees and Mr. Ed's teeth."

"Please tell me this isn't all you've got," Kate said to her father.

"I have a dozen American commandos on standby in Kaiserslautern, Germany. They are armed and equipped for any situation on land or sea," Jake said. "They can immediately deploy to almost anywhere in Europe within two hours."

Kate stopped walking. "Because they're stationed at Ramstein Air Base. Are you telling me you've got active duty soldiers involved in this?"

"They aren't on active duty, at least not officially. Let's just say they're enterprising young men who are ready to handle situations that fall outside the boundaries of usual U.S. military jurisdiction. They're the guys I trained to replace me and my team when we retired."

"They're doing black ops for the Pentagon and the CIA?" Kate asked.

"They wish they were. They're bored out of their minds in Kaiserslautern. Regime change and extraordinary renditions have really slowed down under this administration. So they could use some excitement."

"They could get court-martialed for helping us," Kate said. "If they don't get killed first."

"Who do you think will be deployed for this mission if Jessup is able to push the button? These guys. So they're in either way. Besides, nobody is going to slap their hands for thwarting a terrorist attack on America in their free time. It's their job," Jake said. "It's not like they got drunk one weekend and deposed a dictator for fun."

"You've done that?"

"Let's just say there's a capital in deepest, darkest Africa where you'll find a guano-covered statue of a soldier who looks a lot like your old man," Jake said. "Bottom line, you're in good hands."

"I know that. Keep a close eye on our people. I'll let you know when the virus is on the move." Kate hung up and looked at Nick. "Dad has our backs."

"I never doubted it for a second. It's showtime." Nick took out his phone and dialed Litija.

. . .

Dragan Kovic knew five minutes into Nick's presentation in the apartment on avenue du Maine that he'd made the right decision bringing the master thief into his scheme. Nick made the impossible seem ridiculously easy.

"The labs are primarily designed to keep viruses from getting out, not to keep people from getting in," Nick said at the outset, flanked by his team of Kate, Joe, Gaëlle, and Huck. "The institute has some very elaborate security measures, but they made one key mistake. They built their basement lab in the middle of a honeycomb of tunnels that have existed for centuries. We're simply going to stroll into one of those tunnels, dig a hole into the lab, take what we want, and be on our way."

"During the dig, I'll be in a van on the street and hardwired into the institute's security system," Joe said. "I'll disable the alarms as soon as Nick enters the lab, and I'll hijack the video feed so the guards will see an empty room."

Huck told Dragan it would take at least twelve hours using a $12,000 Hilti DD 500-CA diamond coring rig to tunnel into the lab from within a municipal utility shaft full of electric, fiber-optic, cable, and telecom lines that ran parallel to the basement.

They would have to cut through six inches of concrete, twenty feet of limestone, and finally sixteen inches of heavily rebar-reinforced concrete to create a tunnel just large enough for a man with a pack to crawl through, a *chatière* as Gaëlle called it, a pet door.

"We'll tap the electric lines and plumbing lines that run through the tunnel to power the coring rig," Huck said. "We'll have a second coring rig and a small, portable generator as backups in case the rig fails or we lose power."

"What we need from you are five men," Nick said to Dragan. "Three of them will be underground to help with the drilling and removal of the extracted cores, which can weigh over two hundred pounds."

"The other two will be up on the street, acting as lookouts to alert Joe if there's trouble or any police activity," Kate said. "He'll tip us off. We won't have any radio or cellular signal in that part of the underground. We'll communicate with Joe using a single phone that's hardwired into a telecom line that runs through the shaft. We won't be able to hear a thing with that drill going, so I'll be manning it and we'll install a flashing light to tell us when a call is coming in."

Kate's job, as far as Dragan could tell, was to watch Nick's back. The only equipment that still had to be acquired were the diamond core drills, the track, an air blower to clear exhaust fumes, a backup generator, and three trucks painted to look like sewer and telephone utility vehicles. He could easily acquire all of that within a day.

Dragan was staring at an iPad that Joe, the alarm and video expert, had given him. Joe had already hacked into the institute's surveillance system, and Dragan was watching the lab in real time. He had the sense that the scientists were working on something highly critical today, and that the man in charge was riding them to quickly produce results.

"I think this woman wants to kill her boss," Dragan said, pointing to his iPad screen. "You can see it in her body language."

Litija looked over his shoulder. "That suit doesn't do anything for her figure. You can't tell she has a body at all."

"See how the man in charge keeps looking at the wall clock," Dragan said. "They are racing against time on something."

"Or maybe he just wants to go to lunch," Litija said.

Dragan handed the iPad back to Joe. "Very impressive."

"Joe still has work to do," Nick said. "He has to do the hardwiring he talked about. We'll do that, and the underground prep work, on Friday night disguised as utility workers. We begin the dig on Saturday afternoon, and finish in the predawn hours on Sunday. I'll stroll into the lab, pick up the sample, place it in a secure, temperature-controlled container, and bring it up to the street."

"We'll take it from there," Litija said.

"And then what happens?" Kate asked.

"We celebrate our success," Dragan said, well aware it wasn't the answer Kate was fishing for. "I have to commend you all on your brilliant planning."

The expertise and swift action that Nick brought to the scheme was beyond Dragan's wildest expectations. Now the smallpox outbreak in Los Angeles could happen within a few weeks instead of months or years. Zarko's death was definitely a worthwhile sacrifice.

"My men will arrive tonight," Dragan said. "You'll have the equipment and vehicles you requested by the end of the day tomorrow. You'll all be working out of this apartment until the job is complete. Litija will see to anything else that you might need."

Dragan would talk to her later to work out the details of transporting the smallpox to his lab. He gestured to Nick to join him by the front door of the apartment, away from the others.

"I want Litija in the van with Joe so she can keep an eye on everything," Dragan said.

"You mean on me," Nick said.

"She will work with the lookouts and be an extra set of eyes on the institute security cameras," Dragan said. "Her job will be to keep you safe and assure the success of the robbery."

"Kate thinks that's her job."

"It's her job underground and Litija's job above."

"I've always wanted two women to stay on top of me," Nick said. "When do I begin betting my savings against the market?"

"On Monday," Dragan said. "The attack will happen in six weeks or so in Los Angeles."

"Why L.A.?"

"It's Hollywood. Celebrities are America's royalty. It will be much more terrifying to see the bodies of famous people than complete strangers. On top of that we kill two for the price of one."

"I don't understand," Nick said.

"When a famous actor dies, so do the beloved characters that he plays. But it gets even better than that."

"We'll kill some adorable puppies, too?"

"We won't just be killing actors, but the hopes and dreams embodied in the movies they made. That's certain to terrify and depress the market worldwide, not just in the U.S. We'll be sure to short a lot of entertainment industry stocks."

"You've really thought this out," Nick said.

"And you're making it all possible," Dragan said, clapping Nick on the back. "You're even better at this than you say you are."

"I don't like to brag," Nick said and rejoined his team.

Nick and his people were very talented, and if this wasn't going to be Dragan's final crime, maybe he wouldn't have decided to have them executed immediately after the robbery. He was already feeling a twinge of regret as he left the apartment, and they weren't even dead yet. Dragan went down the spiral staircase and thought about his decision.

If he spared them, could he take the risk that one of them might talk before or after the smallpox outbreak in L.A.? No, of course he couldn't, and he was angry at himself for even considering the notion. It was ridiculous and stupid. Did he feel anything for the thousands of people, perhaps *tens of thousands,* who would perish in Los Angeles? Absolutely not. So what difference did a few more corpses make?

None at all.

Dragan stepped outside, walked across the sidewalk, and got into his black Maserati GranTurismo Sport parked at the curb. It was a good thing that he was becoming a billionaire and retiring soon, he thought. He was beginning to get soft.

22

There were three snipers watching Dragan drive off on avenue du Maine. Two of the snipers were Road Runners in a sixth-floor apartment in the building directly across the street. Their names were Daca and Stefan, and their job was to protect Dragan while he was in the apartment. Now that Dragan was gone, Daca and Stefan began dismantling their weapons and packing up.

The third sniper, on the rooftop of the same building, was Walter "Eagle Eye" Wurzel. He'd also had his eye on Dragan while Jake O'Hare, standing beside him with binoculars, watched the others in the room. Walter and Jake knew about the two snipers on the floor below them and would stay on the rooftop until Antoine Killian, in the shadows somewhere on the street, alerted them that they were gone.

"I hope I don't regret that I didn't kill Dragan when I had the shot," Walter said, lifting his eye from the scope as the Maserati drove off.

He wore large square-rimmed glasses with thick lenses balanced on a bulbous nose covered with red squiggly capillaries. The glasses magnified his eyes and made them look unnaturally large. He lay on his stomach, the rifle balanced on a tiny tripod.

"If you'd killed Dragan," Jake said, "the snipers would have killed Nick and Kate."

"Maybe, but you're talking about saving two people instead of thousands," Walter said. "At a certain point, we may have to choose between our team and our mission."

"There is no choice," Jake said. "I believe in Kate and Nick, but if their con fails, we take down Dragan and stop the attack, no matter what."

"Let's pray it never comes to that," Walter said. "In the meantime, do we have any croissants left?"

Jake reached for the bag next to him and looked inside. "One chocolate and one butter."

"I'll take 'em both," Walter said. "I'm hypoglycemic. My vision gets blurry when my blood sugar crashes."

On Saturday afternoon, Kate parked a sewer department van on boulevard Raspail. It was just north of place Denfert-Rochereau, beside a bus stop shelter that had a large advertisement featuring Johannes Vermeer's painting *Girl with a Pearl Earring.* The ad read *Atelier Vermeer. Apprenez à peindre comme les ancien maîtres. Copies de tableaux.* It was the first thing Nick saw when he emerged from the rear of the van wearing a sewer worker's jumpsuit. "Vermeer Workshop. Learn to paint like the masters. Copy the paintings."

He figured that spotting an advertisement for a school that taught art forgery, at the outset of faking the robbery of a level-four biolab, was probably a very good omen.

He walked to the manhole and used a crowbar-like tool to remove the cover while Road Runners Dusko, Vinko, and Borko unfolded a chest-high yellow canvas pedestrian barricade around the opening. The four men transferred the equipment from the van to the manhole and down into the sewer while Kate remained in the driver's seat with the engine running and watched for trouble. This was the first time they'd entered the sewers so close to the institute and place Denfert-Rochereau, a high-traffic area for cars and pedestrians. Being so visible was a necessary risk, since it was the largest manhole close to where they'd be digging, making it the best place to deliver the heavy equipment. But it was also the moment when they were the most likely to attract unwanted attention.

Once they were done, Nick disassembled the tripod while Dusko and Vinko removed the barricade and put it back in the van. Then the two Serbians went down into the sewer to join Borko. Nick followed them in, slid the manhole cover back into place, and Kate drove off. The operation had taken less than ten minutes.

In the sewer, each man picked up a piece of equipment, and Gaëlle led them single file through several IGC access tunnels to the lighted utility corridor where they would be working. The corridor was about six feet high and six feet wide, and the concrete ceiling and walls were lined with scores of pipes and conduits.

There was a big *X* written chest-high on the wall where they would be drilling three twelve-inch circular shafts, one right next to another, in a tight cluster to create one tubular tunnel large enough for a man to crawl through.

Vinko placed the diamond coring tool on the track. Dusko attached the coring bit and water line to the machine. Borko plugged the rig into the electric line. Nick powered up a twelve-inch flat-screen TV that Joe had mounted on the wall and that was hardwired into the institute's video surveillance feed. Several angles on the lab came up on-screen. There were four scientists working in their inflated suits.

"They are putting in some overtime," Nick said.

Vinko came up beside him and looked at the screen. "Is that a problem?"

"No. They can't hear us digging and will be long gone by the time we punch through the wall at two or three in the morning."

Vinko watched them working with their pipettes of plague for a moment.

"I'm glad you're going into that room and not me," Vinko said. "The air is full of death."

"The room will be clean when I go in," Nick said. "It'll be a lot more sanitary than the sewer we just walked through."

Huck took out the tablet device that operated the computerized coring tool and typed in some data. "I'm ready."

Nick shut off the monitor. Everyone put on their goggles and ear protectors. Huck tapped a key on the tablet, starting the drill. The diamond core bit began spinning, the water-moistened circular face cutting into the concrete with a noise amplified so much by the confines of the tunnel that it became a physical sensation. The men shook with the sound, and the wall wept slurry under the spinning bit as the core driller made its slow progress.

A panel van from Orange, the French telecom company, was parked on a nearby side street that ran along the ivy-covered walls on the southeastern edge of Montparnasse Cemetery. Litija and Joe were sitting in the back of the van at a console watching two monitors.

One monitor showed dozens of thumbnails representing the views of all security cameras inside and outside the institute. The other monitor showed a full-screen picture of the lab they'd be breaking into.

Litija closely watched the scientists in the lab to see if any of them appeared to notice the sound or rumble of the drilling outside their walls. Nothing seemed to break the concentration of the scientists on their experiments. The only thing she sensed was the urgency and seriousness of their work. She glanced at the other monitor. Nothing out of the ordinary was happening elsewhere at the institute either.

"So far so good," Joe said, looking to her for agreement. But she didn't give it to him.

She picked up the radio and called her lookouts.

"Daca, what do you see?" she asked in Serbian.

He was stationed atop a building that overlooked place Denfert-Rochereau so he'd be able to see any police vehicles approaching from any of the intersecting boulevards.

"*Ništa se dešava,*" he replied. Nothing is happening.

"Stefan, what do you see?" she asked.

He was positioned atop a building one block further north, where avenue Denfert-Rochereau intersected with place Ernest Dennis. Between the two men, she'd know if authorities were coming from any direction.

"*Isti,*" he replied. The same.

Litija set the radio down and gave Joe the nod he was looking for.

"So far so good," she said.

That was true for now. But she knew with absolute certainty that it wouldn't last.

By midnight, Huck had drilled through the limestone and was close to cutting his first hole into the concrete wall of the laboratory. In the hours leading up to that, Nick and the three Road Runners had lugged a dozen cylindrical cores of solid concrete and limestone out of the utility corridor and into the sewer, lining them up along the wall. Nick and Vinko had just brought out the last two limestone cores and were drenched with sweat.

"Here you are, working for Dragan Kovic, the man who kidnapped and then betrayed you," Vinko said to Nick. "That makes no sense to me."

"Dragan didn't betray me," Nick said. "Zarko did."

"We both know that's not true. Zarko always followed orders. He took a fall for you."

"A very long one."

Vinko got in Nick's face. "Zarko and I grew up in the same village. We served side by side in the war. He was like a brother to me. He's not a punch line for a smart-ass remark."

"I didn't push him off the cliff. If you have a problem, it's with Dragan, not me."

Vinko shook his head and poked Nick's chest hard with his finger. "Dragan did it for you."

Kate stepped out of the adjoining IGC tunnel. "Huck is about to punch through into the lab. Do you guys want to be there for it or is it interrupting your tea time?"

"We're on our way," Nick said.

Vinko walked away, brushing past Kate into the tunnel. She turned to Nick.

"Do we have a problem?" she asked.

"No, but Dragan might." Nick rubbed his chest. He was lucky he didn't have a collapsed lung. "Tossing Zarko off a cliff probably wasn't a great move for employee morale."

They made their way back to the utility corridor. Huck was crouched outside the four-foot-diameter opening and held the tablet controller for the diamond core driller. The core driller was twenty-two feet further down and digging through the concrete wall of the lab under remote control.

A brownish slurry, from the water that kept the drill bit wet, spilled out onto the floor. Dusko was trying to suck up as much slurry as he could with a workshop vacuum.

"We're close," Huck said. "Any second now."

Nick turned on the monitor, showing several views of the empty lab. One angle showed the back wall of the control room. Kate, Borko, Vinko, and Gaëlle huddled closely around Nick for the big moment.

The first thing they saw was a circular seam opening up in the wall, then water seeping through. An instant later, the diamond-serrated edge of the core bit cut through, looking like the wide open mouth of a metal snake that had just swallowed a huge chunk of concrete. They were in.

The drilling went very fast after that. The remaining two bores were cut in less than two hours, making the hole wide enough for a man with a pack to crawl through. The drilling tool was removed and the track was pulled up. It was time for Nick to go inside. He picked up the small backpack that contained the titanium case for the vial of smallpox and went to the mouth of the tunnel.

"Good luck," Kate said.

"The hard part is already over," Nick said.

He gave her a smile, their eyes met and held for a long moment, and he crawled inside.

In the van, Litija and Joe sat at their console and stared at the image of the empty control room and the hole in the wall. Nick crawled out, his white SAP jumpsuit smeared with wet slurry, and wiped his gloved hands on his suit.

They watched him take off the muddy work gloves, set them on the counter, and pull out a pair of white surgical gloves from his pocket. He put the rubber gloves on, took off his backpack, and removed the container for the vial from inside the backpack. His lips were pursed and he seemed to be moving to a jaunty beat.

"Is he whistling?" Litija asked.

"It's 'Whistle While You Work,'" Joe said. "From *Snow White*."

"How do you know?"

Because Joe could hear him. Now that Nick was in the basement of the storefront, the signal from his earbuds wasn't blocked anymore by tons of limestone and concrete. Nick could hear Joe and Litija, too. But, of course, Litija didn't know that.

"That's what he always whistles when he goes in solo on a break-in," Joe said.

Nick looked up at the camera and pointed to the keypad that operated the air lock.

"Yeah, yeah, I'm unlocking it," Joe said and began typing furiously on the keyboard.

The air lock door opened and Nick stepped inside. Only his face was visible through the porthole window. Joe switched the image on the monitor to a view from a camera inside the lab.

Nick stepped out of the air lock and, still whistling, made his merry way across the lab to the freezer that contained the deadly virus.

"That, ladies and gentlemen, is a natural thespian in action," Boyd said, pointing at the TV. Willie and Tom were in the storefront with him. They were a floor above the lab set, sitting in folding chairs and watching the con unfold on their screen. Chet was down in the basement, outside the set with his tool belt on, ready to spring into action if there was a technical problem.

"Notice how effortlessly Nick expresses his relaxation as well as the joy he derives from his work," Boyd continued. "That is body-language acting. His entire character comes through."

Nick looked up at the camera, pointed to the keypad on the freezer, and whistled some more while he waited for Joe to release the locking mechanism.

"That is Nick being Nick," Willie said. "He's just having fun."

"People thought the same thing about James Garner, Jimmy

Stewart, and Spencer Tracy," Boyd said. "The great actors make acting look easy, as if they are just playing themselves. You're forgetting that this is not a real robbery. That's Nick acting like a thief who is enjoying himself."

"But it is a real con," Tom said. "I think he likes that even more than stealing stuff."

"Because it involves acting," Boyd said.

The keypad of the refrigerator flashed green and Nick opened the fridge door. A fog of frost escaped, dissipated, and revealed the rows of vials inside, each presumably containing a deadly virus.

"Look, he's stopped whistling," Boyd said. "That's because he's staring into the gaping maw of rampant pestilence, misery, and doom. The chill he's feeling on his face might as well be the fingers of Death stroking his cheek. He's learned so much from me."

Nick set his box down on a nearby counter, opened it up, then slowly reached into the refrigerator for a vial.

23

Something on the monitor caught Litija's eye. She nudged Joe and pointed to Nick.

"What is that on his back?"

"Dirt," Joe said.

"No, no, the black thing," she said. "I think it's moving."

Joe tapped his mouse and the camera zoomed in on the black dot. It was a big, black spider and it was crawling between Nick's shoulder blades toward his neck.

"That's a spider," she said. "We've got to warn him."

"How?" Joe said, knowing that Nick could hear every word they were saying. "Besides, what harm could it do?"

Litija picked up the phone. But it was too late.

As Nick turned to place the smallpox vial in the container,

the spider went over his collar and down his bare neck. And bit him.

Nick winced at the sting and reflexively reached for his back with both hands, dropping the vial of smallpox.

The vial hit the floor and shattered.

Everyone in the utility tunnel stared in horror at the screen. Nick was still reaching for the spider, and hadn't realized yet what had happened.

"The spider just killed him," Vinko said, the edges of his mouth curling into a smile.

Nick will live, Kate thought, but the con, and all the work they'd put into it, was dead. She swore, ducked into the opening, and started crawling for the lab.

Vinko looked at the others. "What's she going to do? Read him his last rites?"

Litija couldn't believe what she was seeing and, at that same instant, neither could Nick, who spotted the broken vial on the floor. The full impact of what it obviously meant slammed him. He was infected with smallpox. Nick staggered back from the broken vial, shaking his head, seemingly unwilling to accept the inescapable truth—that he was a dead man.

This changed everything for Litija. All of the plans she'd made would die with him. She couldn't let this happen. There had to be a way to salvage this for herself.

And then, as if Nick were reading her thoughts, he looked

up into the camera and right at her. She could almost see his mind working, desperately searching for a way out of this.

Save yourself, Litija thought. Save me.

She saw Kate crawl out of the hole into the control room. Her first thought was that Kate was crazy to expose herself to the virus, then Litija remembered that the lab had an independent air system and there was an air lock between the two rooms.

Kate knocked on the control room window to get Nick's attention.

In the few seconds that it had taken Kate to crawl from the utility corridor to the control room, she'd figured it out. Nick was a world-class thief and a master con man. And yet, he'd been foiled by a spider . . . a very photogenic spider, one with a Boyd Capwell sense of drama and a Hitchcockian sense of timing.

Nick approached the window with an appropriately shell-shocked expression on his face.

Kate got close to the glass and whispered, "You jerk. You changed the game plan and you didn't tell me."

Kate knew he could hear her through the earbuds they were both wearing, and she wanted to be quiet in case anybody else came through the opening behind her.

"That's cruel," Nick said. "You're not showing a lot of sympathy for my dire predicament."

"The spider was no accident," Kate said. "It's not even a real spider, is it?"

"It's a tiny robot Chet made for me," Nick said. "I put it on my back in the air lock and he operated it by remote control from outside the set."

"You did this so Dragan will have to take you to his lab to harvest the virus. You've made yourself the smallpox sample," Kate said.

"I'm also the tracking device. I swallowed it as I was crawling in. There's another one in my biohazard suit." He tipped his head to the three emergency protective suits hanging on the wall behind Kate. "It's like one of those."

She didn't look behind her. "So you also had Chet create a working bioprotection suit for you, too. Very thorough. You planned to do this from the start and hid it from me. I really thought you trusted me."

"I do."

"You have a strange way of showing it."

"There wasn't time to tell you. I couldn't shake the feeling that you, me, Gaëlle, and Huck weren't going to make it out of the sewers alive. The broken vial was a last-minute decision that will ensure we all make it to the street, where there is protection," Nick said.

"Once Dragan realizes that you're not really infected, he'll kill you."

"I'm responsible for Dragan having the smallpox that he's already got. If this attack happens, all those deaths are on me. I made it possible. I couldn't live with that. This way, I guarantee that I will have a chance to stop him."

She couldn't fault him for having a conscience. In fact, it was nice to know that he did. But it didn't make her any less angry or any less afraid for his safety.

"It's suicide," Kate said. "You idiot."

"Where's your optimism?"

"I prefer being realistic."

"You'll rescue me before anything bad happens," Nick said.

"Don't be so sure. I was too late in Antwerp."

"You made up for it later."

"That'll be hard for me to do if you're dead."

"I think you're missing the point here," he said. "I'm trusting you with my life. How much more could I trust you than that?"

Kate squinched her eyes shut. "Ugh!"

Litija squinted at the screen. "It looks like they are saying goodbye."

Joe shook his head. "I think Nick is up to something."

"How can you tell?"

Because he'd heard their conversation. "He's got that sparkle in his eye."

It was true, he did. Or maybe Joe just imagined it.

"You can see a sparkle?" she asked.

"Can't you?"

The phone rang. Joe hit a switch, putting the call from the tunnel on the speaker.

"Nick is the smallpox sample now," Kate said.

It took a second for Litija to wrap her head around that. At first what Kate said made no sense at all to her, and then she realized it was brilliant. Things could move forward exactly as Litija had planned. The only difference was that now the box carrying the virus wasn't titanium, it was flesh and blood.

"How is he getting out of the lab without infecting everyone?" Litija asked.

"He'll strip out of his clothes and put himself in an impermeable vinyl suit like the blue ones hanging in the control room," Kate said. "The suits have independent air purifying respirators that operate on a battery with a six-hour charge. But there's one thing he needs to know first. Does Dragan have the smallpox vaccine? If Nick can get it within the next seventy-two hours, he has a chance."

"Yes, of course he does," Litija said, though she had no idea if Dragan did or not and she didn't care. It was the only answer Nick wanted to hear so that's what she gave Kate.

"Gaëlle will lead the others out of here and up to the street," Kate said. "I'll bring Nick to the manhole on rue Boissonade. Have the sewer utility van waiting to roll."

Rue Boissonade was a good choice, Litija thought. It was a residential side street that ran along the northern perimeter of the institute, on the other side of the block from avenue Denfert-Rochereau. There was little chance of any cars or pedestrians there at this time of the morning, and there would be few, if any, surveillance cameras. Daca and Stefan wouldn't be able to see them, but the two snipers could still watch the major cross streets and give her plenty of warning if the police were coming.

"There's one thing *I* need to know first," Litija said. "What happens if he tears his suit going through the little tunnel you just dug? He could infect us all."

"I'll tape up any tears."

"Won't you get infected?" Litija didn't care about Kate's health. What she was worried about was Kate starting an outbreak herself in Paris and ruining everything.

"I was vaccinated for smallpox in the military," Kate said. "It was part of our preparation for chemical warfare."

"Okay," Litija said. "Give the phone to Vinko."

Vinko got on the line and they had a quick discussion in Serbian. Litija told him that Nick was now the virus but that everything else was to go exactly as planned. When she was done, she caught Joe staring at her suspiciously.

"Why weren't you talking in English?" he asked.

"He's not very good at English and I wanted to make absolutely sure there were no misunderstandings," Litija said. "Or people could die."

It made sense to him. Joe nodded his approval. "Starting with us."

Definitely, she thought.

Nick went through an air lock in the back of the lab that presumably led to the room where scientists donned their positive pressure suits. Instead, he walked off the set into the basement where Chet was waiting for him with the blue biohazard suit on a hanger. There was an open bottle of red wine and a plate of cheese, prosciutto, and grapes on a table for Nick, too.

"Well played," Chet said.

"The real credit goes to that spider of yours," Nick said, unzipping his sewer worker's jumpsuit and stepping out of it wearing only a T-shirt and Calvins. "You ought to sell it as a novelty item. It would go over big with little boys eager to scare their sisters and mothers."

"Too late. You can buy radio-controlled spiders for twenty dollars on the Internet," Chet said, scooping his spider from the floor. "This one costs two grand. It's left over from a movie I worked on. So is this biohazard suit. It only looks and sounds like the real thing. It's not actually impermeable, and the respirator doesn't purify the air you're breathing or exhaling."

"I'll try not to wear it around anyone infected with a real virus." Nick popped a few cubes of cheese in his mouth and poured himself a generous glass of wine, which he drank like water. "Okay, let's do this."

Boyd, Willie, and Tom came down the stairs as Chet was helping Nick into the suit. It looked like something an astronaut might wear for a moonwalk except with a huge transparent hood instead of a helmet.

"That was a brilliant performance," Boyd said.

"I thought I overacted and made the bite look more like a gunshot," Nick said, stepping into rubber boots with his suit-covered feet.

"You had to. It was a silent movie," Boyd said. "Every gesture and emotion has to be exaggerated to make up for the lack of dialogue. But you conveyed the abject horror perfectly. It really felt like you were doomed."

"Because he might be," Willie said. "Kate's right, Nick. You're an idiot. Making yourself the virus was a dumb move."

"I admire what he's doing," Tom said. "He's risking his life for one chance to save thousands of Americans. It's noble."

"Be sure to put that in his eulogy," Willie said. "It'll bring everyone to tears."

"You're almost as bad as Kate," Nick said.

Nick taped his boots to his ankles with duct tape. He got up and headed for the air lock. "You all did great work, as usual. Willie, you'd better get in your car, we'll be going soon."

"I won't lose you," Willie said, heading back up the stairs.

"Once we're gone," Nick said, "the rest of you get out of here and take the first flight back to Los Angeles."

Nick gave everyone a thumbs-up and walked through the fake air lock into the lab.

"You can find me in Miami," Boyd said. "I'm not going anywhere near Los Angeles until I hear how this turns out."

"That makes two of us," Chet said.

"Three," Tom said. "I'm meeting my family in Walla Walla."

245

. . .

Kate was already in the control room holding a roll of duct tape when Nick entered the lab. He walked across the lab to the air lock and stepped inside. The door closed behind him. He waited for the green light that indicated the air had been sucked out of the tiny room and new air pumped in. It was all for show, of course, none of that was actually happening, but they had a lie to sell if anyone was watching.

The green light went on and Nick stepped out. He modeled the suit for her.

"How do I look?"

"Very stylish," she said. "I'll go through the tunnel first and wait for you on the other side. I'll check you out for tears and tape up any that I see."

"You'll get infected," Nick said.

"I've been vaccinated."

"No, you haven't."

"How would you know?"

"I would have seen the scar," he said.

"You must have missed it."

"I gave you a very thorough examination," Nick said. "I can map every freckle."

"I don't think I am going to be in any *real* danger of infection, do you? I'll see you on the other side of the tunnel," she said and crawled inside.

He waited a moment, then carefully crawled in after her. It was a tight fit, but the diamond core driller had left the walls fairly smooth, and he went slowly. When he got to the end, she helped him out of the hole and checked his suit out for punctures or tears.

She tore off a few pieces of duct tape, putting one on each knee and another on his back, where the shape of the respirator stuck out like a backpack under the suit.

"Were there some rips?" Nick asked.

"I don't think so. I covered the scratches just to be on the safe side," she said. "Follow me."

They walked single file down the corridor, through an IGC access tunnel, and then into the sewer. A sign on the wall read *rue Boissonade*. They reached the ladder to the manhole and Kate climbed up first, pushing the manhole cover up and sliding it aside. She climbed out into the predawn darkness and saw the SAP truck parked at the curb under a street lamp. Litija was in the driver's seat. The three Road Runners, Gaëlle, and Huck were standing a safe distance away on the sidewalk behind the van, as if Nick might explode and they didn't want to get hit by the shrapnel.

Kate climbed out and waved Vinko over. "Help me ease Nick out of here."

Vinko looked like he'd rather have a hot coffee enema, but he came over anyway.

As Nick slowly emerged, they each took one of his arms and gently eased him out of the manhole, careful to make sure his suit cleared the opening without scraping it. The instant Nick was out, Vinko joined Borko and Dusko behind Gaëlle and Huck. It was like the three Road Runners were using Gaëlle and Huck as human shields.

Kate led Nick to the back of the van and opened the doors for him. Nick stepped inside the empty cargo area. Once he was settled on a bench, Kate started to climb in, too.

"What do you think you're doing?" Litija said, turning in her seat to look at them.

"I'm going with you," Kate said.

"No, you're not." Litija lifted a Sig Sauer P239 off her lap and aimed it at Kate. "Get out."

"It's okay, Kate," Nick said. "I don't need your protection anymore. I think I'm way past that now."

"I thought I was more than protection to you," she said.

"You thought wrong," Nick said. "Good luck to you."

"I'm not the one who is going to need it."

Kate stepped out and slammed the door closed behind her. Litija set her gun down on the passenger seat.

"Put on your seatbelt," Litija said. "We don't want any accidents."

24

Kate watched the van drive away before turning to face Gaëlle and Huck and the three Road Runners.

The Road Runners had guns drawn, and Gaëlle and Huck had eyes wide with fear. Dusko moved a short distance from the group and aimed his gun at Kate.

"You really don't want to do this," Kate said to the men.

"It's not a question of what we want," Vinko said. "We follow orders."

Kate stared him down. "I'd reconsider if I were you. If you don't lower those guns, you'll be killed. We have protection."

"You don't look protected to me," Vinko said.

She stayed stoic. "You're making a mistake."

Vinko and Borko aimed. So did Dusko.

Huck took Gaëlle's hand. Gaëlle squeezed it hard and they

both closed their eyes. What they heard next sounded like two sandbags hitting the ground. It took a second for Gaëlle and Huck to realize that they weren't shot. They turned around and saw that Vinko and Borko were dead on the ground, both shot in the head.

Kate didn't hear or see the shots, but knew she had Walter, up on a rooftop somewhere, to thank for saving Gaëlle and Huck. She looked at Dusko now. He stood very still, eyes wide, and then toppled face-first to the ground, a knife in his back. Antoine Killian stood a few feet behind Dusko. Kate had no idea how the enormous man had got there or where he'd come from so fast.

"*Merci*," Kate said to him.

He nodded and offered her a polite smile. "*Je vous en prie.*"

She assumed it was French for "You're welcome" or "No problem." Antoine stepped up, pulled his knife out of Dusko's back, and wiped the blood off on the dead man's jumpsuit.

A black BMW 7 Series sedan slinked around the corner behind Gaëlle and Huck and glided smoothly to a stop beside Kate. Willie was at the wheel and lowered the passenger window to speak with her.

"I've got a strong tracking signal on Nick," Willie said, holding up a tablet device that was plugged into the car's USB port. "They're crossing the intersection of boulevard Saint-Michel and boulevard Saint-Germain."

Kate turned to Gaëlle and Huck, both of whom looked shell-shocked. "It's all over. You're both safe now. Thank you for everything you've done. Now get out of here fast and maybe go on a vacation for a few weeks."

She got into the BMW, and it sped away.

It wasn't until the car was gone that Huck Moseby realized that the fat man who'd stabbed Dusko had disappeared. Now he and Gaëlle were alone with three corpses. Huck didn't know what had just happened or who the fat man was or who the woman in the car was or who the hell had shot Vinko and Borko. All he knew for sure was that he'd barely escaped death and that Gaëlle was holding his hand.

He looked at her and thought she was the most beautiful woman he'd ever seen. She was literally the woman of his dreams. It was hard to believe that she actually existed.

"If you'll have me," he said in French, "I will devote my life to making you happy."

She smiled. "You have a deal."

They kissed softly and then walked away, still holding hands.

"The first time we met," Nick said, buckled in tight in the back of the van, "I'd just emerged from a coffin in a fake diamond vault in Belgium. Now here I am in a hazmat suit, infected with smallpox, and we're driving through the streets of Paris in a sewer van. Who would have imagined that?"

"You lead a wild, exciting life," Kate said.

"You do, too."

"But it's been much more profitable for you than me."

"It doesn't seem like it at the moment," Nick said.

"I'm sure you've been in situations as bad as this." She glanced at him in the rearview mirror. "How many times have you had a gun to your head or a knife to your throat?"

"This is different. I can talk myself out of those situations."

"I've seen you do it and it was amazing, especially the way you played Dragan. Nobody has ever done that before. It's not just what you say, it's also the outrageous risks you take at the same time. You've inspired me."

"Really?" Nick said. "To do what?"

"You'll see," she said.

She remained silent as they headed north through central Paris, along much of the same scenic route that Gaëlle had taken with Nick and Kate during their Uber ride. They hit the A1 freeway, taking the ramp for Lille/Aéroport Charles de Gaulle/Saint-Denis. Nick figured they were going to an airport to board Dragan's private jet for a trip to another country. Suddenly Litija exited off the freeway and drove into an industrial warehouse district miles away from the airport.

"Are we taking the scenic route?" Nick asked.

Litija ignored him and proceeded through the rotting gates of a sprawling abandoned factory. The cavernous brick buildings had multiple smokestacks and were tangled in the gantries, pipes, and conveyors belts that ran through them, around them, and over them. She drove into one of the buildings, which was the size of an airplane hangar, and stopped the van.

"Where are we, Litija?"

"At a turning point for both of us." Her cellphone rang. She answered it and put it on the speaker. "Hello, Dragan. I've put you on the speaker and am talking to you in English so Nick can hear you, too."

"I'm very sorry about what happened to you, Nick," Dragan said. "But I can assure you of two things. Thanks to your quick thinking, you'll survive and our project can still go forward as we planned. You'll be a very rich man when this is over."

"I like that," Nick said.

"In a few minutes, you'll be on my plane and on your way to my lab, where you'll get the best medical care and you can watch our plans take shape while you recuperate."

"Recuperate? I thought I was getting the vaccine."

"You are," Dragan said. "But not immediately. We need to wait for the virus to multiply in your bloodstream so we can extract a potent sample that we can work with."

"You're using me as an incubator?"

"It's not how I would have liked to do things, but you're the one who dropped the vial. So we're turning lemons into *limoncello*, as they say."

"Okay, so what's the delay?" Nick asked. "Why are we sitting in this warehouse?"

"I can answer that," Litija said. "There's been a little change in plans, Dragan. I wanted you to hear Nick so you'd know he was with me and that he's still alive."

"Smallpox doesn't kill instantly," Nick said.

"But I do," she said. "I will kill Nick unless twenty million dollars is wired to my offshore bank account in the next ten minutes."

Litija disconnected the call.

Kate and Willie heard every chilling word through their earbuds as they sped along on the A1 freeway. This was an unexpected complication they didn't need after one too many complications already.

"How far behind them are we?" Kate asked.

"Five minutes," Willie said.

"Make it two," Kate said.

Willie floored the gas pedal and wove through the cars in front of them like the *Millennium Falcon* flying through an asteroid belt. Kate took out her phone and hit the speed-dial key for her father.

"How close are you, Dad?"

Willie leaned on her horn and drove between two lanes, shearing off the side-view mirrors. "Oops. I guess I should have taken the insurance," she said.

"Ten minutes," Jake said. "But we'll make it five."

"Just sit tight, Nick," Litija said, aiming her Sig Sauer at him. "Once I have the money, I'll leave you here. I'll let Dragan know where to find you when I'm a safe distance away."

"That could take hours, and I don't have a lot of hours to spare."

"It is what it is."

"I have a better idea. It's getting stuffy in here. So I'm going to unzip this suit and get some air unless you put that gun down and start driving."

"If you touch that zipper, I'll shoot you."

"That would be stupid, because if you puncture this suit, you'll be infected with smallpox."

"There are three problems with your threat. The first is that I've been vaccinated against smallpox."

"I don't believe you," Nick said. "So I will call that bluff."

"The second is that I'm a dead woman anyway, because whether you live or die, Dragan will hunt me to the ends of the earth. But with twenty million, I'll have a better chance of outrunning him or at least living very, very well until he finds me."

"That just proves how much you want to live."

"Which brings me to number three. You don't want to die. You'd rather take your chances with the virus than risk a bullet in the head from me. Besides, you've got nothing to lose in this transaction. What do you care if I walk away with twenty million dollars? You're going to be a billionaire."

"Assuming Dragan pays."

"He'll pay," she said. "What's twenty million against billions?"

"You might kill me anyway just to spite Dragan."

"Do I strike you as a spiteful person?"

"Isn't that why you are doing this? Because you're mad that Dragan killed Zarko?"

Litija laughed. "I don't care about Zarko. You met him. He was a slug."

"But you were shaking after Dragan pushed him off the cliff."

"Because it could easily have been me if I'd been standing there," she said. "I'm doing this for the money. I want to be rich and far away from Dragan Kovic. The man is insane, in case you haven't noticed."

"I noticed," Nick said.

"But you still went into business with him. You must be crazy, too." She picked up her phone and checked it. "The money hasn't shown up in my account yet. You've got three minutes."

There was a tap-tap on the driver's side window and Litija went pale. It was Kate, tapping the barrel of her gun against the window.

"Put the gun down or I'll blow your head off," Kate shouted through the glass. She was still in her dirty sewer worker's jumpsuit.

Litija stared at Kate in absolute disbelief. "How did you get here?"

"The same way he did," Kate said, gesturing to the passenger side.

Litija turned. A man in his sixties stood outside the window, and he was also aiming a gun at her. He had the buzz cut, bearing, and hardened gaze of a soldier. She'd underestimated Nick and Kate. They'd had a second team of professional killers watching their backs. Her inability to anticipate this move demonstrated why she'd always been somebody's minion. She wasn't clever enough to lead. It proved to her that this twenty-million-dollar play was her last, best chance at changing her fate.

"*You* drop the gun," Litija said. "And the old man drops his, too, or I will kill Nick right now."

"That would be a mistake," Kate said. "Because I'm your ticket to freedom and happiness."

"How do you imagine that?"

"I'll let you go and tell Dragan that I killed you," Kate said. "You won't have your ransom money, but at least you'll be free and won't have to look over your shoulder for the rest of your life. Or you can shoot Nick and die right now. Your choice."

How did Kate know about the ransom? Was the van wired? Was Nick? The fact that she didn't know the answers to those questions was more humiliating evidence that she was destined to a life of servitude and pocket change, never to leadership and wealth. She glanced at her phone, hoping for a $20 million reprieve from her wretched destiny.

The ten minutes were up. There was no alert from the bank that a transfer had been made, and Dragan hadn't called arguing for more time. He didn't pay, and she had the miserable, crushing realization that he never would. He'd rather sacrifice Nick and put off his scheme indefinitely than let her extort a dime out of him.

The bastard.

"You gambled that Dragan's greed was larger than his ego," Nick said. "I could have told you that was a losing bet."

Litija put her gun down on the passenger seat and placed her hands on the steering wheel in surrender.

"You can't blame a girl for trying," she said.

Kate stuck her gun in her jumpsuit and opened the driver's side door. "Come on out."

As Litija stepped out, a jaunty little Alfa Romeo convertible sped into the building and came to a stop behind Kate. The man at the wheel was as jaunty as his car. He had a big smile and wore a herringbone wool driving cap, a red cravat, and a tweed jacket. He was so British he might as well have draped himself in the Union Jack.

"Hello, luv," Robin Mannering said. "Going my way?"

Litija looked at Kate. "Where's he taking me?"

"Out of France," Kate said. "He'll set you up with a passport, credit cards, and some cash, and you're on your way."

"But we'll find a decent cup of tea first," Robin said.

The truth was that he would take her straight to the British Embassy, where she'd be placed under arrest. Her faked death would make Litija the perfect secret informant against the Road Runners and law enforcement's best hope of tracking down the stolen diamonds.

"Why aren't you killing me?" Litija said.

"Because I work for Nicolas Fox and he insists that I only kill in self-defense, never in cold blood," Kate said. "It's a character flaw that will probably cost him his life one day."

"That day will come very soon unless you break that rule with Dragan." Litija got into the car with Robin and they drove off.

Kate climbed into the driver's seat of the van and looked back at Nick, who'd unzipped his hood and pulled it off his head.

"Did you see Litija's double-cross coming?" she asked.

"Nope. I must be losing my touch."

Jake got into the passenger seat and reached over to shake Nick's hand. "Good to see you."

"Likewise," Nick said.

"Your crew is long gone, and Antoine and Walter have cleaned up the mess on the street," Jake said. "The three bodies will never be found."

"Vinko, Borko, and Dusko?" Nick said.

"Walter and Antoine took them out and saved our lives," Kate said. "Your instincts were right."

"What about Dragan's two snipers?" Nick asked.

"They couldn't see what happened from where they were," Jake said. "They were watching avenue Denfert-Rochereau and I was watching them. They left their positions as soon as they saw Litija drive off in this van. They probably assumed the mission was accomplished and are now on their way out of the country."

"We should be, too." Kate picked up the cellphone, hit the speed dial, and waited. Dragan answered on the first ring.

"Have you come to your senses?" he asked.

259

"That's hard to do when your brains are splattered on a wall," Kate said. "Litija is dead."

"Well done," Dragan said. "How is Nick?"

Nick spoke up. "Eager to get to you as fast as possible."

"How much time do you have left on your battery, Nick?"

"Maybe five hours," Nick said.

"No worries," Dragan said. "We'll have everything ready for you when you arrive."

Dragan gave Kate directions to the terminal and hung up.

"Wherever Dragan's lab is, we'll be there five hours from now," Kate said to her father. "You'll strike two hours later."

"You mean I'll come and get you," Jake said.

"I mean blow the place up," Kate said. "Reduce it to ash. Make sure Dragan and his virus do not get out."

"That was the old plan," Jake said. "But things have changed now that you two are going to be inside."

"Not the way I see it," Kate said. "Do you have a set of our earbuds?"

"I do, but I hate wearing them," Jake said. "They are too much like hearing aids. They make me feel old."

"When you're within striking distance, the three of us should be able to communicate with one another," she said.

"See you in seven hours," Jake said, kissed Kate on the cheek, and got out.

Kate drove the van out of the warehouse, past Willie in her BMW and the Renault that Jake had driven, and headed for Charles de Gaulle Airport. Willie and Jake would be close behind them, bound for the private plane that they also had on standby.

"We're in this together again," Nick said.

"We are always in it together, even when we're apart."

"Not to be overly unmanly, but the moment I escaped from you that first time in L.A.," Nick said, "I regretted it two minutes later and was tempted to let you catch me just so we could be together."

She looked at him in the rearview mirror. "Really?"

"Really."

Kate was pretty sure she believed him. "I had no clue."

"Would you have done anything differently if you knew I was enamored with you?"

"No," Kate said. "Zip up your hood, we're almost there."

Damn! He was enamored with her way back then, she thought. It was enough to get her doing a happy dance. She wouldn't, of course, because she was the job. Still, she could happy dance in her mind.

Nick secured himself in the suit again as they reached the general aviation area of the airport and the private terminal. She drove through the gates, escorted by a security officer on a golf cart, onto the tarmac beside the black private jet. She backed up so the rear of the sewer van was as close as possible to the open hatch at the front of the plane. Kate didn't want Nick in his biohazard suit to be visible for long. Fortunately it was dawn on a Sunday and the odds of anybody being around to see him were slim.

Daca and Stefan appeared in the plane's open hatch. She recognized them as the same two men who'd followed them in Sorrento and later took them by boat to Dragan's villa. She got out, held her Glock down at her side, and walked to the back of the van.

"Good morning, gentlemen," she said. "I'd appreciate it if you'd open the van and help Nick into the plane."

"We'd rather that you do it," Daca said.

She shook her head and aimed her gun at them. "I want to see that you're unarmed and I want you out of the plane so I can check it out."

"You can trust us," Stefan said. "We're on the same side."

"Is that why your three buddies just tried to kill me?"

Daca nodded acknowledgment. The two men got out of the plane, and Kate stepped aboard. She quickly checked out the cabin and then watched from the hatch as the men opened the van, helped Nick out, and guided him to a seat on the plane. Kate took a seat near the cockpit, and Daca secured the hatch. They had only about four hours left on Nick's battery.

"Let's go," she said to the pilot. "The clock is ticking."

Kate didn't lower her gun until they'd taken off. She didn't think Daca and Stefan were dumb enough to start a shoot-out in the confines of a pressurized airplane. But she didn't turn her back to them, either.

Daca and Stefan stayed as far away from Nick as they could get, not that it would protect them from infection if he decided to open his suit or if he tore it somehow.

"Could somebody flag down the flight attendant?" Nick asked. "I'd like some peanuts and a Bloody Mary."

25

They landed in Frankfurt, Germany, an hour and fifteen minutes later. The pilots didn't announce their arrival, but Nick recognized the skyline the instant he saw the Trianon, a forty-seven-story office building with an enormous glass diamond that was suspended between three pinnacles at the top.

"I once cracked a safe in that building in broad daylight in front of a room full of executives. I pretended to be an expert hired by the corporate bosses in Berlin to evaluate the company's security measures," Nick said. "I scoffed at the lax security in the Frankfurt office and took the diamond-studded Egyptian antiquities that were in the safe with me to a place where they'd be better protected."

"Your living room?" Kate asked.

"A museum in Egypt," Nick said. "I would have kept them, but they clashed with my recliner."

The plane taxied to a stop a few yards away from a black helicopter.

"You're taking the helicopter the rest of the way," Daca said.

Kate aimed her gun at them. "I want you both to go in the bathroom and shut the door. Don't leave until we're gone."

"Why?" Stefan asked. "Are you afraid we're going to shoot you in the back?"

"Yes," Kate said. "Now get inside. No peeking, or the last thing you'll see is the bullet in your eye."

"I bet you aren't half as tough as you think you are," Daca said.

"How ironic," Kate said. "Vinko expressed the same sentiment to me. Now he's dead."

Stefan and Daca squeezed into the bathroom and closed the door. Nick and Kate got out of the plane and walked quickly to the helicopter.

The only person inside the helicopter was the pilot, who acknowledged them with a nod. Kate helped Nick get up into the chopper, then she climbed in and slid the door shut.

"The other guys won't be joining us," Kate yelled so the pilot could hear her over the sound of the rotor blades. "They got airsick."

The pilot gave them a thumbs-up and they lifted off. They headed southeast across the Main River toward the wooded mountains in the distance. They passed over several picturesque, storybook villages of half-timbered buildings and Gothic towers, and finally over a dense forest.

"That's the Spessart forest down there, home of *Snow White and the Seven Dwarfs*," Nick said.

Kate wouldn't have heard him over the sound of the rotors if it wasn't for the earbuds in their ears.

They came to a valley where a clearing had been cut into the woods. In the center of the clearing was an immaculate lawn and a medieval stone castle surrounded by a moat full of dark water. A gravel road ran alongside the edge of the clearing to a crushed gravel lot where two black Range Rovers were parked.

The castle walls were topped with battlements and so was the circular tower that rose high above the tree line. As the helicopter came in low over the castle, Kate could see four men armed with rifles patrolling the battlements and another man atop the tower scanning the forest with binoculars.

The helicopter landed in the grass in front of the drawbridge, where Dragan Kovic stood to welcome them. Nick and Kate got out of the chopper and walked up to Dragan.

"Welcome to Schloss Gesundheit," Dragan said.

"'Castle Good Health' is a strange name for the place where you're producing smallpox," Nick said.

"We inherited the name," Dragan said as he led them onto the drawbridge. "The castle was built in the 1400s and was a ruin by the 1880s, inhabited by nomads and bandits. That's when it was rebuilt as a sanitarium for people with horrible diseases. It was the ideal place to exile the poor souls, presumably for their health and well-being, because it was remote and the walls were thick. They even sent lepers here. Schloss Gesundheit closed in the 1950s and was abandoned until I came along. Nobody wanted to get near it."

"I can't imagine why," Kate said.

"The same qualities that made it an attractive sanitarium made it perfect for our needs," Dragan said. "It seemed right to keep the name."

They reached the iron lattice gate that sealed the passageway into the castle. Dragan stopped and held his hand out, palm up, to Kate.

"I'd like to have your gun before we go inside," Dragan said.

"I'm sure you would," Kate said. "But it's not happening."

"We're on the same side."

"That's what your people keep saying," Kate said. "It would be easier to believe if Vinko and your men hadn't tried to execute me and the rest of our crew after Litija drove off with Nick."

"I'm certain that I would have faced the same firing squad if things had gone as planned and I hadn't been infected," Nick said.

"I had nothing to do with it," Dragan said. "This news comes as a complete shock to me."

Dragan wasn't very convincing, but Kate figured he didn't have to try very hard. He knew Nick wasn't going anywhere.

"That's twice you've double-crossed me after a robbery," Nick said. "I should kill you, but self-preservation and extraordinary wealth mean more to me than revenge."

"Vinko, Dusko, and Borko were obviously in league with Litija," Dragan said. "She tried to double-cross us both."

"If what you say is true," Nick said to Dragan, "then your employees aren't very trustworthy. So I'm sure you can understand why I insist that Kate remain armed. She can protect us both."

"Well, when you put it that way, how can I argue?" Dragan said. "I'm glad to have someone of Kate's proven skills protecting us from further treachery."

Dragan nodded to a camera mounted by the entrance and the gate rose, creaking with age. He led them into a passageway leading to a courtyard with a wishing well in the middle.

Nick pointed up at the arched ceiling of the passageway. "I see you kept the *meurtrières*."

Dragan smiled. "I love charming architectural details like those. Every home should have them."

Kate looked up and saw sunlight spilling through six large holes in the stonework. "What are they for?" she asked.

"They're commonly known as murder holes," Nick said. "They're for pouring cauldrons of boiling water or hot tar on invaders."

"I prefer cauldrons of lye," Dragan said. "It makes cleanup so easy. You just hose what's left of your unwanted guests into the moat."

"Have you had the opportunity?" Kate asked.

"Not yet," he replied. "But you never know when unexpected guests might show up."

Kate did. They'd be coming in four hours, and she'd be sure to warn them not to come in through the front door.

They crossed the courtyard and entered the foyer of the castle. A burly Serbian with a gun in a shoulder holster sat at a console similar to those found in office building lobbies. He had a phone and several screens showing security camera views.

There were three doors off the foyer, and one of them was an air lock. Dragan went to the air lock, held a card key up to the reader on the wall, and they heard the lock open.

"After you, Nick," Dragan said.

Nick stepped into the air lock. After a moment, the door on the opposite side opened and he stepped into a corridor.

Dragan gestured to the door. "Proceed."

"We'll go in together," Kate said, worried that he could lock her inside and have all the air sucked out. She wasn't sure that was even possible, but she didn't want to find out the hard way.

"It will be a tight fit," Dragan said.

"We'll manage."

"As you wish."

She held the door open for him and, once he was inside, she stepped in behind him. He opened the next door and they joined Nick in the corridor. It was almost identical to the corridors inside the Institut National pour la Recherche sur les Maladies Infectieuses that Kate had seen on the security videos. Same walls, same floor, same hospital ambiance.

There were two air locks, one on each side of the corridor, and three large observation windows that looked in on the labs. Another burly armed guard was also waiting in the corridor, presumably to prevent Kate from taking Dragan hostage and demanding the vaccine for Nick.

She'd toyed with a similar scenario, except that she'd demand the smallpox sample instead of the vaccine. The problem was that she had no idea where the smallpox was or if it had already been used to create new supplies of the pathogen. Even if she did, one of the snipers would probably shoot her and Nick before they could leave the castle. Kate couldn't take any action until she knew where every last microbe of the virus was in the facility and her dad had arrived to back her up.

Dragan gestured to the air lock on their left. "Go through there, Nick. It's laid out just like the institute. Go straight through the locker room, the dressing room, and the suit room, where we have the positive pressure suits. You'll see three air locks, each with a number on them. Take the air lock marked number one. That's the lab that we've had repurposed as your quarters. Remove your suit and all of your clothing. Leave everything on the floor. You'll find new clothes waiting for you."

Nick peered through the window into the lab. Amid the workstations, dangling air hoses, and other equipment, he saw a cot with a set of surgical scrubs, slippers, and a towel laid out on the blanket.

"It's a good thing I'm not bashful," Nick said.

"You can draw the blinds if you want privacy," Dragan said and passed his card key over the reader, opening the air lock.

Nick stepped into the air lock and into the next room. A few moments later, Dragan and Kate saw him come through one of the two air locks in the back of the lab. He unzipped the suit and got out of it, stripped off his T-shirt and briefs, and put on the scrubs. He left the suit and clothes piled on the floor.

The other air lock in the lab opened and two technicians entered in positive pressure suits just like the ones Boyd, Willie, and the others had worn, and attached themselves to the air hoses hanging from the ceiling. They each carried large bags and stuffed his suit and clothes into them, sealed them with zip ties, and carried them out again.

"Everything he wore is going into the incinerators in the basement," Dragan said. "The microbiologists who came in will step into a disinfectant shower in their positive pressure suits, then once they've removed the suits and their undergarments, they will shower themselves. We're very serious about safety protocols here."

Nick walked up to the window, faced them, and pressed the intercom button on the wall. His voice came out over a speaker in the corridor. "What happens now?"

Dragan pressed an intercom button on his side. "Make yourself comfortable and get some rest. If you need anything at all, just press the intercom button here, by the air locks, or at any of the lab stations and a technician will handle it."

"What if I need to use the bathroom?"

"There's a bucket, wet wipes, and a roll of toilet paper under your cot," Dragan said. "Call for service and the bucket will be taken away."

"Not exactly the Four Seasons, is it?"

Before Dragan could answer, Nick shut the blinds. Dragan released the intercom and frowned.

"Moody, isn't he?"

"He gets that way when he goes without sleep for twenty-four hours, spends twelve hours digging a hole in a sewer, and then gets infected with a virus that will make him spew blood from every orifice."

"Nobody said that becoming a billionaire is easy," Dragan said. "Let me show you to your room. I'm sure you'd like to change and freshen up."

"I'd like a tour first," Kate said. "I won't feel comfortable until I get the lay of the land."

"Your uniform is filthy and you smell like the sewer. Clean up, then we'll have brunch and I'll show you around."

He led her out of the air lock, back to the foyer, past the guard, and through one of the other two heavy wooden doors. This led to another corridor that, unlike the lab area, felt like a castle should. It was entirely stone, rough-hewn on the walls and polished smooth under her feet. All that was missing to complete the authentic ambiance were torches to light their way instead of a series of LEDs in the ceiling. Dragan stopped at one of the doors.

"This was Litija's room," Dragan said. "She was more or less your size. You can wear her clothes or the scrubs that we've left on the bed. I'll see you in the dining room in an hour. It's straight down the hall and to your right."

She didn't have the hour to spare. She needed time to see the layout, come up with a plan, and then execute it before her dad showed up, guns and rockets blazing.

"Let's make it thirty minutes," she said. "I'm starving."

"Very well," he said and walked down the hall.

26

Dragan wanted to smash Kate's head against the wall until it splattered like a ripe melon. *Nobody* talked to him like that. This wasn't a hotel and he wasn't her bellboy. But instead of acting on his impulse, he'd walked away. It wasn't her gun that had stopped him but some practical considerations. He needed her alive. Nick would remain cooperative as long as he was under the delusion that Kate guaranteed his security and eventual vaccination.

But in two weeks, once Nick was sick enough that a nice, virulent sample of virus could be taken from him, then Dragan would kill Kate and take the time to thoroughly enjoy the experience. Maybe he'd use her to try out the lye. *That* would certainly be entertaining. The thought made him smile. Now he had another good reason to wait.

. . .

Kate closed the door and surveyed the room. It was a dungeon decorated like a bed-and-breakfast. The four-poster bed and armoire were hand carved, very old, and rich with vintage charm. She went to the window, barely more than a slit in the wall. It looked out over the moat and the lawn, where the helicopter was still sitting. She turned back to the room. There was a set of scrubs neatly folded on the bed, but Kate chose to check out what Litija had in the armoire instead. She couldn't holster her Glock on scrub pants.

"How are you holding up?" Kate asked Nick via the earbud.

Nick put his head in his hands so that Kate could hear him without the cameras in his room seeing him talk. "I'm trying not to fall asleep. I'm in position to take decisive action once you find out exactly where the virus is. It must be in one of the rooms or labs within this biosafety area."

"But it's a high-security area and you don't have the card key."

Kate opened the armoire. It was stuffed with Chanel ready-to-wear. Silk dresses, embroidered blouses, miniskirts, and lambskin slacks that were extremely colorful and meant to stand out. Whatever Kate picked to wear would make her an easy target to spot.

"You're forgetting something," Nick said. "I'm already past security. Dragan graciously escorted me in."

"But you're locked in a lab."

"Actually, I'm not. The biosafety area is designed to lock

people out, not to lock them in. I have complete freedom of movement within these labs, once you tell me where to go."

"You make it sound so easy." Kate grabbed a multicolored silk blouse with a busy design, cream lambskin slacks, and a large black belt and tossed them on the bed. The only shoes in the armoire were high heels, so she decided to stick with the mud-caked boots she'd worn in the sewer. "How am I supposed to find out that information? I don't have time to sneak around."

"Ask Dragan where it is."

She slipped out of her filthy jumpsuit and left it on the floor. "Why would he tell me?"

"Because he likes to show off," Nick said.

"It's one thing to brag about his villa and his castle, but there's no reason for him to tell me what he's done with the smallpox."

"So give him one," Nick said.

She tossed her underwear on the bed and stood naked in the middle of the room. "I'll think about it in the shower."

"I'll think about you taking a shower."

"I'd rather you thought of a plan for destroying the smallpox and escaping," she said.

"I'm on it," he said.

Nick got up from his cot, went to the intercom on the wall, and pressed the button.

"I have needs," Nick said.

"What can I get for you?" a man's voice answered.

"A box of cigars. The best Dragan has. And bring me bottles of vodka, scotch, and rum. The highest proof you've got. I intend to get smashed."

"Completely understandable," the man said.

The dining room was huge with a long table under two elaborate chandeliers that resembled upside-down Christmas trees. A large window overlooked the moat and the forest beyond.

Kate was admiring the chandeliers when she spotted the fresco on the ceiling. It was a copy of Michelangelo's *Creation of Adam* from the Sistine Chapel, with a robed, bearded God reaching out from the heavens to touch the outstretched hand of a lounging, naked Adam. But unlike the original, this Adam had Dragan's pockmarked face and an enormous penis. She was still staring at the disturbing image, not really believing what she was seeing, when Dragan walked into the room.

"What do you think?" Dragan asked.

"I'm surprised that your face is on Adam and not God."

"God doesn't have a dick," Dragan said.

"God doesn't need one," Kate said.

"It's not necessary if you're going to rule the heavens, but it is if you're going to conquer the world," he said. "Metaphorically speaking, of course. That's the point this painting is making."

"I wish I could see that painting," Nick said in Kate's ear. She almost replied *No, you don't.*

Dragan waved her to a seat at the end of a table that was set with smoked fish, sausages, fruit, and an array of pastries, along with coffee, juice, and water.

"Is that the point of the smallpox, too?" Kate asked. "Metaphorically speaking?"

"I suppose it is," he said.

"To pull off your biological attack, you're going to need someone who can slip into the United States to plant the device. You're going to have a hard time doing that with one of your Serbian Army buddies. But it would be no problem at all for an American citizen born and raised in California. Lucky for you, here I am."

"Brilliant," Nick said. *"I knew you'd come up with something."*

"You would do that for me?"

"I would do it for the twenty million you're going to pay me now and that I'm going to use to bet against the market," Kate said as she chose a croissant and poured herself a cup of coffee.

"That's the same amount Litija demanded as ransom for Nick."

"Yes, I know," Kate said. "Right amount, wrong play. You'll be glad to pay for this."

"You have no qualms about launching a terrorist attack against your own country?"

"My country is wherever I happen to be at any given moment," Kate said. "Right now it's Germany. In a few months, it will be the private island in the Bahamas that I am going to buy with my windfall."

Dragan smiled. "You didn't accompany Nick here to protect him. You came to strike a deal for yourself."

"You've hooked him," Nick said. *"Now slowly reel him in."*

She took a bite of the croissant and almost swooned. It was unbelievably flaky and buttery. She licked her lips and nibbled off another piece.

Dragan rapped his knife against his water glass. *Clang, clang, clang.* "It's just a croissant," he said. "We eat them every day. Can we move forward?"

"Yes, but this is a *really great* croissant," Kate said. "It's flaky and buttery. How do they get it to taste like this?"

"Focus!" Dragan said.

"Jeez," Kate said. "I was enjoying a moment, okay?"

Dragan looked like he was running out of patience, but Kate could hear Nick laughing at his end. She put the croissant down, took a sip of coffee, and dragged herself back to the task at hand.

"Having me around makes Nick feel like he's got some control in this situation, that he'll get his vaccine and his money. But we both know that's a fantasy. You're going to kill me as soon as you can get the virus out of him, and then you're going to let him die naturally because it'll be fun to watch."

"If you know that," Dragan said, "why are you still here? Why haven't you left?"

"Because it won't change anything. I know too much. You've got to kill me. You already tried once, and you'll keep at it until you get it done. I'm giving you a better option, one that benefits both of us. Or I can shoot you now and probably get myself killed trying to get out of here."

She took another sip of coffee and looked at him over the rim of her cup as if they were casually discussing a change in the weather and not her life expectancy.

"I can see why Nick is so fond of you," Dragan said. "Killers are easy to find but you're almost as good a talker as he is."

"He still thinks he can talk his way out of this," she said.

"He's wrong. However, you make a convincing argument for your life. I won't kill you. I believe you're too valuable a resource to waste."

"I knew you were a man of reason."

He was also a man without a woman now that Litija had got her brains blown out, and he'd gotten hard watching Kate eat her croissant. He thought she might be of short-term use to him.

"We can use the couple weeks or so that we're waiting for Nick to die to figure out the operational details of the attack," he said.

"That's fine, but there's only so much we can accomplish from a castle in Germany," Kate said. "After Nick is dead, and while you're cooking up batches of the virus, I can make a dry run into the U.S. and work out the kinks in the field. Nothing beats boots on the ground. I'll come back with what I've learned and we can fine-tune the plan."

"That's an excellent idea," Dragan said. "Would you like to

see how the virus is coming along and the delivery system you'll be using to spread it?"

"Why not?" she said and finished her coffee. "I've got nothing better to do."

Dragan and Kate entered the biosafety corridor as a scientist passed them pushing a cart that carried a box of cigars and bottles of vodka, rum, and whiskey. The scientist went through the air lock with the cart.

"Looks like the reality of the situation is sinking in for Nick," Dragan said.

"It had to happen eventually," Kate said. "Be glad he didn't ask for a gun or a bottle of sleeping pills."

Dragan led her past the closed blinds of Nick's lab window to the next window down the hall. Inside, she saw four men in positive pressure suits diligently engaged in their scientific tasks at various workstations.

"This is our second lab, where we're using an old-school method to grow enough smallpox to create a weapon. You see those chicken eggs?" Dragan pointed to a scientist sitting at a table in front of dozens of eggs resting in a tray that looked like the bottom of an egg carton. The man was using a syringe to inject a milky substance into the eggs. "We inject the virus into live chicken embryos. I won't bore you with the science, because frankly I don't understand it all, but the virus thrives in that goop. What you're looking at is our smallpox production line."

Kate desperately wanted to take a step back from the window. There was something unnerving about being that close to something so unbelievably deadly, no matter how many safety protocols were in place. She watched as another scientist, a Chinese man, took a tray of eggs to an incubator and opened it. There were four other trays in the oven-like machine.

"If you're already producing virus from what you got in Antwerp," she asked, "why did you need to steal another sample?"

"The one from Antwerp was small, and production would have dragged on," Dragan said. "The additional virus we've just acquired will speed things up exponentially. Plus the virus in Nick's system is derived from a more recent, and far deadlier, strain smuggled out of a weapons lab near Novosibirsk, Siberia, by a rogue microbiologist in the late 1990s. The smallpox Nick carries is a chimera."

"What's a chimera?"

"It's from Greek mythology. A fearsome monster made of parts of many different animals. In this case, it's a pathogen composed of more than one deadly virus. The smallpox that Nick is infected with is mixed with Ebola. You could call it 'big pox.' It embodies the worst of smallpox and Ebola. It's one hundred percent fatal and incurable."

"You neglected to mention that detail to us before," she said.

"Oops." Dragan shrugged. "My mistake."

"What was the institute in Paris doing with a smallpox chimera?"

"They're studying it to find a cure," Dragan said.

"In the center of a densely populated city?"

"There are level-four biolabs in major cities all over the world," Dragan said. "The institute is just one of many secretly hired by governments to find cures for the worst possible bioweapons in case an army, a terrorist group, or an enterprising investor like me decides to unleash a plague."

"So how do we do this?" Kate said. "I presume we aren't just going to throw those eggs at people."

"Once the eggs are teeming with new virus, we extract the goop and turn it into an aerosol spray." Dragan led her to the next window. Inside that lab, she saw more workstations and freezers. "This is lab number three, where we will be creating the spray and storing it for the weapon."

"Where's the weapon?"

Dragan reached into his pocket and took out a small breath freshener dispenser. It was roughly the same shape and size as a keychain thumb drive.

"It will look like this, only it will be equipped with a small timer," Dragan said, admiring the device. "It releases a mist of micron-sized virus particles. One of these placed in an inconspicuous spot in an airport terminal will infect thousands of people in just a few minutes and spread 'big pox' all over the globe. But I prefer a more targeted approach."

"That shouldn't be hard to smuggle into the U.S. or to hide

in a movie theater or an enclosed shopping mall," Kate said. "But you'd have to prove to me that the timer works before I set one up. One spritz and I'm dead, too."

"We've created some harmless mock-ups that you can test."

"How many scientists do you have here?"

"Six scientists in the labs and two engineers who run the air filtration and decontamination systems."

"Where do the scientists come from?"

"England, China, Russia," he said. "There's no shortage of disillusioned, underpaid, ethically challenged scientists out there who aren't getting the respect or salary they want from their country or their profession."

"How many Road Runners are here?"

"A dozen," he said. "Why do you ask?"

"I'm wondering how many people we have to kill to cover our tracks."

Dragan smiled. He liked her answer. "Then you also have to include the two maintenance workers who run the castle's heating and electrical system."

"That's a lot of killing," Kate said.

"There's enough gasoline stored in this castle to power a small town, not to mention the oxygen tanks in the filtration system," Dragan said. "With a few well-placed explosives, we can kill them all on our way out the door."

"I'm glad we're good buddies now."

"Me, too," Dragan said. In fact, he was getting hard again at the thought.

"I haven't slept in over twenty-four hours. Now that we're friends, I can take a nap without worrying you might slit my throat as I sleep."

"I doubt that you ever sleep without worrying about that," Dragan said, leading her back to the air lock. "I certainly never do."

27

Nick lay on his cot, enjoying a tumbler of scotch and a good Cuban cigar. It was relaxing.

"Even though it's not the smallpox chimera, it's still one hell of a scary virus they're hatching next door," Nick said through Kate's earbud. "It's a good thing I fortified myself with cigars and plenty of strong liquor."

Kate entered her room and closed the door. "This is no time to get drunk," Kate said.

"I meant it literally," Nick said. "Dragan not only escorted me through security, he kindly provided me with a lighter and an accelerant to set the place on fire."

"Can you do it without infecting yourself and still escape?"

"I certainly hope so." Nick blew smoke rings up at one of the cameras aimed at him. "But I'll need you to knock out the cameras and create a distraction so I am not disturbed."

"I can take care of the cameras," Kate said.

"I'll create the distraction," Jake O'Hare said.

"Dad?" Kate went to the window in her room and looked outside. Everything was the same as before. "Where are you?"

"In the woods," Jake said. "I can see you in your window. You're wearing the perfect camouflage for hiding in a jar of jelly beans."

"You're early," she said.

"The traffic was light," Jake said. "Is that a problem?"

"No, it's not."

"Good, because I've got ten men in the woods and two more in the Apache attack chopper that will be here in ten minutes," Jake said. "I'm aware of two men walking the grounds, four more on the battlements, and one in the tower. How many more are we up against?"

"There's one outside the labs," Nick said.

"And one more at the security desk," Kate said. "I don't know where the others are."

"Perhaps they're manning the cauldrons of lye," Nick said.

"The *what*?" Jake said.

"Just don't come in the front door," Kate said. "It's a trap."

"We won't be coming in at all," Jake said. "There's smallpox in there. The fireworks start in eight minutes."

. . .

Kate slipped out of her room, walked down the hall, and passed the security guard at the console. She was heading for the third door off the foyer. It was the only one she hadn't been through yet.

"Halt," the guard said, standing up at the console. "You can't go there."

Kate stopped and turned to face him. "I'm Dragan's very special guest. I can go anywhere I want."

The guard stepped out from behind the console and came toward her. "That's Mr. Kovic's private wing. You can't go there unless you are summoned."

"Maybe I want to surprise him."

"Surprises are forbidden," the guard said.

"Okay, if you say so."

As Kate walked past him, she lashed out at the back of his knee with the flat of her left foot. His knee folded and so did he. As he tumbled, she spun around and kicked him in the jaw, snapping his head back and knocking him unconscious. She took his gun and dragged him back behind the console, where she sat down, studied the switches, and began shutting down systems.

Dragan was pondering his extraordinary good fortune as he sat at his office desk, watching the video feed from the lab where the once great Nicolas Fox was mumbling drunkenly to himself and blowing smoke rings at the ceiling.

The Paris job had gone completely wrong in so many ways

and yet, inexplicably, it turned out to be an extraordinary success. Instead of getting a mere vial of smallpox chimera, Dragan had lucked out and acquired an infected man, a living factory of the virus. On top of that, Dragan had also acquired Kate, an American who could easily deliver the viral weapon to Los Angeles. Now he had the means to create a global genocide if it pleased him, either by spreading the virus himself or by selling the means to others. It felt good.

But he was a businessman, not a madman. He gained nothing from a worldwide pandemic except proof of his power and a certain sense of accomplishment. He was content to settle for a few thousand deaths, billions of dollars in profit, and an early retirement. However, it might be time to paint his face on God on the dining room ceiling after all. He was imagining how that might look when the video screen went dark.

Nick had just finished his tumbler of scotch when Kate spoke in his ear.

"The cameras are down," she said. "Make it quick. I'll be waiting for you outside the main air lock."

Nick got up, set his cigar on the cart with the bottles of liquor, and stripped the bedding off his cot. He stuffed the sheets into the bottom shelf of the cart and wheeled it through the air lock into the suit room, where he was greeted by a bloodcurdling scream of sheer terror.

The scream came from a Chinese scientist who was already

in the room, preparing to get into a pressure suit. The scientist scrambled backward so fast that he tripped over his own feet and landed hard on the floor.

"I thought you might like a drink," Nick said, gesturing to the cart. "Whiskey, perhaps?"

"Who are you talking to?" Kate asked in his ear.

The scientist covered his nose and mouth, got to his feet, and rushed into the air lock leading to the showers.

"You'll be seeing him soon enough," Nick said.

Nick put on a pressure suit, attached an air hose to it, and waited to see if there were any leaks that became obvious when it inflated. Satisfied that his suit was airtight, he detached the hose and pushed his cart through air lock number two and into the lab.

The four scientists were intent on their work and paid no attention to him at first. Nick snapped an air hose to his suit and wheeled the cart up to the incubator. He opened the incubator, picked up the bottle of 140-proof Habitation Clément Rhum Vieux Agricole, and began splashing the eggs with the rum.

One of the scientists behind him stood up from his seat. *"Halt! Arretez! Stop!"*

Nick turned around, his lighted cigar between his gloved fingertips. "Anyone want a smallpox omelet?"

He tossed the cigar into the incubator, igniting the rum in a flash of fire that made an audible *whoosh*.

The scientists got to their feet and stood frozen for a beat, mouths open in shock. Nick picked up the Stolichnaya bottle by the neck and smashed it on the edge of a workstation, splattering 100-proof vodka and glass shards all over a tray of eggs. He held up the jagged edge in front of him.

"One tear in your suit and you're infected with plague," Nick said. "Who wants to take me on?"

Okay, so he wasn't sure if they understood English. He thought they would understand the tone and the gesture.

"Time for Nick's distraction," Jake said. He was deep in shadow in the forest with Willie, who was holding a shoulder-mounted rocket launcher and aiming it for fun at the helicopter on the grass. She started to hand him the weapon when he shook his head. "No, you do it."

"I've never fired a rocket launcher before," she said.

"Then you've been denied one of life's greatest pleasures."

"I've never denied myself any pleasure, and I'm sure as hell not going to start now," she said. "What do I do?"

He handed her a set of earplugs and gave her quick instructions on how to release the safety and fire the rocket.

"A child could do this," she said, took aim, and fired.

The rocket shot out and the backfire from the launcher blasted chunks of bark off the trees behind them. An instant later, the helicopter blew apart, sending rotors flying in all directions.

"Hot damn," Willie said. "That's a rush. What can I blow up next?"

Jake shoved her to the ground just as a barrage of machine gun fire from the castle shredded the trees and branches above their heads.

Dragan was about to call the security desk to find out what had happened to his video feed when there was an explosion outside, followed by the sound of automatic gunfire from the ramparts above. His radio crackled. A guard spoke in frantic Serbian.

"This is the tower. The helicopter is destroyed. We're under attack."

Dragan grabbed the radio from his desk and spoke into it. "From who? From where?"

"I don't know," the guard said. "The rocket came from the woods in front of the castle. We're returning fire."

Those facts immediately raised a crucial question in Dragan's mind. If everybody's attention was focused on the front of the castle, what was coming from behind?

"Zone four, report," Dragan said, addressing the guard patrolling the southern rampart. "What do you see?"

Some initial crackle came over the line. "I see nothing unusual." There was the sound of the guard gasping in surprise, and the gasp was followed by swearing in three languages, an explosion, and gunfire.

An Apache helicopter gunship is a fast, lethal, and versatile flying arsenal designed to destroy armored vehicles, bunkers, and buildings. It's typically equipped with thirty-eight Hydra rockets, nineteen on each side of the aircraft, and a 30mm automatic chain gun loaded with 1,200 explosive armor-piercing rounds mounted on its nose. That was what the Zone 4 guard saw heading toward the castle.

The next thing the guard saw was the Apache fire a Hydra rocket that zoomed past him at 2,425 feet per second. So at almost the same instant he was aware of the missile firing it had already slammed into the castle's tower, shearing off the top in an explosion of fire and stone.

A cascade of rubble tumbled into the moat as the Apache streaked past the castle, the guards along the battlements firing at the gunship in futile fury.

The two explosions rocked the lab. Beakers and test tubes fell to the floor, providing enough incentive for the scientists to forget about Nick and rush for the air lock. They bunched up in front of it, only able to go through one at a time in their inflated suits. One of scientists slapped the emergency alarm button, setting off a shrill siren.

Nick struck a match and tossed it on the vodka-soaked eggs. The tray of eggs went up in flames. There was a notebook on the table. He tore the notebook in half and tossed some of the pages into the incubator and the others onto the tray to keep the fires going.

He opened the freezer, doused everything with whiskey, struck a match, and set the contents on fire. He reached for the nearest air hose and sprayed oxygen on the fire, fanning the flames.

There was one last thing to do. Nick yanked the bedsheets off the cart, draped them over some of the workstations, splashed the remaining whiskey on everything, and then tossed a few lit matches on top. The sheets ignited.

Kate sat impatiently at the security console, waiting for Nick. She could hear the gunfire, even over the wail of the alarm, and could feel the rumble of the Apache passing overhead. There was a lot of action going on and she was sitting it out. The guard on the floor began to regain consciousness so she kicked him in the head, more out of frustration than her legitimate need to keep him down.

One by one, beginning with the terrified Chinese guy, the scientists ran out of the air lock, through the foyer, and across the rubble-strewn courtyard in a mad flight out of the castle. Even two guards ran past Kate without giving her a second look. They were all rats leaving a sinking ship. But where was the king of the rats?

Kate hadn't seen Dragan since the grand tour, and that concerned her. As far as she knew, there was only one way out of the castle, and he hadn't come out yet. Where was he? She was tempted to hunt him down, but she didn't want to leave Nick unprotected in his escape.

"Hurry up, Nick," she said.

"My work is done," he said. "I'm on my way out."

28

The Apache gunship swooped around the castle, raking the battlements with its armor-piercing bullets, obliterating the parapet and killing two guards who tumbled into the moat. A handful of people with their hands raised in surrender spilled out of the castle and ran for the woods.

Jake grabbed his radio to relay orders to the strike team. "Apprehend those people when they reach the woods. Nobody gets away."

The Apache came back around and fired two Hydra missiles into the castle walls, blasting huge holes in them. One of the missiles hit something extremely flammable, perhaps propane or gasoline, Jake didn't know what, but it set off a chain reaction of explosions that moved like a blazing zipper along the eastern wall. It looked to him like the choreographed sequence of blasts used to demolish a building. That wasn't supposed to happen yet, not while Nick and his daughter were still inside.

"The castle is coming down," Jake yelled, hoping Kate and Nick could hear him on their earbuds. "Get the hell out of there now!"

Kate got the warning just as she saw Dragan dash across the courtyard from some unseen doorway and climb into the wishing well.

"Oh crap," she said. "Dragan is getting away."

"Go after him," Nick said.

"I'm not leaving you."

"I'm right behind you," he said. "Don't let him escape!"

Kate grabbed her gun and ran to the courtyard. The castle walls were cracking, huge slabs of stone tumbling down as the fissures widened and spread. She climbed over the rim of the wishing well and set her foot on the first rung of a ladder that descended thirty feet down the shaft.

"The wishing well is an escape tunnel," she said. "I'm going in after him."

It was true that Nick was behind Kate. Saying he was *right* behind her had been a stretch. He couldn't leave his area without decontaminating his suit first or he could infect himself and others.

He left the lab and stood in the chemical showers in his

pressure suit, thinking it was like standing in a car wash during an earthquake. Disinfectant spray doused him from every angle, thoroughly drenching his suit, while the floors and walls shook. Cracks rippled across the walls, popping off tiles. He could hear the explosions deep in the bowels of the building.

"It sounds like you're in a shower, Nick," Jake said. "Tell me you didn't stop to clean up."

"I couldn't leave like this."

"You're going to be buried alive. Get out of there. You've only got seconds left."

He hoped he'd been in the decontamination showers long enough. But it was either go now or die. Nick peeled off the suit, ran out of the showers, through the locker room, and out into the corridor. The labs were engulfed in flames, and the windows were beginning to rupture, spider-webbing with cracks. He hurried through the main air lock and into the foyer.

Bits of stone were raining down on the entryway as he stepped out. He looked out at the courtyard. The castle's front wall had collapsed like a sand castle kicked by a petulant child, smashing the wishing well and blocking Nick's only way out.

Kate reached the bottom of the thirty-foot pit just as the castle wall collapsed above. Huge stones poured down the shaft, demolishing the well and forcing Kate to take cover in the tunnel. It was about six feet high, four feet wide, and, from what she could see, about a hundred yards long, maybe more. A string of naked lightbulbs and a ventilation pipe ran along the ceiling. It was a straight shot in front of her, and she could see Dragan about forty yards away and running.

She aimed and fired and missed. She adjusted her aim and fired again, hitting him in the leg. He went down to one knee.

"Stay down!" Kate shouted. "I'm an FBI agent. You are under arrest."

"Go to hell," Dragan said, getting to his feet, opening fire on her.

Kate flattened herself against the side of the tunnel and shot back, but he was already on the move, shooting as he limped away.

Her back was soaking wet, and water was dripping on her head. She looked around and saw that the ceiling and walls in this section of the tunnel were seeping water at an ever-increasing rate. The moat was probably right above her head, and the castle was collapsing into it. That couldn't be good news for the structural integrity of the tunnel. She charged forward in a crouch, closing the distance between them. Dragan whirled around to fire off another shot, but she got her shot off first. He cried out in pain and tumbled backward, splashing into the mud at his feet.

Kate got up and approached him warily, her gun out in front of her, feeling big drops of water hitting her head. The lights were beginning to flicker. They'd short out from the water soon.

Dragan was on his back, bleeding from wounds in his right thigh and upper left arm. His foot was twisted at an impossible angle. Probably broken when he slipped in the mud, she thought. Muddy water was raining on him. He wasn't going anywhere on his own and there was no way she could carry him. She picked up his gun, ejected the clip, and tossed the weapon away. She took hold of the foot that wasn't broken and attempted to drag him. She slid in the mud and went down on her back. The floor of the tunnel was too slick to get any kind of traction.

"What's at the end of the tunnel?" she asked him.

"Another dry well," he said, grimacing in pain.

"I'll come back for you with medics and handcuffs. Try to hang on."

Nick didn't know where to go. He chose the door to his left and ran down the corridor. Another explosion shook the castle, throwing him off balance and nearly knocking him off his feet. He staggered forward, turned a corner, and found himself in a grand dining room, the chandeliers dropping and crashing onto the table.

He saw a window overlooking the moat. It was his last, best hope. He grabbed a straight chair and was about to toss it through the window, when something caught his eye. Nick looked up at *The Creation of Adam* and was astounded to see Adam with enormous genitalia and Dragan's face. It was so bad that it was mesmerizing.

Another explosion jolted the castle, and a huge crack opened up on the ceiling, cleaving the fresco in half. That got Nick's attention. He heaved the chair through the glass and then took a running leap out the window as the dining room caved in behind him.

He plunged deep into the murky, ice-cold moat, followed by enormous chunks of stone that hit the water like depth charges.

Kate was about ten yards from the shaft at the end of the tunnel, and her eyes were fixed on the ladder bolted into the wall. A stream of water hit her heels and she heard a deep, jagged rumble, the sound rock might make if it were being torn in half.

She looked over her shoulder and saw water gushing out of the ceiling. The moat was collapsing into the tunnel. The tunnel ceiling caved in and an enormous surge of dark water poured in through the opening. The lights went out, plunging the tunnel into total darkness. Dragan screamed, a sound that was immediately drowned out by the powerful flood of water.

Kate ran forward into pitch-darkness, arms outstretched so she wouldn't take a header into the ladder. If she tripped, she was dead.

She hit the wall hard, grabbed hold of the nearest rung, and started climbing. The water slammed into the wall below her and surged up the shaft. She couldn't escape it, and took a last, deep breath. The wave swallowed her completely, yanked her from the ladder, and propelled her upward. She banged against a cover that splintered on impact, and she bobbed to the surface sputtering and splashing, reaching out for something solid. She found the stone wall of the well, heaved herself over it, and flopped onto the ground. Water continued to surge out of the well and swirl around her. She got to her hands and knees, breathing hard. She stood and took a minute to steady herself. The water was no longer gushing over the rim of the well and was gently lapping at the interior wall. The rotted piece of plywood that had capped the well had been tossed onto the mud and grass a couple feet from her.

"Holy crap," she said. "Holy cow. Holy moly."

The well looked like it hadn't been used in a hundred years. It was positioned a short distance from what might have at one time been a caretaker's cottage. The cottage itself was in a patch of woods. There were no roads leading out so she walked toward the smell of smoke and the sound of activity. It didn't take long to break out of the woods into the open field that surrounded the castle.

Kate stopped and stared at the ruins, pushing her wet hair out of her eyes, leaving a smear of mud across her face. The castle was a pile of smoking rubble, an occasional tongue of flame licking out over the moat, which was half as deep as it was before.

Oh man, Kate thought, this wasn't going to look good on form GS205.

Jake and Willie had military-style rifles trained on a clump of men who were sitting on the grass, their arms zip-tied behind them. There weren't any U.S. soldiers in sight and the Apache was gone. Kate's heart skipped a beat when she realized Nick wasn't there.

She slogged across the field and saw Jake smile with relief when he saw her. Her boots squished water, and her clothes were plastered to her and clogged with mud. She was shivering from cold and adrenaline withdrawal.

"You look like you went swimming in a frog pond," Jake said.

"T-t-tunnel leads to a w-w-well," Kate said. "Dragan is still in the tunnel." She looked around. "Where is everyone?"

"You just missed the strike team. They wanted to get back to the military base before dinner. It's steak night."

"Where's Nick?"

Jake tipped his head toward the parking lot. "He borrowed one of the Range Rovers. He didn't want to be around when the police got here."

"Good thinking," Kate said. "We shouldn't be here either."

"We're just hanging out waiting for our ride to show up," Jake said.

Kate heard the familiar *wup, wup, wup* of a chopper, and a six-seater Bell rose out of the woods and landed a short distance away.

"Thank you for being here for me," Kate said to Jake and Willie.

"Well, I wouldn't be much of a father if I didn't occasionally blow up a castle for you."

"And I fired off my first rocket," Willie said. "It was life changing."

Jake looked toward the chopper. "Are you coming with us? Or are you going to stay behind to try to explain this to the authorities?"

"I'm coming with you," Kate said. "No one is left who actually knows who I am. And there's no good way of explaining this. Better to just chalk it up to terrorists. Plus, I need to call Jessup and give him a fast debrief so he doesn't fall off the wagon and start drinking again."

"Good idea not to hang around," Willie said. "You wouldn't want someone taking a mug shot of you right now. Your hair is like ... *yikes.*"

After weeks in Europe, digging a hole in a sewer, and nearly drowning in a flooded tunnel, Kate was eager to go back to her one-bedroom apartment in Tarzana, and sleep in her own bed.

She flew into Los Angeles on a red-eye and walked in her door at nine in the morning. She followed a trail of Toblerones into the kitchen where Nick was waiting.

"Originally I was thinking of leaving a trail of rose petals, but that didn't feel right," Nick said.

"Toblerones are good," Kate said, peeling the wrapper off one and eating it. "What are you doing here?"

"I thought you'd be hungry so I stopped around to make you breakfast. I have Frosted Cinnamon Roll Pop-Tarts, Cocoa Krispies, and Cap'n Crunch's Crunch Berries, Eggo waffles, and Jimmy Dean sausages."

"No champagne?"

"I went with Coke and Folgers crystals."

"My kind of guy," Kate said.

"Go figure."

He was wearing a loose-fitting T-shirt, khaki shorts, and flip-flops. She gave him a head-to-toe appraisal and wondered how fast she could get him out of his clothes. Probably pretty fast.

"Is this a con?" she asked him.

He grinned at her. "Does it matter?"

ABOUT THE AUTHORS

JANET EVANOVICH is the #1 *New York Times* bestselling author of the Stephanie Plum series, the Fox and O'Hare series with co-author Lee Goldberg, the Lizzy and Diesel series, the Alexandra Barnaby novels and Troublemaker graphic novel, and *How I Write: Secrets of a Bestselling Author.*

evanovich.com

Facebook.com/JanetEvanovich

@JanetEvanovich

LEE GOLDBERG is a screenwriter, TV producer, and the author of several books, including *King City, The Walk,* and the bestselling Monk series of mysteries. He has earned two Edgar Award nominations and was the 2012 recipient of the Poirot Award for Malice Domestic.

leegoldberg.com

Facebook.com/AuthorLeeGoldberg

@LeeGoldberg

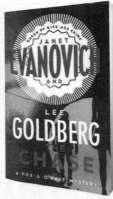
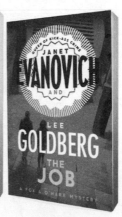

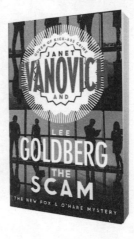

Coming this autumn . . .

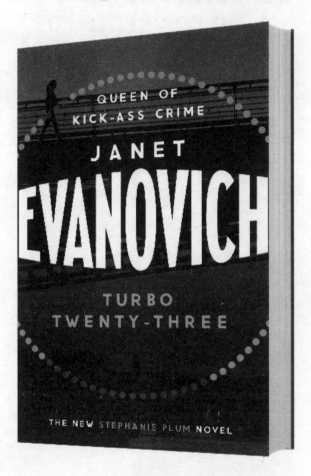

Speed is the name of the game as
Stephanie Plum returns in
Turbo Twenty-Three.

Order it now at
www.headline.co.uk

Join JANET EVANOVICH
on social media!

Facebook.com/JanetEvanovich

@janetevanovich

Pinterest.com/JanetEvanovich

Google+JanetEvanovichOfficial

Instagram.com/janetevanovich

Visit **Evanovich.com**
and sign up for Janet's e-newsletter!